TO THE DOOMSDAY BEACON

" 'Tis a thousand times better to stay clear of the affairs of those who rule the affairs of stars and worlds beyond number. Still, you deserve to know."

And so I told him, all of it. Of Drusus Base, of Eden Valley and the colonies. I explained the death of Earth and how the refuge of Avalon had been denied us all by some as yet unsolved mystery. I told him of the terrible council decision and the CT nova-warhead, and how even now it was coming to annihilate all his world unless I could somehow get to the blinker light and complete the task set me by Avalon's *whisperer* who'd brought me to do just that.

"I've just two months and a few days to reach that beacon," I finished. "The answer to the problem of whether this world will live or die is precisely there—and I mean *all* this world, not just the chunk of it with which you're familiar."

DAW BOOKS

by Arthur H. Landis

A WORLD CALLED CAMELOT
CAMELOT IN ORBIT
THE MAGICK OF CAMELOT

HOME - TO AVALON

Arthur H. Landis

DAW Books, Inc.
Donald A. Wollheim, Publisher
1633 Broadway, New York, N.Y. 10019

FIRST PRINTING, NOVEMBER 1982

1 2 3 4 5 6 7 8 9

DAW TRADEMARK REGISTERED
U.S. PAT. OFF. MARCA
REGISTRADA, HECHO EN U.S.A.

PRINTED IN U.S.A.

One

There was nothing singularly different about the ship. Indeed, its very familiarity evoked a certain numbing dullness. It was an Argos, Class III, an armored merchant; the standard two-thousand-year-old product of Terra's genius, give or take a few years, and it had hit Drusus' thin atmosphere at 14:00 hours. Planetfall had been across a portion of our southern hemisphere, where it came to rest within the arc of the Malvian sand mountains.

At no time had it come within range of our simple base weapons. We could have taken it out with a Sonsine. But no Terran colony had loosed a precious Sonsine missile in the last three hundred years. And this, with our own Drusus Base having been raided at least twenty times in the last hundred.

No need to anyway. And therein lay the true oddity. For aside from a pocked and graying skin, reflecting but the faintest of atmospheric wear—a singularity in itself, considering the years—all sensor reports showed the *Argos'* weapons to be inactive; nor was there any sign of life aboard. This last being impossible to accept, we were indeed faced with the proverbial mystery within an enigma.

I'd therefore flown a squadron of sixteen floater-skimmers some eight hundred miles from Base H.Q.—a full fifth of the small planet's diameter—and to within a thousand yards of the silent visitor without ever breaking a military skyline. My four captains, representing a good half of the command of Drusus' fleet, were even now positioning themselves as per my orders, to cover its cardinal points.

"Just here will be good," I said. "I'll personally give it a target, stir things for a proper readout."

The young lieutenant in charge of my command-craft—his name was Kardis—saluted briskly and dropped the floater the last few feet to settle on the opposite slope of one of the largest dunes shielding the armored merchant. Suited up and combat ready, as the situation demanded, I waved to our twelve-man warrior crew, slid open the air panel and stepped to the coarse sand. They snapped to attention in deference to my *Warlord*'s stars and circle. And, too, they recognized a sacrifice situation when they saw one. . . . Except that even then *I* knew better.

Bellerophon, Drusus' sun, shone weakly at some three hundred million miles. The reddish soil of our arid little world reflected into a mostly nitrogen atmosphere, what there was of it, to give it a pastel pinkish glow—this, at 140° below.

Free of mag-line gravity, I reached the dune's summit in a few low-trajectory leaps. At the military skyline, and with only my helmet visible to whomever or whatever might be aboard the *Argos*, I image-shifted—a trick, achieved with the aid of small prisms attached to same. The effect was a ghostly, three-dimensional projection of myself to anywhere within a three-hundred-foot radius of the real me. It was a simple diversionary tactic, useless against any knowledgeable colony warrior. Somehow, however, I'd guessed that our opponent, this time, was anything but that.

To do this, my helmet obviously, and of necessity, had remained above the skyline; therefore, the suggested danger.

Nothing.

The image shifted, followed the exact movements of my body as I walked here and there below the skyline. At one point I drew my blaster and aimed it directly to where the ship would be were I on the other side of the dune. The image, mine, would seem to any *Argos* observer to be within a perilous few yards of the merchant's command hatch.

Again, not the slightest reaction.

The ship continued motionless, silent. More. I could now see that both its cargo and command ports were open; yawning, as it were, to the elements.

I flicked my eyeshield to ten mags so's to see even within the airlock. Nothing. I then killed the projector, stepped to the skyline, crossed over, went down the dune's far side and walked deliberately to within a hundred yards of the enigma; this, with my suited arms lowered and my gloved hands flat out in the universal sign of peace.

It was just then that I saw a weathered name above the command hatch. *Scot's Leap* it said in an amateurish attempt at ancient runic script. A subliminal memory tugged sharply at my mind; indeed, sought desperately to tell me, or rather, to warn me of something.

Adrenalin charged; it didn't register.

I instead shouted boldly, "Hail *Scot's Leap!*" while simultaneously opening all command com-lines and hitting the amplifier so that my voice would assume the proper stentorian qualities. "This is Commander Jarn Tybalt, *Warlord* of Drusus, Bellerophon system. You are on Eden Colony territory. Unless you have Central Council business and can prove it, you are subject to the penalty for trespass. Either way, you will step down now and surrender your ship!"

Again I waited. Nothing.

I grew impatient. The eyes and ears of two hundred of the toughest floater warriors of the quadrant were now upon me, as were those at Command Center. Damn! All right! I'd try one more time to coax out with words that which I was sure had never been in the *Scot's Leap* in the first place. I shouted fiercely: "This is your last chance. Come out now, else we'll board and destroy the lot of you."

Silence.

A familiar voice then sounded off, insulting, challenging— but from my audio, not the ship. "That's an *Argos*, Jarn. And it's a bloody damn original with all its parts. So what the hell are you stalling for? Seize it, *Warlord* (my title, mouthed in that way, was an ill-concealed curse), and bedamned to your stinking protocol."

I fought to control my anger. The voice belonged to Vice Commander Arne Telles, ranking officer at Base H.Q., tucked safely away in our domed and protected crater of Eden Valley. That the man's hatred of me should have peaked at this particular moment was insufferable. I'd known he would attempt a power play sometime, and probably in just such a situation. That it had finally happened and at a crisis point embodying an ambiguity wherein my leadership could be safely challenged was no accolade to my precognitive abilities.

The question now was how far would he go?

That Telles was ambitious was the least of the problems we had with him. He was also an anachronism which, under any circumstances, was bound to put the two of us at opposite poles. He was also both visibly and vocally an omnipresent re-

minder of the Council-sponsored theory that inevitable disso-
lution would eventually destroy our remnant colonies if we
failed to fight to retain each shred of civilization left to us.

Odd paradox that that same Council, so right in most positions, had also approved the annihilation of beauteous Avalon,
the sole planet so far discovered in all the galaxy to be capable
of human life support; excepting, of course, our long-dead
Earth. . . .

Across the two thousand years since that unthinkable happening, that catastrophic destruction of the birthplace of humankind, we of the despairing colonies, while longing for
Avalon, had been denied its promise; and this, despite all efforts at communication and to reestablish the proper coordinates for warp. Thus the Council's decision: That the
continued existence of the planet Avalon *without access to it*,
is deemed totally destructive to the Colonies' ongoing struggle
for survival. . . . Their verdict had been death—Death for
Avalon!

And even there our Telles had committed the unforgivable
sin in the eyes of Drusus' colonists. For *we* had opposed Avalon's destruction. Our three delegates had been pledged to a
no vote. But Lars Aiken, our warlord of that far time of
twenty years before, had died en route to the Council Base on
Holbein IV. Commander Herrin, our second—killed in a raid
on Rafael Base at a later date—had voted no, accordingly.
Arne Telles, however, a young captain-delegate then, had simply betrayed his pledge for whatever opportunist reasons and
had voted *yes* with the slim majority. *I*, to my everlasting
pride, as an eighteen-year-old lieutenant-alternate to our Warlord, had dared to demand the right of proxy. I, too, had
voted *no*!

But still we lost.

And so the largest of our remaining starship freighter hulks
had been armed with a nova-force, C.T. warhead and warped
on automatics to the twenty-light-year barrier of the Persei
system; from there to continue at speed-of-light to Avalon,
and to effect its total destruction.

Nineteen years and ten months had passed since that insane
decision; which meant that Avalon still lived—but not for
long. Moreover, there was no way now to prevent the hap-

pening. Such a miracle would require our being there—which involved the eternal enigma of the chicken and the egg. . . .

The question of the why of it all remains unanswered. That there were reasons goes without saying.

Telles, our neo-Neanderthal with whom, by the very laws of inertia, we were fast beginning to emulate, lived only for himself and Drusus Base. The great mystery of where we'd come from and where we were going, if at all, was completely lost on him. So, were the fine points of our history on Earth and later, in the horror of the abandoned work places. For we were never colonies in the truest sense, but rather just the crews and engineers of this company or that who'd been attached for but a few years to mines and whatever where all accommodations, excepting a control center, were at best *tentative*. The C.C. could be used again, but *not* the accommodations. Life then had become a simple continuing, ghastly struggle to stay alive; this, in domed barracks on airless planets; at the bottom of the churning seas of methane and other noxious gases—or on the dead gray shores of Dantean lakes of molten metals—and all of it in the stone-cold corridors and amid the forever sickening stench of the hydroponics.

To Telles and those he attracted to him, all this was but a transient inconvenience which he and they would eventually overcome—at the expense, of course, of other humans in other remnant colonies. Courage he had, in vast quantities. For a back-to-the-wall firefight in a tough situation, there was hardly a better man than Telles. But the amoral streak was too much.

The thing that kept a colony alive was the individual's concern and responsibility to the collective. I had it. He didn't. Our men and women, in their majority, knew this. So they preferred my leadership to his . . . Chalk one up for the sand-grit common sense of our tightly knit, save-every-drop-of-water culture, as opposed to his opportunism.

To bloody hell with Arnes Telles!

I'd hesitated, listening to the excited breathing of my two hundred warriors aboard the floaters. Then, deliberately ignoring him, I gave my orders to the captains. The floaters, responding, arose to a height of fifty feet, their weapons trained solidly on the encircled *Scot's Leap*. With the lines open, it was as if I stood with each man at his post, and this amid a whispering of chuckles at my "non-handling" of our "second-in-command," Arne Telles.

"We'll play it by ear," I told them flatly. "We got a weird situation. No one's to open fire, therefore, unless *I* say so. And that, sirs, is a direct order!"

Lieutenant Kardis had settled my personal floater to the sand some fifty feet to my rear. "We'll be the boarding party," I told him after he'd hit ground and quick-trotted nine of his crew to where I waited.

He saluted, stared wide-eyed at the open hatches. "What do you think, Warlord?"

My eyes, too, had been hard on the yawning portals. "Our first scan at pre-entry could have erred," I told him. "That being possible, dulled sensor-sentience factors and all, our second scan, what with that—" I gestured toward the hatches, "could simply mean that whoever or whatever was aboard is now somewhere in the dunes."

"Do you really believe that, sir?" His blue eyes through the face shield twinkled above a broken nose.

"No," I said brusquely, "I do not; nor do I believe in ghosts either."

He squinted hard, amid a shuffling of sand boots all around. "Well at least the ship's no ghost." Then he frowned, lifted his head, looking for all the world as if he were somehow sniffing the nonexistent air around us from the inside of his helmet. . . . He'd heard what I'd heard, what all of us had apparently heard.

A great roaring had come suddenly from nowhere to beat upon our eardrums; this, though its form seemed more like a monstrous *whispering* than, say, a maelstrom. It was all around us, too; not just from the audios. Alarmed, I tapped the master com-stud. The sound continued, banshee-like, pervasive. I was suddenly and oddly reminded of the sick-bay of our lone Taurus destroyer, where my father had been placed to die during the battle for Anubis. He'd been desperately trying to tell me something, whispering hoarsely, the sound very much like what I was hearing now. . . .

"You will hold your positions," I cried harshly against the beat of the sound. "My original order stands. Are you ready, Lieutenant Kardis?"

Kardis nodded. Upon which six of his nine stalwarts trotted to our front with drawn weapons—high-energy blasters and lasers. The remaining three swept their two-handed kuri-swords from their backs and moved to the immediate rear of the arc of six. Whatever might happen between here and the *Scot's Leap*'s open portals would be taken care of by the handguns. Entry, however, would be forced by the kuri-swords. If this sounds boastful or stupid, considering the power of lasers and such as opposed to bare blades, hear this: With rare exception, nothing to date in the history of Earth and the thousand colonies has withstood the rush of kuri-swordsmen at close quarters—unless it was *more* kuri-swordsmen.

Kardis' gleaming eyes awaited my final attack order.

Instead, I held up a hand. The whispering had suddenly changed to a moaning, an agonized howling. And with it now the ebon parabola of sky beyond the fragile film of pink-white atmosphere became a vague translucence so that a grayness crept in everywhere. It was as if we'd been suddenly caught in some swirling methane twister, intruding in all the space above and around the saucered parabola wherein set the armored *Scot's Leap*.

The sound then coalesced, drew tight in upon itself so that it was suddenly a repetitious gibbering of unintelligible—*words!* Try as I would, I could liken it to nothing but a scene from an ancient film-clip which I'd viewed in my youth. It was a cameo, actually, from some elder play—a spot wherein the murdered father of a distraught son—a prince, I think he was—returns to demand vengeance upon his murderer.

And *that* was the voice we heard, a great *whispering*, a word sound, with each syllable suggesting an effort born of an unendurable, hellish agony.

Words followed one another in drawn-out waves, became discernible. First there was my name—said again and again— "Jaaaarrrrrnnnnn Tyyyybbbbaaaaaaalllllt— Jaaaaarrrrrrnnnn-nnn Tyyybbbaaaaaalllllt— and then— Ennnnnnteeeeerrrrrr thhhheeee shhhhhhiiiiiippppppp! Ennnnnnnteeeeeerrrrrr thhhh-eeeee shhhhiiiiip, Jaaaaarrrrrrnnnnn Tyyybbbbaaaaaalllllt. . . ."

The horror of it, the ghastly sound of it, the very fact that it had singled me out, literally froze the blood in my veins. I looked to Lieutenant Kardis. His foolish smile was gone. His face beneath the burn was white, his eyes were staring.

I managed a hoarse laugh, but barely. Words stuck in my throat, choked me. Still I forced them through strictured muscles. "Whatever the damned thing is," I told him, "it wants *me*."

Kardis cursed. If he could have, he would have spit. If for no other reason than to show me he could do it. "Give the word, sir," he said tightly. "I've still more curiosity than fear."

"No," I repeated. "It wants *me*. And, if that's the case, I doubt much that it intends to harm me, at least not right away. So you'll hold your men just here, Lieutenant. And that," I called to my captains, "goes for the four of you, too."

I loosed my own kuri-sword, knowing even as I did so that any weapon would be useless against whatever it was that called. I stepped out deliberately toward the *Scot's Leap*.

"JARN!" Telles' voice broke through, raging, insistent. "Just what the hell do you think you're doing?"

I unconsciously hesitated. The whispering continued. It seemed now like an echoing, enveloping, tactile wind. "Jaaarrrnnn— it called. "Yoooouuuuuuu— wiiiiiillllll— noooooottttttt beeeee haaaaaarrrrrrmmmmmeeeeeddddd. Ennnnnteeeeeerrrrr thhhhheeeeeee shhhhhiiiiiip— Jaaaaa-rrrrrrrrnnnnnnn. . . ."

To hell with Telles. I brushed aside the arc of blasters and kuri-swords.

At his challenge, however, Lieutenant Kardis had plunged forward to join me. "Allow me," he begged, "to at least accompany you."

"Go back!" I grated. "If I don't return within ten minutes, you'll place yourself under the orders of Captain Aars of the fourth unit. Do you hear that, Aars?" I raised my voice. "You will then be in command. *However!* If there's a liftoff, if this ship chooses to take me to wherever it wishes to go, no one is to interfere. It has obviously come for a purpose. I *mean* to see it through."

"Jarn Tybalt!" Telles yelled again; though this time his fury seemed more controlled—and therefore was more dangerous, "I demand, in the name of Drusus' Colony, that you cease all efforts toward entering that ship. More! That you blast it, now, taking care so's not to hit the converter pods, or any section of the engine room, especially the Hua-Tsing drive, the accumulators and the like. Do you understand me, *Warlord*?"

"I do. You through?"

"No."

"I think you are."

"Damn you, Tybalt." Arne Telles' breathing was heavy. I pictured his face as a coronary red. "What kind of a game are you playing? Better yet—who are you working for? Calsis Base? Maybe that filthy gang on Rafael's Third? They still got two ships, I hear. Or maybe you've tied in to that three-base hook-up on Capella? Real nice—except there's a lot of us who don't forget that they killed *sixty* of ours in that damned sneak eight years ago. . . . Or, perhaps," and he let his words become measured, deliberate, so as to have the greatest effect on our now breathless audience—"just *perhaps*, our Central Council's gone and done it, opted for confederacy controls over all of us. Is that the game, Jarn? Is that *their* ship, sent to pick you up and cinch the deal? We know it's on automatics, right? Maybe for you to make a quick run to Heilbron Center."

"You're insane, Arne." I broke in as strongly as I could.

"Could be. But I'll tell you something: You're not going anywhere, Warlord! If that ship lifts off with you aboard, then, by the gods—I'll fire a Sonsine!"

I said coldly, "I order you, Telles, to step down, now!"

His reply was mocking laughter. Others joined in. He wasn't alone. Damn! Had he stacked Base H.Q. with his supporters? My anger was fast becoming white hot.

By the level of resonance in his delivery, he'd long ago switched to full participatory-open, so that all scanners, intercoms, every suited warrior, was on him, and vice versa. I hastily switched, too. Odd that he'd do that. Conceit, arrogance? I had cause to wonder, for he'd never had the vote, nor could he win a popularity contest. Whatever. I, too, would now speak directly to the six hundred of our dwindling population. . . .

For I wanted them to hear; indeed, it could already be too late. I knew now that he'd seized on the chance to orchestrate this little psycho-drama from the very beginning; set them all to watching the moment our small fleet had left—when the *Scot's Leap* had first entered atmosphere! Still, it was a game that two, or any number, could play.

"Now hear this!" My voice was harsh, authoritative in the old way—the way whose disciplines had kept us civilized despite our wars and the constant raiding of each other—"It is I, Jarn Tybalt, your elected Warlord who speaks to you. The situation is as follows: In conformance with my duties, I am about to board a Class III Argos which has breached our space in violation of Council codes.

"Its purpose remains unknown; this, though I've been asked to come aboard." My eardrums were instantly hit by an immediate blast of ooohs, aaahs and angry exclamations, all forcing the realization that none but my two hundred warriors aboard the sixteen floaters were aware of the great whispering voice—inclusive of Arne Telles. I'd no choice but to continue. "This invitation is not, in my opinion, life-threatening. Whatever our opponent, if he is that, has in mind, the answers to his presence here are in the ship, not in the dunes. Moreover, if I'm right in that it means no harm to us, why then, conversely, we can only gain from such a meeting.

"That's the first part," I finished calmly. "You've all heard the second, the slander; the insane accusations of our vice-commander. Who?" I demanded sharply, "is now at Base H.Q.? I order you to call out your names at once."

They began to do so, immediately. Point one for me. I'd caught Arne off balance. A good half of the twenty present were in no way Telles' men. I felt a sudden relief; especially when I heard Commander Hardis Donnert say his name.

Telles, the bastard, was bluffing!

I called out strongly, "Telles! I'm going to ask you just once more to step down."

"*No waaaay!*" he roared to crack the intercom. "You've lied to the people, Tybalt. There's *no* invitation. That goddamned *Argos* is on automatics."

"Wrong! And you've my word on it. Indeed, you'll eventually have the word of every officer and man of the floater fleet who surround the *Scot's Leap*. How does *that* grab you, mister?"

He was silent.

"Say now that you'll step down."

He hesitated.

"Say it, damn you!"

He continued silent.

"Commander Donnert?" I called.

"Aye, Warlord." Donnert's voice was calm, in control.

"On my order, sir, you are now in command of Drusus Base. And in that capacity you will place Vice-Commander Arne Telles under immediate arrest, to be held until such time as I return or, if I do not, until the full council of Eden Valley decides the matter."

"Aye, Warlord."

"And I mean close arrest, with no contact beyond the base." I'd ordered this last for the simple reason that the supposed sins that Telles had accused me of—could be quite true where he himself was concerned. In any event there was no harm in hedging one's bets.

"Damn you, Tybalt!" Telles was shouting. "You've no right. By the gods, when—"

"I—have—every—right, you traitorous bastard," I grated back. "Commander Donnert! I charge you, sir: At the slightest hint of trouble from Mr. Telles—*Cut him down!*"

"Aye, Warlord. But a point, sir. Explain, if you will, this *invitation*."

I cursed, and told him, briefly, for time was running out. Moreover, I'd no way of knowing what exactly was happening in the command room—unless I reboarded my floater for scanner view. Action being the proverbial father to the thought, I sent Kardis racing to the little ship and the scanner.

"I'm going in now," I yelled after him, "else I'll never find the goddamned hatch in all this mist." (A mist on Drusus?) At the time, when I think about it now, there had been some sort of fast-forming misty cloud which we'd both regarded as but a stirring of the sand by the floaters overhead. Anything else as the cause would have simply been unacceptable. Mist or sand-dust, at the time I could barely see the *Scot's Leap*'s profile.

Through it all the whispering had never ceased, except that now an urgency was evident above the pain— "Ooooooooooo-hhhhhhhh Jaaaaaarrrrrrnnnnnnnn. . . . Thhhheeeeerrrrrr isssssss noooooo tiiiimmmmmmeeeeeee. Goooooooooo—Ennnnnttttteeeerrrrrr—"

But there was time. Sufficient at least for me to wonder if the whole insane charade was not just some form of budding madness inside my head. Rough sand crunched beneath my boots at each long, low leap. The distance had been two hundred, then a hundred, then fifty. Then, with but twenty feet to go, it happened! A high energy bolt smashed down between myself and the open hatch to turn the sand to glass. More! It had been preceded by audio sounds of scuffling, rip-ping explosions and a medley of screams and curses from all com-line outlets.

Above the bedlam I heard the frantic voice of Kardis, yelling, "Warlord! Quick! The airlock! We've a damned traitor here."

Even as he warned me, and while I threw myself forward, half-turning the while to glance over my shoulder, the pencil beams from a number of floaters reached out to needle the culprit, the command ship of our east unit. Damn the bastard! I'd always suspected Captain Marjian; but like Telles, battle-wise, he was a man. As if on signal, my loyal units, taking no chances, hit Marjian's group with everything they had so that my last view of the space around and above the dunes of the Malvian Sand Mountains was that of a kaleidoscope of falling, riven ships, bursting color and an ongoing medley of screams and curses from every source.

One voice, fully amplified, roared wildly above the others: "You've had it, Tybalt! By the gods, you'll get a Sonsine now. I swear you will. And there'll *still* be salvage!" Great laughter followed, Telles' laughter. Then the outer hatch slammed of its own accord. . . .

Physically and mentally numb, I literally dived through the inner hatch, heading for the *Scot's Leap*'s bridge—*And the inner hatch swung shut behind me.* The mystery continued. For where normally there'd be a crackling flow of communications, there was now but a dead silence. I ran my fingers over the com-lines. They'd been full open. I phased them out, then in again—Silence! The *Scot's Leap*, for whatever reasons, had become an effective insulator against all communications. But more. Since the hatches had been open, we should have been airless and with a temperature to match that of Drusus, i.e., 140° below. But such was not the case. Indeed, every readout on my sleeve showed a normalcy in all things—pressure, heat, and the exact ratios of oxygen, hydrogen and nitrogen. A paradox, in truth. And why had *it, they* or *whatever* even bothered to shut the hatches, considering?

In the master swivel—I'd hastily divested myself of the unneeded suit, retaining only my weapons and harness—I sampled the control panel response. Nothing. Still, though dead to my fingers, all standard in-transit factors had been activized. Readouts were registering and the scanner-viewer was at work. It seemed stuck, however, in one position, attuned only to the positional view as already seen through the transparency of the *Scot's Leap*'s bow. And we were already off-planet. Odd. I'd felt absolutely nothing; and this, apparently, while the anti-gravs had been at full.

Dammm! Just now was the time to scan in on Drusus Base. For I could tell by the hum that the Bensons had cut in. It would be now or never for Telles' Sonsine missile to come out and blow me and the *Scot's Leap* to bloody ions. But there was still nothing. Either he hadn't, or he couldn't. But then the Bensons weren't humming—they were screaming!

And then—and *then*, at some millions of miles, six by the readouts, and that was impossible time-wise under normal thrust, there was the weird, chuckling shift to the Hua-huas and the first shower of flashing, elongated, sleetlike snowflakes, plus bursts of light to run the gamut of the rainbow.

By the bloody gods. We'd "hole punched," gone in and out of hyperspace, and were now—somewhere else. Cold sweat bathed my face while a strange sickness touched all my body. *The time sequences were all wrong!* We'd used up ten minutes since the beginning of liftoff, no more. Yet we'd passed from mag-line anti-gravs, gone six million miles under Benson iondrive, and had then managed a coordinate warp through hyperspace. The Benson six million alone should have taken an hour!

Resting my head on the great control panel, I breathed deeply to regain composure; talked, as it were, to my body. The sickness left, but slowly. My normal feeling of well being returned at the same pace. Again I tried for communications power. Nothing. From the new star patterns, as seen through both the bow and the scanner, we'd obviously leaped a considerable distance. I tried for a dimensional backward traverse, an inverse balancing method to tell us where we'd been so that we would then have the coordinates to tell us where we were. Nothing! But! The *Scot's Leap* was now slowly turning, the star patterns shifting. A sun star appeared—and I mean within a hundred million miles of us. It was young, a beauteous yellow-white, comparable to Sol, or Bellerophon.

And then, to starboard, there came the first thin edge of a disc which grew to be in its entirety the most beautiful thing I would ever see in my lifetime. . . . It was not just another planet, but rather a blue-white water world, with the kind of atmosphere that promised everything. The readouts showed its content to be exactly what I was already breathing. Clouds, great masses of them in swirls and high-piled cumulae were everywhere; especially in the northern hemisphere wherein, as was evident by the planet's axial tip, bleak winter would soon be on its way.

Beneath those clouds, all sparkling in a crystal clarity of great open patches of azure sky, were primal, blue-purple seas, a myriad of cobalt lakes and silvered-emerald rivers. The snowy peaks of great mountain chains were everywhere. Beneath them verdant valleys extended to great open savannahs, to shimmering grasslands and on to forests the like of which I could not believe. . . . Tropical, deciduous, coniferous—they stretched to the world's end and back in literally tens of millions of square miles of breathing, pulsing—*life!*

Hypnotized, I still sought to tear my eyes away to check the readouts. I couldn't. For I was a human who'd lost his world, the birthplace of my species; a human, descended from generations of humans who, by cataclysmic catastrophe, had been denied for two thousand years even the smallest part of his natural birthright. My fathers and their fathers before them had never walked on anything but the pyrite dust of meteors, or the churned and frozen lava of ten thousand times ten million dead volcanoes. To even imagine a soil which of its own both harbors and produces life, and to think that I would soon be able to walk upon it, to smell it, hold it in my hands with the full knowledge that it was everywhere beneath me, the true *Earth Mother* of my ancestors—well that is but the barest beginnings of what I felt.

Bleak Winter? By the very gods and the tears that had begun to stream down from my eyes, the bleakest of winters on a world such as this would still be paradise to us of the colonies who had spent two thousand years in hell!

The scanner went in and down. And it was not my doing, though assuredly, had the controls been given me, it is exactly what I would have done. For I was an *historian* as well as Warlord. Indeed, the former was *the* prerequisite to being the latter. I knew what the readouts would say without my seeing them. They would but corroborate what every human of the colonies knew by rote. This planet was even more than Earth had been. Half again its size and with but two-thirds of its surface covered by water, it had twice the land mass of our ancient Terra. I knew what I saw. More. I felt it in my guts and in my soul, if such a thing could be. For here before me in all its pristine, unsullied beauty was our lost world.

The very last one that we, the last of humankind, had condemned to ghastly death!

This world was *Avalon!*

The minutes passed. In the meantime the *Scot's Leap* had actually entered atmosphere, had switched from ion to magline, anti-gravs. Even the descent was slowed—to deliberately allow me, or so I mused, to observe a particular continent which was fast swinging to the planet's night-side. Considering the planet's size, the continent was not all that big—two thousand by three thousand miles, perhaps. Great seas washed all its shores. The nearest land anywhere was at least two thousand miles away. It lay mostly in the temperate zones, was heavily forested, with a number of mountain chains, alluvial plains, great rivers and a series of lakes, all diamond blue in their purity.

It also had something that existed nowhere else. Here and there, though by no means in abundance, there was a town, or a village, or a startling craggy castle or great keep. This is not to say that the other areas were completely void of such. It is to say, however, that the villages, towns and castles on the continent were alive with *life*, whereas elsewhere they were but collapsed and moldering monuments to another time, long gone, long dead. For Avalon, too, as I well remembered, had had its catastrophe. The remnants were but stones on stones, great crumbled walls, fallen towers, strange and beautiful temples, invaded, choked with brush, gigantic trees and the endless writhing ropes of raging vines. . . . I saw monstrous animals, great lizards atop those destroyed walls and lichen-grown blocks of granite. Creatures quite alien, I'm sure, to the life that had once walked there.

We came in on a northwest tangent toward what appeared to be a blinking signal light. It was the only sign I'd seen so far of a modern service device. I marked its position in my memory as I'd been trained to do. Its beeps had also locked in on the readout scanner to give a series of diminishing distances; the last one being some sixteen hundred miles in round figures.

Three silver moons arose in the equatorial sky, the more brilliant for the fact that we were now on the night side. Each moon was but half the size of Earth's Luna. And all were within but two hundred thousand miles of the mother planet.

I watched in wonder.

And because of this, my hypnotic reverie, I saw only the flash of the massive energy bolt as it struck—*and not its origin!*

A great crackling touched all the hull of the *Scot's Leap*; an unleashed, metal-destabilizing blow of tremendous blue-white power. After that I had only the sense of a hurtling drive toward the primal black beneath us.

Then there was nothing.

I awoke to more stiffness than pain. I awoke, too, to cold air on my face; not freezing cold, just cold, like at fifty degrees. Odd. . . . Then I remembered. Laughed with relief. Two things were immediately obvious: 1) I was alive and on Avalon! 2) The air and its coldness was Avalon's, not the ship's.

Ahead, the entire bow was crushed. A large section to port had been torn away by granite boulders against which we'd hit, caromed, and hit again in the automatic's try for a landing. It was as if I looked through a picture window without a pane. The view was of a gently sloping grassy glade between two lines of granite outcroppings. Trees and underbrush were everywhere. Beyond the slope the upper boles of blue-green conifers were massively impressive.

The command swivel, with me in it, had been hurled against the rail of a bridge entry-ramp. Fortunately the "give" had been sufficient to halt my progress toward a lee-side bulk head, else I'd have been smashed to a bloody pulp against it. So, no broken bones, no lacerations. Just a lump on the left side of my head, a dull throbbing headache and one exceedingly bloodshot eye.

"All right!" I called to the entity whisperer. "Show yourself. What happens now?" No answer. There was only the wind in the trees; which in itself, to me, was fantastically wonderful. I sensed then; indeed, I *knew*, that for whatever reasons it was gone; that I was completely alone. I went to the control banks, began punching for manuals, readouts, power—anything.

Again, nothing; the same with the auxiliaries. I gave up. The *Scot's Leap* was dead.

Repairs? Perhaps in the minor areas, yes. But there could be none on the great hull, the converters and the like. That had forever been the problem of the colonies. For the creation of a starship's hull requires a massive engineering staff, computer banks the like of which only Earth possessed—and a planet with myriad minerals, space, and an unconscionable amount of air and water with which to work.

So "later" to the *Scot's Leap.* As of now I had but one priority. A blinker-light some sixteen hundred miles to the north was, hopefully, still blinking, *i.e.,* I'd apparently been chosen to be a part of something big. To quote a cliché: I had a date with destiny. . . . The voice had known *my* name; knew of me! Indeed, however impossible it seemed, the fact that in that far time I'd been one of those who'd voted a *no* proxy to Avalon's death had now made me prime material for Avalon's savior. I'd been chosen, apparently, as the Launcelot, or the Arthur to do the job. I wondered briefly how they'd done it— put names in a basket? Drew straws, perhaps?

To hell with it! *How* they'd done it was beside the point. The irrevocable bottom line was that I was here, and alive. Moreover, if *I* had made it to Avalon, however the means, it simply meant that there was a way—had always been a way—for others, too. But this last, of course, would only be possible now, if Avalon was saved.

I scavenged whatever I could from the suit. What I wore underneath was what I always wore when not wearing the suit. The standard woven half-boots, blue and pleasing to the eye; a light thermal undergarment, a body-suit, metallic, to turn the finest blade, hopefully—and a jacquarded, silken, full-sleeved tunic, reaching to just mid-thigh and string-tied at the throat with a bit of lace peeping from the edge. The tunic was standard Eden Valley, *golden.* It had my blazonry: a bright red dragon against the blue-white tail of a comet. This last, the dragon, had been traced, I think, by some ancestor of antiquity, from an old encyclopedic flag of a forgotten land of Terra.

My belt with its holstered blaster and laser around my waist, and with various miniaturized medi-pacs, mag-scanners, vites, power units and the like tucked in appropriate belt pockets, I then slung my kuri-sword in its gold-worked scabbard to its place across my back. I checked the gold coin contents of my belt-purse, too. Its weight was assuringly comfortable. A last thing was the salvaging of that small colony luxury, a tiny packet of super concentrated bath lotions, perfumes and such which, when you think about it, considering our circumstances, were in no way just a *luxury*. . . .

I then stepped over the buckled plates of the crumpled bridge to lower myself through twisted girders to the soil of *Avalon*. . . .

Would you believe that I could actually feel it as being *alive* beneath my feet? Well it was. And to me it will always be so.

The sharp bite of the morning air caused an exhilaration in all my body. Birds sang, insects hummed. I knew this because there they were, singing and humming and resembling the filmclips and artwork so treasured in our archives. I sang, too; whistled, even. Instead of thirty-eight, I felt like a boy of fifteen. Even Avalon's mass—despite its larger size it was still less than that of Earth—had conspired to elevate my mood. I could step higher and livelier.

The glade ended at the edge of a small cliff with a hundred-foot drop. Scrambling down it, I found the ground to again be grassy but more profuse with flora of every kind. I smelled water, too—and heard it before I ever reached it. But a short distance across what seemed as a cart path, I found it to be a sparkling stream just a few feet deep in some places and as wide as twenty. Trees, wildflowers and undergrowth lined its banks.

I bent to drink, trembling at the prospect. The taste was ambrosia, nectar. I then lay flat, breathed deeply—and put my head beneath its surface. I looked around, saw fish and other living things staring back at me. I almost drowned with the euphoria of it, forgetting that I was not suited. My ensuing coughing spell over, I lay back to contemplate the effect of it all, forced myself to begin *now* to accept it rapidly; take things in stride. For there would be no time to fully savor or to experience each happening.

At the cart path again, I sat down with my back against the trunk of a large deciduous tree; this, after first loosing my sword against whatever animals might seek to attack me. In my scanning they'd seemed everywhere and in all shapes and sizes. Persei's heat touched me, warmed me; indeed, even my fantastic empathy with the life around me seemed like a soothing, warming blanket. I slept. Dozed is a better word. For though asleep, I was still a part of both worlds, with my subconscious active and alert to whatever might be coming down the path from either direction. . . . And down it something came, but only after an hour or so of peaceful, dozing slumber.

The sound that preceded its coming was akin to the trot of some four-footed beast, or beasts. It was accompanied by a humming, the kind a human would make since it had both tune and meter. Instantly wide-awake, I drew my legs to me so's to be able to rise quickly—and again loosed my sword.

They came into my small deer-meadow in single file. First the horse, for that's what I thought it was, and the human; for that's what I thought he was. I was wrong on both counts, though not completely. Three more horses trailed the first, except they weren't. For they had clawed pads, not hooves. More. As I would quickly learn, they were smart, as a Terran wolf had been smart; noble, too, and courageous. They also, when aroused, had the most vicious temper imaginable. I had occasion at a later date to thank the gods that they were not carnivores—else pity the established ecology.

Neither the lead horse—or *kaole*, as was its proper, Avalonian gen—nor its rider had expected me. Indeed, the kaole, a blue-black animal, raised instantly to its hind legs, clawed the air, spit wildly at me and rolled its blood-red eyes. All this while growling a vicious equine challenge.

The rider fought hard to keep his seat.

Since I'd made no move except to watch, the kaole soon quieted. The rider then nudged him forward to pull up before me, with the others strung out behind.

As the kaole was not a horse, neither was the rider a man in the truest sense. Dressed all in untanned leather, from boots to jerkin and excepting only a linsey-woolsey shirt, he was at best but four and one half feet tall. His torso was barrellike, his shoulders at least three feet across. Other than a portly paunch, there was no fat on him. Even his short legs were heavily muscled. So were his arms, but long and with great gnarled hands the like of which could rip a gold seam from a solid quartz block. His head matched his body. It was huge, stern-visaged, *scarred*, and with black hair, thick, smiling lips and the bluest, most penetrating eyes I had ever seen.

The eyes held to mine, smiling, amused. The smile reached to his lips exposing square teeth sufficient to crack any nut that nature could create. A brazen shield was slung across his back. One hand held to the kaole's reins, the other caressed the haft of a three-foot, double-bladed axe. . . .

"My lord," he called gently, honoring my blazonry, "you were upwind of my kaoles and therefore surprised them. And, too," he sniffed, grimaced, and shook his head, "You've a damnable musk there, sir, to boil a caaty's nose." He stared at my belt.

I'd just barely understood him. Indeed, I'd expected it would be that way. His words had been strongly accented, as was the idiom of his dialect. Two thousand years could easily have created a linguistic babel among the remnants of the colonists we had known to be on Avalon.

I glanced down. Sure enough, a phial of something had broken. I'd not noticed it for the simple reason of the new smells around me. I removed it from its case—it was the size of a very small pencil—and gave it to him.

And smiled. . . .

As odd as he seemed to me, I doubted not but that I seemed the same to him.

At a height of six-feet and a weight of a hundred and eighty pounds, I hadn't an ounce of fat on me either. And, what with gymnastics as a way of life for all colonists, to be pursued stubbornly until the day we died, I was as trim and fit as any athlete in his prime. More. *His* face seemed seldom touched by the sun. *Mine*, on the other hand, was a space-burnt brown; my body the same. The domes of our fortressed Eden Valley were crystalline, allowing for the passage of ultraviolet, infrared and the like; each in its proper, Terran, proportion. As a rule we went about our business with clothing, or with a simple loincloth.

To touch off this mahogany coloring, I'd a veritable mane of red-gold hair and the famed emerald-green eyes that only Drusus Base produces.

Indeed, he was as startled as I was.

He glanced at the phial. "What shall I do with it?"

I shrugged, nodding toward the stream.

"Nay, lord." He frowned. "I doubt the fishees would survive." He produced a linen kerchief, wrapped the vial in it and thrust it into a leather pouch. His right hand returned deliberately to the haft of his axe.

I arose slowly, stood straight up. At no time had I made any move toward my weapons. If I had, and with *intent* to use them, he'd have been a dead man. But he didn't know this and I'd had no reason to prove it.

Following my eyes with his own, he laughed, shrugged and held out his hand to me. "One hardly knows just whom he'll meet in the deep woods; especially on the roads. Allow me, my lord. I am Hulok Terwydd, master stonecutter, at your service." He bowed his head in simple courtesy and I shook the out-held hand.

"And I am Jarn Tybalt, a lord of our southern isles, come north to see the world," I told him. I'd spaced my words slowly, enunciating each syllable so that the span of years would not make them too gibberishlike to his ears.

Hulok Terwydd looked around, at the empty cart path, the deep and somber woods, and at myself, standing alone and without so much as a backpack. "To see the world?" He repeated my words. "I know not of your southern isles, sir. But 'tis plain that you're here in the middle of nowhere with neither retinue, mount, nor traveling gear. Nor," and he grinned widely again, "do you seem to care a fig that that's the case."

The kaoles, nervous at my strange word sounds, were pawing the ground and making strange whinnyings at each other.

I said, "Well now, my lord—"

He held up a hand. "Just wait," he said seriously, "and hear me out. First off, I'm not a lord. As stated, I'm but a master stonecutter. Second, since you seem never to have seen or heard of me, I, sir, am a *dwarf*. I am on my way to the seaport town of Vils, in this land of Sierwood. From there, comes spring, I'll take a ship north—to my homeland."

I couldn't help it. My eyes narrowed at his words. "Where, in the north, sir dwarf?"

"Why, to Olfin, of course, for that is our land. Surely you've heard of it?" He cocked his great head, his eyes gone suddenly flat.

"I have," I improvised. "It's just that you're here now, sir stonecutter, and Olfin's not that small. I meant—to what part of Olfin?"

"Did you now?" He laughed without humor. "Enough of talk. I've a spare mount as you can see. You can either journey with me to Vils, or just to the next inn—as you wish. What say you?"

"That I accept on one condition."

"Which is?"

"Why, that you allow me to pay the inn tab." I jingled my purse of colony gold. "And, too," I chanced, "I've heard, sir, that all dwarves are great eaters. Mayhap you'll give me the opportunity to prove that out. . . ."

"Against whom?"

"Why me, of course. Let not this slim waist fool you. I've a way with pastries and such as to frighten any innkeeper."

The humor returned to his eyes. He put out his hand again and I shook it. He said, "Done, my lord. But let us be off for we've a full eight hours to ride."

He whistled the spare mount to him, removed what seemed to be a blanket roll from its saddle, then ordered it to me. A large, roan-colored stud, it whinnied and eyed me meanly for the alien it knew I was. But I, having a certain familiarity with telepathy, made haste to project a calming feeling of *goodness*. I then took a deep breath and leaped aboard under Hulok's scrutiny.

Within minutes, and highly pleased with myself, I was riding the kaole as if I'd been born to the saddle. Hulok, for whatever reason, but shook his head and sighed.

We rode for hours, stopping only for food, which my companion shared without question. It was a heavy, grainy bread, with cheese. He also had a large skin of wine, similar, but far better than that which we of the colonies have made for generations from our hydroponic fruits and such. The taste was akin to Avalon's water. Delicious. I reveled in the very freshness of it, the *life* within it. I savored it, actually, in a way to again cause Hulok to shake his head in pleased puzzlement.

While we ate, I learned a number of things: that my dwarf was as close-mouthed as myself; that he'd been supervising an engineering project, the building of a large, decorative stone bridge for the moat of the castle of some great southern lord; that he was overly cautious of me to a point of not questioning me at all.

The forest was conducive to silence anyway. We forded the stream three times in its meanderings. Once I saw a nightmare beast. Its fangs and claws dripped blood. It was feasting. It saw us too, but stayed beneath its tree. Hulok's hand had strayed again to his axe haft.

Two

Night was fast falling when we arrived at the inn; a chilling rain had begun, too. Made of tree logs, it had a large common room, a combo dining and sleeping room for special guests, a number of upstairs sleeping cubicles, plus an additional large room for the innkeeper's family and built on hovels for servants, ostlers and the like. Our mounts were stabled in a great lofty outbuilding. A stubbled, harvested field was to the rear, extending to a bluff, beyond which, by the sound, there was a much larger stream than the one we had followed; or maybe it was the same one, just grown in size.

Upon our entering, the door to the special room had been quickly closed, but not before we'd seen four lords or knights taking food and drink in a far corner.

A few peasant types were in the main room nursing their purchase of the night, a tankard of thin ale, as peasants are wont to do, or so I have read. Traveler-guests besides ourselves were a silent merchant and his two sons. They doffed their caps as we entered, as did the woodsy peasants. Their seeming awe of Hulok, though suggesting honest respect, also betrayed a certain fear. The same applied to me, too. For I immediately became something to stare at, to wonder about. No one, however, chose to speak to us.

Seeing them all, my first Avalonian humans, descendants of those engineers and workers of the Anglo-Celtic Development Company, the discoverers of Avalon, I was strongly aware of a difference between us. Other than the innkeeper's slender daughter, all else at the hostel, males and females, tended toward stoutness if not obeseness. Moreover, they had a certain unhealthy, unwashed smell about them. There were none such in the colonies. Food there, though substantial and with all the proper balances of vitamins, minerals, protein and the like, was never wasted. To us obesity and ill-health went hand-in-hand. . . . It was also *ugly*!

Forestalling any attempt by Hulok to pay, I'd quick approached the innkeeper while bouncing my fat purse from hand to hand. That worthy, he appeared as a bold and hearty man, appropriately judged its contents in midair—and made instantly to welcome us.

"Sir," I asked, while he bit the first small gold piece I'd given him for our bill, "I've also lost my cloak. I need another, for the weather. Perhaps you've one that someone's left as pay, or maybe one of your own that could fit my needs. . . ."

He did, a furred beauty, for which Hulok took me aside to whisper hoarsely that I should pay but one more coin, no more; this, since Hulok's eye was also quite good at the figurative weighing of such. In his enthusiasm Hulok actually snatched my bag and peered into it, exclaiming upon the purity of the pieces and the perfection of the minted edges. He then slapped my back in a new expansive camaraderie. Dwarves, I was to find, have a healthy respect for money and for those who possess it. In the end the innkeeper was no match for Hulok. The cloak became mine for the single coin—along with a fur cap with a bright red feather.

I'd guessed right as to Hulok's love for the table. Indeed, when we'd finally sat down at the very end of a huge but empty board for eight, he'd almost immediately gobbled up a full loaf of grainy bread before ever the entree was served. He'd sopped it in his wine bowl, the better to hasten its passage—and dared me to do the same. He knew very well that my suggestion for an eating bout had been but a friendly gesture. Still, the idea had apparently so pleased him—for it did afford an opportunity for blameless gluttony—that he felt bound to hold me to it.

The landlord's daughter, young, beauteous and smelling of heather, brought in the huge bowl of steaming stew. She gasped prettily as she put it down—and deliberately leaned the full weight of her slender body, belly and breasts, against my back. That she was attracted to my muscular slimness, I had no doubt; nor did I discourage her. Indeed, I welcomed the chance for such intimacy so soon. It was one way, I knew, to get to know the country.

On Drusus, though I'd had my share of liaisons across the years and between raids and "wars," I'd never *paired*; legitimized a union, as it were. Indeed, I'd found nobody in our limited population with whom I'd wanted to. Besides, I'd continually told myself, there was always time. . . .

Hulok worked on his second bowl while I was still on my first—my tastebuds were already drunk with the alien condiments of that tastiest of stews. The breasts of the innkeeper's daughter again touched my shoulder as she leaned to refill our bowls with the pungent wine. For the briefest of seconds she breathed heavily in my ear. I, in silent response, seized a rounded forearm and ran my lips along its length. Then, as a courtesy to mine and Hulok's "game," I refilled my stew bowl with a mountain of the stuff. . . .

It was just then, I think, and though unbeknownst to us, that the inn door opened silently, allowing the entry of three knights in hauberk and plate, a robed priest and two ladies in traveling gear; the first, blonde, beautiful and pale as a fresh-drawn corpse; the other, black-haired, blue-eyed, slender and with an apparent haughty contempt for the inn and everything in it. A last member of the party, a dark-visaged lord, tall, heavily muscled and garbed in a jacquarded silk cloak over surcoat and hauberk, looked fiercely around him.

The priest called out, and so announced their presence to us. He was old and had a thin voice to point up a pale and bloodless face. "Sir innkeeper," he announced, "we've need of this place for the night. I speak for the Baron Hordee Dagar of Weils, his wife, Jocydyn, and her sister, the Princess Meagan Anne. We'll need your common room now. Whatever you have above must be cleared as well. Do you understand me, sir? Our men-at-arms are already in your barn."

The innkeeper, aghast at the highness of such guests, could barely murmur in fear. "Aye, Lords. 'Twill be as you say."

He immediately cast a hard eye toward the shivering peasants to send them pell mell through the still opened door and into the rain. A muttered word to the merchant and his sons sent them hurrying for their gear, and then out the rear door to the barn. The baron then hissed a question. The innkeeper nodded toward the closed special-room door in answer. He made then as if to move away, but the baron—he now stood with the two ladies, holding his hands to the fire—roared out: "Hold! We'll have meat, bread and wine, and *now*, sir! And the wine's to be heated!"

The innkeeper hurried to order his lackeys back to work in the kitchens. I, in the meantime, had finished my second bowl and filled a third. Hulok was working on his *sixth*. And, too, somewhat euphoric on the wine I'd already drunk, I'd ordered up a third jug while gratuitously proclaiming Hulok as the winner of our game. The wine brought by a trembling lackey, I seized the innkeeper's lissome daughter around the waist and begged her to drink with us.

She fell deliberately, but oh, so softly into my lap.

Hulok, unaware, or uncaring of the "play within a play," as suggested by the baron's arrival, had fallen to licking the grease from a particularly large chunk of meat before popping it into his mouth. He then refilled his stew bowl and went to work, despite the fact that I'd conceded and leaned to whisper hoarsely: "If you've a desire for pleasure, my lord, why say the word. I'll spend an hour or two just here—with that." He gestured toward the wine and the remnants of the still steaming pot.

"I'll think on it," I murmured. "Still, I'd best retire when you do. For I, too, will be going on to Vils. We'll be rising early, right?"

Hulok smiled an avuncular smile above his well-filled bowl, saying, "Right on both counts, my lord. And you're certainly most welcome."

I arose shakily, bringing the clinging, nuzzling daughter with me. The movement caught the eye of the baron who, squinting through the wavering light, cried, "Hey, now! There's a dwarf fellow!"

The others, staring, said nothing.

The innkeeper, hurrying to us, groaned as he saw his daughter put her red lips to my throat. A pretty cameo. "My lords," he began—but choked in horror as my doughty Hulok downed the dregs of a last cup and started a lazy umpteenth spooning of more stew from the pot to his platter. "You heard the priest," the innkeeper continued fiercely. " 'Tis the baron's wish that the inn be cleared."

"And I, sir, am a dwarf." Hulok answered for all to hear. *And he wasn't drunk.* "What applies to others, innkeeper, does not apply to me. I am protected by the code."

"Are you a true dwarf, sir?" the priest called.

"Would you measure me, father?" Hulok called back.

The three knights laughed coarsely and moved to confer

with the baron, who asked loudly, "Well what of your companion, Sir Dwarf? He seems, indeed, as tall as me."

"*You* said it," Hulok laughed. "That's what he is, my companion, and therefore protected, too. For the code reads: Dwarves and all members of their households are beyond the laws of Sierwood, Weils, Lothellian and the lands beyond— unto the ends of the world itself. . . . Your health, my lord Baron." He smacked his greasy lips and raised his cup.

"By the gods!" Dagar roared, sensing an insult.

"Nay, nay." Princess Meagan Anne called in a small but clear voice. "Our little man speaks like a statesman. So let him be. Still—" and she narrowed her blue eyes to stare through the poor light of the tapers and directly into my own—"I do suggest, dwarf, that you leave now for your sleeping quarters, lest your lubricious 'companion' offend myself and my sister with his rutting lust." She then laughed contemptuously and turned her pretty back on us.

Damn! I would not have had it so. For with that one glance, she'd effectively knocked me full off balance. A thing I'd not experienced since I was fourteen, and with a girl who'd later been killed in one of the myriad raids.

Hulok, prompted less by what she'd said than by a thing he seemed suddenly to remember, arose abruptly, seized the jug of mulled wine and said *sotto voce* to me, "Let's go. The less we've to do with the problems of lords, the better. Lead on!" he told the innkeeper. "And see that we're not disturbed. We'll leave at cock's crow."

I followed after. The girl still clung to me. But more sober now, I whispered, "No. Another time," and put her off. Still I was overheard. We'd had to pass the baron's group to get to the stairs. One of the knights, but a few feet away, said abruptly, "Here. I'll take the whore."

He reached for her.

She cringed, paled, and looked at me.

I'd no choice. A brawl was the last thing I wanted. I told him softly, "Nay, sir. She's not for you either. And she's *not* a whore."

"By the gods, you'd interfere?" He stepped forward, a hand on his belt dagger.

I raised my two hands, palms flat, for attack or defense, and looked toward the baron, who, not wanting trouble for reasons of his own, hissed angrily, "Desist, Arrin. We've more important things to do this night."

But Arrin, dagger drawn, simply laughed and lunged; upon which I seized his wrist, pulled him *by* me, whirled him and hit him a lightning blow just below the nose; this, with the hard edge of my palm.

He screamed. Blood gushed from both his nose and mouth. His eyes crossed and he fell. Actually, he'd been quite lucky. For if I'd not "pulled" the blow, it surely would have killed him. Two things happened then. Seizing the moment, I yelled to that black-haired haughty princess who'd watched it all. "*I* think you could use a serving girl, my lady. She'll at least be safe with you."

Her eyes narrowed, then softened. A smile touched her lips. She called sharply, and beckoned: "Come with me, girl, and leave *all* whoremongers to their stupid games."

The second thing was that hearing the scream, those knights in the special room opened the door, looked, caught a glance and a negative shake of the head from the Baron—and closed it again. The Baron, turning, had caught Hulock staring straight at them.

The daughter safe, the innkeeper thanked me as we climbed the stairs, telling us, too, that the baron was here no doubt for the harvest fair at Tag-Afran town. "I suppose," he grunted—the stairs had that effect on him—"that that's where you'll be going."

I asked, "To *where?*"

"Why, to the yearly fair of the Lord Oldus Finley at Tag-Afran. It runs for three days. Tomorrow's the last."

I looked to Hulok, who said nothing. Whatever he'd remembered had deflated him completely. The surfeit of food and wine, too, had reached him. In our room, the innkeeper lit a pair of candle stubs and withdrew. I slammed the double door-bolts shut.

"So what do you think, dwarf?" I pressed Hulok. "I'll surely go with you to Vils, but this fair seems interesting."

He groaned, held tight to the wine jug and threw himself upon the nearest rusk-filled mattress. Looking up at me, he gasped, "If you've seen one fair, my lord of the Southern Isles, well you've seen 'em all. Now go to sleep."

I tried to take the jug from him, fearful that he'd break it and perhaps hurt himself on the shards. But no way! I gave up, doused the candles and laid back upon my pillow.

The *whispering* began in some hidden part of my sleeping mind; for I swear that I heard it first as nightmare, a moaning intrusive crying to plague what might have been the soundest sleep I'd ever known. Again, as to description, I can compare it only to the mouthings of that ghost of the dead king in his ancient land of Denmark.

Unlike the final moments before my entering the *Scot's Leap*, however, it was now just gibbering insanity. No part made any sense. But it did awaken me so that I knew that it was not just in my head. Indeed, it was here; *in the far corner of the room no less*! Wraithlike and all limned by silver moonlight, it was tall, so much so that even crouched on shadowy knees its head and shoulders were necessarily bent forward to avoid the beams. In life—if it had ever lived—it would be nine feet in height.

It wrung its hands and even seemed to threaten me. The floor-planks vibrated to its crying. On Drusus, when I'd heard it, I'd felt no fear. *Now I felt fear to the very marrow of my bones!* The rain had stopped, thus the moonlight. Indeed, one of Avalon's three fat moons peeped through our single window. I wondered. Didn't the thing know that I knew it had come to Drusus to fetch me to do a job which it could not do—to destroy that damned C.T. warhead before it obliterated the last hope of all mankind? Did it perhaps think that *I* had destroyed the *Scot's Leap*?

In the minutes on Drusus, I'd come to feel at ease with it. Now, it was something else. I sensed; indeed, in my very guts I knew it would seize me if it could. Why the change? On second thought, since I'd heard only a voice before and seen nothing, was this then the same thing that had sent the *Scot's Leap* to Drusus?

Dammm! I felt for the tape belt stud. This time I'd get him!

I arose from my mattress to point a finger at it and say firmly, "Speak to me, and clearly. For I'll not have your damn mewlings disturb my dreams a second longer. Say what it is that you've come to say, and go. And know before you threaten that it was not me who destroyed the Argos."

Then, from the main room below, I heard the sounds of an argument to even drown out the creature's moanings. At one point I heard swords drawn and even a clash of blades that died almost as soon as it began. The argument continued. The baron's bellow, the thin voice of the holy man; his title was more vicar than priest, and the sound of a woman crying, plus the voices of the knights. And then, above it all, I heard the haughty tones of the princess, accusing, demanding!

My eyes, in the meantime, had never left the thing. Now, it grew more wraithlike as its mewlings and cryings lessened. To hell with it! I reached for Hulok's wine jug and tipped it to my mouth. It was empty, as I should have known it would be. Angered, I threw it at the wraith; saw it pass through the ephemious substance and shatter against the door frame.

I took a chance and glanced to where Hulok lay. He was no longer sleeping. Indeed, he sat flat up against the wall, his expression stone-cold sober. I lit the candles. The *whisperer* then disappeared altogether.

From below came a crash, as if a chair or some other article of furniture had been hurled across the room. Then a loud female oath. Meagan's? It must have been, for I then heard her shout in unbridled hatred: "Damn you to hell, my lord! Try it again you bastard and I'll have your stinking heart, whatever my sister's fate!"

The words were punctuated by masculine laughter from more than one voice. Then nothing.

I looked to Hulok. He hadn't moved.

Our eyes met. I said bluntly, "Well now, stonecutter, I find this world to be more interesting by the minute."

He said, "I agree, my lord. And I'd thought that I'd seen everything." He then laid down again, turned his back to me and was soon sleeping.

I doused the candles. But this time sleep was slow to come. I was plagued with thoughts of what might have happened to my fleet of floaters; whether my happy Lieutenant Kardis had survived; whether Commander Donnert had been shot down by Telles in his attempt to seize Drusus' Base H.Q., and if so, what had then happened to my six hundred comrades in Eden Valley. . . .

I wondered too, about what had happened here tonight, and whether some kind of extraordinary scenario was even now developing, with the blinker light, the oncoming CT warhead—and the phantom whisperer who'd been so unlike the original. Could it just be, I mused, that Avalon's ubiquitous elder gods had simply painted me into the scene as Devil's advocate?

Then a faint tapping came at the door. I drew my sword and padded softly over. . . . It was Gwladys, the innkeeper's daughter (I'd finally learned her name), clothed in a simple shift. I took her in my arms to stop her trembling, kissed her, patted her so soft buttocks, and attempted to send her away again. But she was insistent and so we retired to my mattress and lazily, sleepily made love. When I awoke the rain had returned and she had gone—leaving a disturbing smell of heather and wild roses.

Three

We set out before sunup, with but a bowl of mush and a stirrup cup of hot spiced ale to see us off. The rain persisted. Which was all right with me. Indeed, just to experience it, to smell it, taste it, participate in the very fact of its being was a sheer delight. Moreover, like the artificial fibers of the rest of my garments, the fur cloak I had purchased also shed water. Its warmth was a tactile pleasure.

Hulok, preoccupied with hidden thoughts, rode silently, which was all right, too. I'd deliberately refrained from mentioning the *whisperer* to him, hoping he'd bring it up himself in his own time. And so I rode, relaxed and with a feeling of well being. . . .

But not for long. An hour or so along the cart-path my reverie was interrupted by an on-and-off subliminal pic inside my head of an awesome red-eyed beast with fangs and claws sufficient to rip a kaole from tail to thumping heart. More! In my mind's cye, I literally saw it crouch to leap. And I knew, in the act of seeing, that it was to my rear and on the fifteen-foot bluff to my right, The thing was *real*! And it had chosen my kaole, thinking, perhaps because of my furred cloak, that I was a part of the animal.

In sheer reflex, I'd already drawn my kuri-blade. I now turned hard in the saddle—and swept the blade in one lightning blow to catch it in midair! I halved it; this, though its girth was twice that of a man. The two parts fell to the road, to be leapt upon in turn by the maddened kaoles. They killed it three times over, my first introduction to both their courage and ferocity.

I couldn't believe it. To know where it would be before it got there? That, indeed, was a new experience. With a cloth from my scabbard I cleansed the length of the shining blade and returned it to its home. The kaoles, their muzzles and clawed pads bloodied by the work they'd done, looked to me and actually bowed, a sign, apparently, of respect in shared victory. I nodded back, as was expected, I'm sure.

Only then did I glance toward Hulok. He was grinning, leaning on his saddle horn. His blue eyes were shining. His shield was on his arm; his axe held firmly, a thong from its handle wrapped tightly around his wrist for added purchase.

"Well done, oh lord who speaks to whisperers." He raised an eyebrow. "Tell me, since you seemed as startled as no doubt the beast was startled when you hewed it asunder—what did you see immediately before?"

"Why, I saw *it*," I replied honestly. "How did you know?"

"How could I not know? You obviously have the power."

"Oh? If I do, then tell me of it."

Testing me deliberately, he insinuated, "Merlin's Eyes? The *Whatzit*?"

I shrugged and shook my head.

"You've never heard of the Whatzit?"

"No, sir stoneshaper, I have not."

He chucked his Kaole into a slow trot again. I joined him. The others dutifully brought up the rear. . . . He explained curiously, "Yesterday, when I took the blanket roll from Huchlan—that's your mount, lord—didn't you know why?"

"No to that too. Get to it, Hulok, what's the power?"

He grinned and pointed to what seemed like a leather canteen dangling from the saddlehorn of his own steed. *"That,"* he said, "is the blanketroll of yesterday."

I waited, for I truly had nothing to say.

"That is the Whatzit, my lord," he confided, "Merlin's Eyes."

I continued to wait.

He looked at me keenly. "You truly don't know, do you?"

I laughed. "No I don't. But I'll be eternally grateful when you tell me."

"It's a living thing, Lord Tybalt," Hulok said solemnly. "It can change to anything it wants to, within the logic of its size. 'Tis like the changeling lizard one sees at fairs, except more so. This last, because it can tell of danger inside the head of *he* who has the *power*. 'Twas the whatzit, my lord, that warned us of the great caati."

"I see," I grunted, careful not to tell him what it was I

saw. . . . I quick shot a mental probe at the Whatzit. Nothing. Who knows? Perhaps it was asleep.

"Where," I asked, "did you get it?"

"It likes coarse sugar, can even live on it. Most dwarves have one, for only we among humans have the power. They seem to like us, to search us out. It's the only way to have a Whatzit, my lord. *They* must choose you. You can't choose them because you wouldn't know one if you saw it—except, perhaps in its original form, which it seldom uses."

Curious, I asked, "And how long have you had yours?"

"For many years." He was noncommittal.

"What is its original form?"

He frowned. "Nay, Lord. 'Twould be unfair."

"To whom?"

"Why to the Whatzit, of course."

But at that very moment the canteen and stopper became a round little puffball the size of a large bladder. It had six pseudopodal feet, a tiny pink nose and ears, and big blue eyes. The form held for at least two minutes while it looked straight at me. Then suddenly it was a canteen again.

Hulok could only stutter. "Well, now. For whatever reason, you've been honored. Few indeed are those who've seen Merlin's Eyes."

"Why do you call it that?"

"Merlin was a great wizard of the old world. 'Tis said that he, too, had a Whatzit. . . ."

"I've never heard of him."

"So, my lord? There are, without a doubt, a lot of things you've never heard of—in the world, that is."

"Quite true. Such as the thing of last night," I suggested boldly. "Tell me of *that*."

He chuckled. "Hey, now. I thought that you'd tell me. For it moaned at you, sir, if I recall correctly."

"Agreed," I confessed. "But still *I* know nothing of it, whereas you—well I doubt me not, sir dwarf, that you could tell me a thing or two."

He sighed, shrugged. "They are the ghosts of the 'old ones.' We see them only in the great ruins at night. And of course," he eyed me slyly, "no one in his right mind goes *there*, at *night*."

And he would say no more.

Nor would I have had the time to listen if he did. For it was just then that we heard a great clopping of Kaole paws, all coming in our direction. A glance at Hulok's eyes and I knew without asking that it was the Baron Dagar and his entourage, making up for lost time. I pulled quickly to the lee of the bluff—the narrow cart path at this point sloped off to our left some forty feet to the fast-flowing stream below—yelling, "Line the mounts here, lest we be run down by those fools of last night."

"Aye," he answered. "But hear me. If they seek a quarrel—and I'm bound to think they might—why let it be with me. Do you understand, sir? Do not allow *yourself* to be involved. . . ."

"Do you know something I don't?"

He grinned, showed all his square white teeth. "Mayhap I'm only guessing. Still, I am what I am, and if they press me, then they'll rue it. And that's a fact." His brow went suddenly black as a thundercloud.

Hearing the rush of steeds coming at them, our kaoles were understandably nervous. We fought to keep them where they were. And around the bend they came, two abreast on a path with a width of but fifteen feet from where we were to where it fell off to the stream below.

No matter the rain or the puddles; no matter anything. Four young sergeants led them, then the fifty men-at-arms—all roaring in glee as they saw us, while literally drenching us with the splatter of mud and water from the great paws of their mounts. . . .

The Baron Dagar himself brought up the rear; this, with his knights, the skinny priest, his wife the lady Jocydyn Tremaine and her sister, the lithe and arrogant Meagan Anne. Holding back from the end of the main body, Dagar was thus able to see us before he arrived at where we were. When he did, however, he broke instantly into a fit of insensitive laughter, grabbing his sides and pointing at our mud-drenched, bespattered state. We were almost, but not quite, unrecognizable beneath the muck.

He caused his mount to rear, yelling out as if in surprise: "Why! 'Tis the dwarf fellow and his strange companion. See? No mind the mud. You can tell 'tis him by the half-size legs and the bloated gut. Ho! *Sadan's imp!* Speak up! Why are you here, sir? I'd thought dwarves to be cunning; smart enough to flee the road when their masters rode the wind."

Hulok, wiping stoically at his face with a bit of pocket cloth, replied calmly, "Why the insults, Sir Baron? There's no call for such childishness. 'Tis beneath your honor, sir. Indeed I'd say you've forgotten the rules and decencies of office."

The red came up out of Dagar's neck like a flood. His dark eyes bulged. He leaned across his saddle to shout, "Shut your mouth, devil's spawn. One does not lecture a master thusly. You go too far."

Hulok then deliberately hawked and spat, to show that he could do it. He studied the faces of the baron and his knights and said flatly, "That's three times you've referred to a mastery of me. I repeat, sir, that it's long been agreed by code guardians that dwarves have no masters—and most certainly none from Weils. . . ."

There was a hiss of indrawn breath from the gathering men-at-arms, and a subsequent chorus of mutterings. Hulok, I perceived, had apparently, if not deliberately, thrown down a gauntlet of some kind which Dagar would be forced to acknowledge.

The great Lord of Weils, white-faced and trembling in rage, cried out, "All right, you misshapen bastard, you'll have your chance. . . . Horvil!" He called. A man-at-arms then came forcing his way from up the line. He was huge, a half-foot taller than myself. His body was massively muscled. His beady black eyes beneath a single eyebrow across his forehead, suggested an animal cunning, if not intelligence.

"I'm here, my lord," he called out.

"You've a challenger. What say you?"

The beast-man simply grinned, hauled a great two-handed sword from off his back, tossed it, caught it—and rode straight toward me and my doughty half-man.

But the skinny priest called out, "Nay, nay! Unfair! The dwarf is the challenged. *He* has the right, therefore, to choose weapons, ground rules and site."

Hulok roared instantly, "A'foot! And on grass. And let him use what weapons he prefers, as I'll use mine. As for challenges, were I to make one, 'twould be with the master, not the man."

"DAAAMMMM, you!" Dagar roared again. He stood high in his stirrups. "Find me a clearing! We'll see this business through, right *now!*"

In but a few seconds the word came back that there was a

clearing just a hundred yards or so ahead. We all rode toward it. Not liking one bit what was happening, and aside from the fact that I now considered Hulok my friend, I also needed him. A chord of empathy had been struck between us. I suspected that even the blinker light could perhaps be discussed with him. I did not *want* to lose him!

"Friend," I whispered, as we rode. "You've addressed me as Lord, for which I thank you. Still, avoiding titles, I am a swordsman, among other things; perhaps the best in all my land. Allow me then to take on this small task for you, for I deem it that even your prowess (I thought to stroke him a bit) can scarce succeed with this man-mountain. What say you, Hulok? 'Twill be my pleasure."

He looked up at me, his great blue eyes all shining with a nova's glow. His smile cracked his face from ear to ear. He said, "By the gods, Lord Tybalt, you've spoken words which I've not heard from any *man* in all my life. I'll remember your offer. You can count on it. But do not fear for me, sir. I've a few tricks to part this idiot from his entrails, and that's a fact. Would it were Dagar. Whatever. Again I thank you. Just watch our mounts and the pack kaoles, for I trust no one who would follow this Weilsian bastard."

"A question."

"Be quick then."

"You expected this. Were you forewarned?"

"Nay. As stated, I guessed it. Last night, in the special room. Those knights there were of Sierwood, not of Weils. 'Twas a meeting, sir, between them and Dagar; and a clandestine one at that, else why the secrecy? Then, when we passed to go upstairs and that fellow screamed when you hit him—well, the door opened. It was not so much that I saw them, but rather that Dagar *saw* me see them. He saw that I recognized them. . . . What I truly expected this morning was an ambush . . ."

"Hulok. You must tell me—*why*."

"Nay, my lord. It's too late. I'm sorry. But don't worry. I *will* survive."

At the meadow Hulok asked for but one thing from the priest—that he be allowed a dip in the stream to get the mud off. I joined him; even dunked my cloak which, as stated, was water-repellent, as were all my other garments. But the mud was something else. Cavorting naked in the ice-cold water was another experience, enjoyed by me, and I think, the princess, too. Hulok then dressed with dry garments from his pack— and stood forth to take on Dagar's Horvel.

The meadow a small one, was made smaller still by the close ring of men-at-arms and knights who pressed in on them. Still, it was sufficient for the job.

Horvel stood a full six-foot-six, and without an ounce of fat on him. He weighed some two hundred and fifty pounds. He wore hauberk, plates and helm. His weapons were a sword and shield. At Dagar's signal they moved stoically to stand about ten feet from each other; this, in an awesome pall of silence. The rain had lessened, fortunately. There would be some purchase on the grass. A sergeant then blew a single blast on a hunting or battle horn; and again at Dagar's signal.

For what seemed an interminable length of time neither contestant so much as moved a muscle. Then the Weilsian, with a battle roar, rushed upon Hulok, who'd been quietly studying him as a woodsman would a tree. Horvel's left arm was to the fore with a rounded shield; his sword arm raised on an angle with his shoulder. With his shield he sought to beat our halfling to the ground where he could then be chopped asunder. Hulok withstood the onslaught, attacked shield with shield. The resultant unearthly clang reverberated through all that river valley. No headway made, Horvel paused, attacked again.

This time his sword wove a devilish pattern of blued steel around Hulok's squat figure. But all blows were caught and turned. More. Hulok retreated but three paces, dropped to one knee and, protected by his own shield, rose suddenly beneath a mighty blow to catch the Weilsian square in the belly—and hurled him over his head!

Hulok then arose, spun and crouched with the agility of a kitten. But Horvel, too, was agile. He sprang instantly to his feet, sword poised, shield covering, *to fend the first screaming slash of Hulok's scammersaxe!*

And the sound was exactly that. For near the haft of each of the axe's blades was a series of holes which caused it to whistle and hum when Hulok whirled it through his intricate patterns of attack and defense. Now he caught Horvel's shield in dead center, split it, drove it in on the arm and crushed that too. Catching Horvel's massive counterblow upon his own shield, he crouched—then savagely and with terrible strength to sweep the axe around in one great glittering arc, to take both Horvel's legs below the knees!

His blow was so swift, the blade of the axe so sharp, that Horvel did not fall; stood there instead on his bloodied stumps and on a new eye level with our dwarf. The Weilsian's mouth opened, strained wide. He roared his pain and fear. For he saw his death and he wasn't ready for it.

A ghastly silence settled upon all of us while we stared, wide-eyed, scarcely breathing. The dripping scammersaxe whirled again, once, twice . . . Then Hulok paused before that quartered, blood-spurting, screaming corpse-man, to gaze solemnly, and to then leisurely, but deliberately, take the head with one last sweep.

So died Horvel, the champion of Baron Hardee Dagar of Weils, a swordsman, one might add, who never knew what hit him.

A rapt silence followed wherein Hulok simply nodded his satisfaction toward Dagar, sheathed his bloodied axe and returned to where I waited with the mounts and gear. I, being somewhat familiar with Dagar's kind, was ready for anything—even to a use of my colony weapons if I had to.

Dagar, still white-faced, ordered his men back to the road. The priest had already accompanied wife Jocydyn there. She'd left in horror at the killing. Then the baron, his poise gone, directed his attention to me, shouting, "And what of you, sir? You wear a weapon of high birth, the *sword*. If you rightly own it, then 'twas your duty to halt my men till I came up. If you'd done so there would have been no trouble and none of *this* would have happened."

I stared straight at him, flat-eyed—and said nothing.

He rose again in his stirrups. "By the gods, you'll answer me. You've blazonry on your chest, and you're bound to tell me who you are right here and now."

I continued silent, hoping that he'd get tired of blustering and leave. To engage him in argument could only lead to trouble.

Hulok, swinging into his saddle, began the round-up of the two browsing pack animals.

Then Meagan Anne intervened. She'd been watching me, too. The revealed glory of my furs, drip-dry surcoat and body tan had caught her eye before. The color of my eyes and hair did so now. "By the gods," she blurted in surprise, "this brave dwarf's companion has the very eyes of a *Sadan*. Speak up, sir companion, or lord, as the case may be. Answer our Lord of Weils before he becomes ridiculous—or has the pictil got your tongue?"

Her jibe at the baron and the fact that she'd driven her mount deliberately between myself and his lordship was an indication, I thought, of her intent. She would stop it once and for all by questioning me herself; this, in the hope that I'd have sense enough to say the right thing—whatever that was.

"Since you ask, my lady," I nodded in courtesy, "I am called Jarn Tybalt, *Warlord* of Eden Valley!"

Instant horror swept over all their faces, excepting Meagan's. They backed their mounts while making what looked like a Terran *tau* cross, an "x," upon their breasts. A glance toward Hulok showed him coming hurriedly toward me. His hand was on his axe haft, his eyes large in a worried face.

Lord Dagar, too, had seized the chance to withdraw, while shouting a last insult. "Blasphemer! Stay clear of Tag-Afran, both of you! Else by my soul, I'll have you quartered." He dashed off to join his lady. Two of the knights hung back, eyeing the lagging princess uneasily.

She simply scratched a dainty nose and stared at me with twinkling blue eyes. "You do have a sense of humor, my lord," she said. " 'Tis apparent. Either that, or you're abysmally stupid. Whatever. Were I you, green-eyes, I'd stay clear of Tag-Afran Castle. Believe him. Our Lord of Weils has sufficient skill and courage, despite his boasting, to carve your gizzard."

She then turned her mount in a graceful swirl of beast and woman, joined the knights and dashed off after Baron Dagar's train.

I smiled. I couldn't help it. For her words were assuredly more dare than warning. . . .

As we, too, came up onto the road again, I asked bluntly of Hulok, "What, sir dwarf, was *that* all about?"

Casting a pleading eye to the heavens, he grunted, "Jarn, my lord, your southern island must be far away, indeed, for you to have forgotten that *Eden* is the name given the deadlands by our ancestors before the unleashing of the death-magic. Those living in Lothellian, *or* Deadlands-Eden were then changed in form. Some to be like *myself*; the majority to be the moodan horrors and the sadans. Some even say that the Whatzits were born in this manner, but we dwarves believe differently."

I asked suddenly, "Tell me of the 'world,' Hulok, as you know of it. For 'tis obvious to you by now, I'm sure, that I know little of it."

Looking straight ahead and with never a question as to why I lacked knowledge, he told me. "The land you're in is the southernmost of the world," he began. "It is called Sierwood and is ruled by a hierarchy of nobles, among which the young Lord Oldus Finley is the first among equals. To the north, as stated, is Weils, the guardian of the Lothellian border and of the horror-hordes of moodans and sadans. Always a kingdom, gossip has it that its king is now imprisoned and its lord chancellor murdered. Moreover, the only son of the chancellor, a bastard, the young Shan Duglass, has disappeared. Perpetrators of this double deed of infamy are the barons of Weils, among them being, and again, the first among equals, the bastard that we've just been forced to deal with. Rumor says that they have done this so's to divide the kingdom between themselves. Their purpose, so *they* say, is that they may better fight the moodan hordes now gathering again upon the borders of Lothellian.

"Lothellian, of course, is the land of the moodans and sadans. Beyond it, the Deadlands. And beyond that just snow and ice."

Hulok fell silent, his history apparently completed.

I sighed. I had no choice. "Tell me of the moodans and sadans."

He couldn't help himself. He glanced at me from the corner of one eye and shook his head. "The moodans are the beastmen who came with the great magic. The sadans, the same, except they've been changed more in the head than in the body. The sadans lead the moodans—rule them. That is the gist of it."

I'd known when he'd first mentioned the Deadlands, the death-magic and the change in form of humans, that Earth's fate had in some way struck Avalon's original colony, too. The Deadlands were what they were—contaminated territory; the moodans and sadans—mutants.

"And where," I pressed softly, seeking to catch him off balance, "do you really come from, sir dwarf?"

His brow darkened, became a thundercloud above eyes that were now twin pools of darkness. His gnarled right hand—it seemed possessed of a life of its own—reached straight for his axe's pommel—and hovered there. He grated between clenched teeth. "You go too far, green-eyes. You know I'm a dwarf, for I've told you so, and events have proved this out. Yes! I *am* of the dark people; or of the *least accursed* as some define us, for we, too, were touched by the death-magic. My land is where I said it is, to the northeast of the Deadlands. It is a land free of moodans. sadans *and* lords!"

"And now, sir," he finished calmly while halting his mount and laying his hands on the reins of my own, *"You will tell me where you come from!"*

"All right," I said. "I will. But first, I must warn you that such knowledge could mean your death. Until now I have called you friend. After? Well who's to say? Do you wish to risk it, Dark One?"

"If you'll first tell me why there's a risk involved."

I breathed deeply. "Last night you thought it best to stay clear of the affairs of lords. Well allow me, sir: 'Tis a thousand times better to stay clear of the affairs of those who presume to rule the affairs of stars and worlds beyond number. Still, you deserve to know. What say you, *friend?*"

"All right. If the word *friend* means the same to both of us—then tell me." I could not help but note that the blue had come back to his eyes.

And so I told him, all of it. Of Drusus Base, of Eden Valley and the colonies. I explained, too, about the death of Earth and how the refuge of Avalon had been denied us all by some as yet unsolved mystery. I told him of the terrible council decision and the CT nova-warhead, and how even now it was coming to annihilate all his world unless I could somehow get to the blinker light and complete the task set me by Avalon's *whisperer* who'd brought me here aboard the now destroyed *Scot's Leap* to do just that.

"And so that's it," I finished. "I've just two months and a few days to reach that beacon. The answer to the problem of whether this world will live or die is precisely there—and I mean *all* this world, not just the chunk of it with which you're familiar."

I then leaned forward from my saddle to stare into his eyes

and say, "Hulok! Nothing must prevent me from accomplishing this deed. *Nothing!* Do you hear?"

"I hear," he said.

"Well then, I now frankly beg your aid, too. What say you, sir?"

He chucked the kaoles to trot forward again so as to conceal his hesitation by a need to watch the road, the clouds—these were fast disappearing—and the great forest, so that if a monster beast was near (and the whatzit was asleep), why we'd know it.

He shook his head finally to say, "My lord, I'll help you, of course. I promise it. But even if 'tis true, what you say, then by your own words we've already lost. . . . By sea, in winter, the trip's impossible. No ship ever built could withstand even the smallest of our *winter* storms. By land—well, one must go through Lothellian and the Deadlands. We'd have to literally cut our way through a thousand times ten thousand horrors. Forget it, Sir *Warlord*. Our battle's lost before ever we begin."

"Just like that?"

"Aye. Just like that."

"But you'd help me if it was possible."

"I promised."

I could see that he was playing it. A stormcloud swept my own brow. "Hulok," I grated, "I do not lie. This world will surely die if I fail the task."

He responded with a certain Sophic smugness. "I've not said you've lied. But 'tis known, as you'll agree, that each man oft' has his own truth. To end your quest victoriously, however, is impossible; therefore your truth is simply flawed. Still, if you find a way, I will help you."

He began to whistle.

"Hulok!"

"Nay, lord." He'd become impatient. "Don't *Hulok* me. Put yourself in my place. If you were me, now that you know me somewhat, would you accept such an unlikely tale?"

"Hulok!" I roared. "By the bloody gods of Ilt, whoever *I* was, if an honest dwarf or man warned *me* of 'world death,' I'd damn well extend to him the benefit of the doubt until he was proven false."

"But I've said I'd help you."

"Daaammmm you!"

He grinned. "Am I still in danger?"

"Blast. You never were."

"But if I had been, how?"

"Like this, you meat-brained stubborn bastard." And in one fluid, practiced movement, I swept my blaster from its holster and split a boulder the size of four stacked kaoles right down the middle, and this at a distance of a hundred yards.

The blue light, the unleashed energy had had its effect. I returned the weapon. "That," I told him, "came with me from the colonies; the same who devised that bloody thing which will soon blow *you* and all this bloody world to hell!"

Lips pursed to belie a sudden paleness of his face, he asked quietly, "Why didn't you show me this before?"

"It would have been blackmail. You had to answer freely. To hell with it and to hell with you. I'll take my chances at Tag-Afran. I've sixteen hundred miles to go and by the gods, I'll find a way to get there—in time."

He looked at me sharply. "Where did you get that figure, my lord?"

"Where else? Aboard the ship I came on; from the *Scot's Leap*; its scanner charts, the readouts. All of them said that from the point where we'd entered atmosphere to the blinker light, it was exactly sixteen hundred miles, give or take a dozen."

His eyes gleamed with an ill-concealed excitement, the meaning of which, I could only guess. My profession being war, and that being similar to chess, I could assume that his agitation was derived from the fact that he too knew of something of importance which lay in the exact latitudinal area of which I had spoken. In effect, my story now had a new meaning for him, for I'd accidentally come up with a salable fact to which he could actually relate.

"I've told you the difficulties," he mused pensively. "They're actually worse than that. Knowing as little as you do, then just how in the name of Og to you propose to make it on your own?"

We'd mounted the crest of a small hill. On its far side, however, a great plain was suddenly disclosed. It spread in all directions for as far as the eye could see. Excepting for a village here and there and for a town and castle some four miles to the south—an intersecting road cut into our own at about two hundred yards—the whole was still heavily forested.

We slowed at the intersection. "Well," I said. "The Baron's

down there. Maybe I can make my peace with him and in so doing at least reach Weils safely. Come to think of it, I could even volunteer for his stinking army, if he's truly off to fight the moodans. *That* should get me halfway through Lothellian. Nay, good dwarf, your difficulties bedamned. Look, sir, on the positive side of things. Here, with but a few idle thoughts, I've come up with a way to get me a good half of the sixteen hundred miles already. And I daresay that's the half that'll be most difficult. I've but one thing left to do with you."

"What's that?"

"Why to purchase Huchlan here from you. He's served me well so far. I'd like to keep him."

"You know, of course," he said icily, "that your chances of surviving the baron for even twenty-four hours are simply nonexistent."

"You are right and I agree," I told him. "I've therefore changed my mind again. Since you've said you'll help and have sealed that with your *promised* word, why then I'll take you with me. That at least should raise the survival percentage by one. Moreover—I'll have even saved myself the price of a mount."

Hulok, his piercing blue eyes reflecting a medley of thoughts wherein both anger and amusement were obviously dueling, said wryly, "Count not your pookies before they're in the stewpot, sir. If I now turn south with you to Tag-Afran—and I note that that's what we're doing—'twill not be because of your badgering, but rather for the fact that dwarves are oft' times as curious as they are stubborn. Moreover, it makes little difference when I arrive in Vils. I have the whole winter to wait in any event."

We rode for awhile, and again we followed a stream. It was very pleasant. Flights of strange birds flew above us, heading south, too, for whatever reason; this, with the continuous murmuring of the water made me quite sleepy. I shook myself, talked to Hulok to stay awake. "One thing's been proven," I told him. . . .

"What's that?"

"That across the years dwarves have not changed a bit. There are books about you, you know, for you existed on Old Earth too. You're a true man, not a mutation. Whatever," I finished. "Historically, you've remained as ignorant and stubborn as they were."

Hulok said, "What a pity. I was about to compliment you. For a moment you sounded almost like a dwarf yourself." He chuckled, and for some weird reason the kaoles joined in, snorting, hacking and looking back at us to roll their great red eyes.

Four

Seen still from the height of the hills, but at a closer distance, Tag-Afran was surrounded by a number of villages, extending to varied distances and with their connecting roads and cart paths looking like so many spokes on a wheel. There was a lot of animal husbandry, imported Terran cattle and sheep. There was also an Avalonian meat-animal called a hottle. It was large, fat and abysmally stupid. How they'd survived at all in, as I would later find, a world simply alive with carnivores, was a mystery. There was also a rodent somewhat like the Terran rabbit, except that its ears, instead of being elongated, were round and leathery. Imported Terran chickens had mated with Avalonian chickens to produce a fantastic hodge-podge of cacklers.

I was tempted to think that whatever the vicissitudes of these new Avalonians, descendants of those few thousand workers of the Terran English conglomerate that had discovered the planet and had then sought to develop it while the great Terran council debated the question of opening it for colonization on the grand scale, and this across almost fifty years of time—they had survived them well. Even the names had generally retained their Anglo-Saxon-Celtic base; their flavor, too.

Odd, however, that with the loss of science, a direct result of the miniature holocaust that had destroyed the original northern base, they had retrogressed to what their forefathers had been—but as free men, thanes and cottage craftsmen rather than the serfs that existed in the parallel peasantry of the countries of Terran Europe during that same period.

The kilt, as an article of clothing, had returned, too, along with the sporran and the tam. Each lord, as I was to find, was based on a clan; each clan had its own singular tartan, or plaid—and bagpipes were everywhere, along with the hand-held harp.

The brilliant autumn sun, though not all that warm, still gave to his pastoral charm a certain semblance of summer . . . We reached the meadowed lee of the castle an hour before high noon, entrusted our animals to the keeping of ostlers and the stables and pens provided for such by the castle's seneschal—and went off to the fair.

Tag-Afran, according to Hulok, was the center of Sierwood's largest holding. Innumerable villages were under its protection, as well as a number of towns, the seaport of Vils being one of them. This being the case, Tag-Afran's three-day harvest festival was the largest in the south and the one to which many a lesser lord had come with his entourage to be entertained, and to participate in the festivities of tourney and wassail.

The great field was bright with the banners and tents of this lord or that who'd failed to find housing in the castle itself. The many-hued booths of tradesmen and those who offered games, goods, and a chance to wet one's throat, plus food of all kinds, were also representative of other towns and holdings.

I confess that I walked in awe of the whole thing. *People* were everywhere. To me, a man of the far-flung colonies, among which my own with its six-hundred cadres was equal to the largest, the sight of ten thousand humans massed in one square mile of space, was *trauma!* I choked at the oppressive closeness of it. Only a quick bowl of barley-beer with the rusks still in it, plus a table cleared of oafs by Hulok's dark glares and the sight of my own blazonry, sufficed to bring me around. Indeed, this, a few quick pulls at the bowl plus certain breathing exercises, had me back in control again in short order.

Hulok had helped. Noting my dismay and guessing the reason, he'd begun a ridiculous patter on things to see and do. "Why, look there, my lord," he'd suggested with false levity. "That's the booth of a cloth merchant from Coody-South (as opposed, perhaps, to a Coody-North?). It's on the coast, sir. Close by to that Isle of yours, perhaps. And there's some rattan chairs, too—from *Lools*, the only place they make them. It's another seacoast town. Surely the vendors there should have the same accent you do. It would be wise to speak to them. . . ."

"Hulok. Don't bait me."

"Bait you? Bait you, indeed! How better to learn of the south than to talk with those who live there?" In disgust he kicked a stone from the dirt floor at his feet. It then skittered and bounced from beneath our tarped overhang to finally hit a fierce kaole's privates so that it roared, reared, pawed the air, and came down to clear a circle for fifty feet around. Its rider, a husky young knight with an almost illegible bit of blazonry on his quite ragged surcoat, was hard put to control the raging beast. When he did, he drove right at us to shake his fist and yell, "Stay where you are, sirs. I've to stable my Primrose here. But by the gods, I *will* be back!"

"We'll be here," Hulok said courteously.

I grunted. "Enough of games." I was in no mood for nonsense. "I must somehow meet this Lord Oldus Finley, and quick. It's the last day, Hulok. And I mean to be on the road to Weils tomorrow—and with swords to back me."

He snorted and became curious. "And just how," he asked, "do you propose to do that?"

I sighed, sipped my beer. The concept of war as being an extension of politics, though on a higher level—an ancient Terran dictum for all who would command—had apparently been lost to Avalon's "Dark People."

"How?" I repeated his question. "Well for one thing, sir, young Finley's lord here. You've said yourself that his holdings are the biggest in all of Sierwood. Now. A Baron of Weils is also here, one of those who has overthrown his king, imprisoned him, and who now seeks to divide his kingdom between himself and his cohorts. Moreover, the king's two daughters are in this man's power. He's married one and stupidly made an enemy of the other. This baron is also and *obviously* here for a purpose other than a run of the lance in tourney, or for Lord Finley's southern cuisine. Lord Finley and the Baron of Weils, my good dwarf, are central to all that is happening in this so-called 'world' of yours. This being so, we cannot afford to while our time with ale and pot-pies. If I'm to go north, I must now, *today*, find myself a place at Finley's table. I must, in effect, become a part of the decision making process as it involves these two—so as to, hopefully, direct it toward getting me to the place of the blinker lights in the shortest possible time."

Enthralled by my delivery, if not my personal magnetism, his great blue eyes had been on me all the while, expanding, growing. With my inspired ending, therefore, he could not help but pound a fist into a leathery palm and shout, "By the gods! You've got it. And *I* have the answer. No one, my lord, can ignore the man who wins today's tournament—or what's left of it. You're a lord. You wear surcoat and blazonry. You carry a lord's weapon, that curious sword. Enter yourself, sir. And *win*! Indeed, announce this entry to the gathered throngs. If all goes well, sir, 'tis a guarantee that we'll be at Finley's table before the sun sets. . . ."

I sighed disgustedly. "Only in romance do such things happen. You've a head, sir dwarf, like a hollow gourd."

He quipped slyly, "Nothing ventured, nothing gained."

"You mock me, Hulok."

"No, I do not."

"There are things that you hold back."

"As do you, sir—as do you."

I sighed. We were wasting time, and I *did* need him. I said softly, "I still call you friend, Hulok."

"And I you."

"Well then, we'll play the thing by ear—and still go north together."

He grinned. "Why not? I'm pledged to you."

Even as we talked, I'd spotted two things that could be used to get me Finley's attention. The first was that Lord Oldus Finley himself, and entourage, had left the castle on its hill to the west and were now wending their way down toward the field. The tourney grounds with the knights' pavilions and viewing stands were to the east of our field; ergo, he would have to pass a certain spot where the second thing was taking place, *i.e*, a large crowd had gathered around a roped-off circle wherein were a group of acrobats. These were amusing the throng with simple handstands, back flips and the balancing of one or more of the troupe upon one or more of the other's shoulders.

I arose, downed the last of my beer, husks and all, signaled Hulok to follow and strolled casually over to force my way through the crowd. Timing now meant everything. In the archaic, I'd have to play it cool and hope for the best.

At the ropes, I sized up the members of the troupe. There was a "catcher," an older man; their leader perhaps, five tumblers; one of them a catcher too, two girls, also tumblers and a couple of juggler-tumblers who were now moving out to work while the others rested.

In the background there were a couple of older men and women, a spate of children and a few wives. By their tartans, the adults, though mostly unrelated were still of the same clan. They were, I mused, the standard traveling troupe.

As I made my way to the older catcher, one of the jugglers, a young man, began to do wonders with a dozen fruits that looked like oranges. The second young man did the same with a dozen more items that looked like apples. Completely apart the two dozen apples and oranges were two separately whirling cascades of red and orange fruit. But then they suddenly faced each other and began a rapid medley of an exchange of fruit so that the cascade, though single now, was red-orange, red-orange. A final trick was to speed up the hurling of the fruit at each other so that at the count of twelve the apples and oranges were back with their original juggler. Quite neat. I'd seen nothing like it in the colonies so I joined in the applause.

Having reached the catcher, I said a few words to him, received his puzzled but curious nod of agreement, put a gold piece into his hand and returned to Hulok. My dwarf then watched stoically and with a certain pained displeasure as I stripped down to shorts and nothing else. I'd put everything in a pile, cloak, clothes, harness, guns and sword. Hulok stood over it. He'd drawn his axe and now leaned upon the handle. The folk, accordingly, had withdrawn to a safe distance.

With an eye to Lord Finley's train—it was now quite close—I alerted the catcher. That worthy stepped forward, swept his green cap from his head, bowed, then held up both hands for attention. "Now hear me all," he shouted. "I've a young lord from our southern Isles who'd like to show you how they exercise each morning. He tells me that it sharpens the appetite, makes the blood flow and keeps one's weight down—a result most pleasing to the ladies. For your pleasure. . . . The Lord Jarn Tybalt!"

Not knowing exactly what to do—they'd never been entertained by a lord before—they shuffled, looked at each other, stared, and waited. In the meantime the leading edge of Finley's pride was already thrusting toward the rope. . . .

Good timing! I stepped out a few feet, raised my arms, turned slowly so that all could have a look at me—then took three leaping steps toward the circle's center, bounded almost straight up into the air, went into three full body turns, landed on my hands and instantly went into three more of the same.

Amid the ensuing applause, I beckoned the catcher, placed him in the circle's exact center and had him assume the catcher's stance, muscular legs half-bent at the knees and hands cupped with fingers joined and resting on the pelvis. I then whispered a word or two and he nodded.

This time I bowed slightly, holding both hands wide while I circled the catcher. In this way, I literally milked the crowds' total attention while commanding their silence. *And now, too, all Lord Finley's train was watching!* I went to the circle's edge, breathed deeply, turned, with my arms out, took four great bounding leaps and again hurled myself straight into the air, where I made four full body flips, with the first and second being made with a dazzling twist to left and right, respectively. The last of the four was completed in such a way that I came down feet-first, directly into the cupped hands of the catcher. His arms gave for about a foot. He then heaved with such power as to toss me over his head to attain even a higher arc. I made *five* complete turns with a left-right, right-left twist to the first four and landed with the last upon my shoulders—and rolling in such a way as to achieve a series of lightning-smooth somersaults and come to my feet exactly where Hulok stood guard over my clothes. The landing on one's shoulders, suffice it to say, is quite a trick. One can easily break one's neck that way.

The applause was thunderous. To add to it, and to the troupe's purse, I boldly and in full view, tossed the catcher another golden coin; this, to show that *I* had paid *him*, and that I truly was a lord! While I quickly donned my metallic body suit, lace shirt and golden jacquarded tunic with its blazonry of bright red dragon against the blue-white tail of a comet, the crowd continued to roar its pleasure. My catcher, whom I'm sure had never believed I could do it, could only stare in absolute awe and bow and bob to my mastery of the art.

And then it happened exactly as I'd hoped it would.

A young, commanding, voice rang out: Lord Finley's voice, from where he sat his mount at the rope's edge. He was perhaps twenty-two, slight of build—no warrior—a scholar, perhaps, and had a pair of extremely intelligent, light-blue eyes in a nondescript face. His hair was a bit redder than mine. "My lord," he called, "since you seem so truly that in style, grace, raiment and sword. I beg your courtesy, sir, to attend us to the tourney viewing stands and to our table, too, this night. For," and he smiled, "I would learn more of your southern isles and what it means to fly, and how it's done. . . ."

I bowed my head slightly in respect. " 'Tis indeed my pleasure, my lord," I told him—"If you'll allow myself and my companion here to retrieve our mounts. . . ."

Lord Finley looked keenly at Hulok and his smile became a happy grin. "Why, he's a dwarf. And dwarves, I've heard, bring luck to all who can stand their insolence. By all means, sir. You're welcome, both of you!—And luck to all of you and yours," he called graciously to the catcher. "And here's my surety of that."

He, too, then tossed a gold coin upon their spread-out canvas. A veritable shower followed his gesture; this, from his knights and followers. Then he led the final dash toward the waiting stands.

And while he'd talked and before they trotted off, I'd had time to see that quite close to Finley; indeed, as a part of his inner circle, was the Baron Dagar, at least two of his knights, the Lady Jocydyn—and my blue-eyed, raven-haired loudmouth in a pants suit of some kind (they must have ridden directly to the castle and changed for we, Hulok and I, couldn't have been more than an hour behind them), of a velvet blue and white with half-boots, broad belt, a shirt with the whitest lace collar I'd ever seen and a tartaned, pomponed tam of the royal house of Tremaine to keep the long black hair from flowing in the wind.

I could not but note, too, that when they'd moved to leave, she'd held back; indeed, had caught my eye and dared to wave and to boldly smile. Upon which Dagar seized the reins of her mount and literally pulled her after them. Her hand had gone instantly to the dagger at her belt. But her sister, so ethereal, so wraithlike, put out a hand and stayed her. . . .

Taking our time, we returned to the eatery's tented tables, ordered more ale, cheese, bread and shared what I knew to be an absolutely poisonous meat pie. Those of the crowd around us who'd watched it all made much of the fact to those who hadn't. That I, an obvious lord, still condescended to sit with them increased my standing more.

"You forever surprise me, my lord," Hulok told me, after he'd halved the pie to our mutual satisfaction and we'd each gobbled our share. "Indeed, I'm more and more inclined to believe your story. Who else could attract the notice of the greatest of Sierwood's lords by fluttering about in the air and without even wings to make the feat seem reasonable? I still think, however, that a run of the lance—providing you know how to hold one—will nail the project properly down. . . ."

"Hulok," I snorted, "is it that you *wish* to see me lose?"

"Nay, lord. Not at all." Honest alarm showed in his eyes, that he'd gone too far in jesting.

"The first part of the game's won, dwarf. We've but to find where it leads us, and to press our luck. Now tell me of your gods—so I'll not be the fool that your humor would paint me."

And he told me. And I found them to be Father Abram, his son, Og, and Abram's wife, the Lady Easter. All quite familiar. Leave it to Anglo-Saxon Celts who have lost their religion, to invent one from the mythology at hand. Father Abram was the "Green Man" of Celt antiquity, coming no longer from the Sinai, but rather from somewhere in Old Ireland. Eostre, or the Lady Easter, was the Earth Mother transposed, to be honored at the spring planting of the summer solstice. As for Og, well he was the ubiquitous type, precocious, brilliant and jealous at times of his father so that storms, heavy snows and earthquakes to rival those of Poseidon Earthshaker, were visited upon the peoples of Hulok's world.

And, though these three were the most honored, a recognition of the existence of other gods afforded many outlets for additional religious expression. . . . Heaven existed. It was something like the "world" in full summer. Hell existed, too. It was the *Deadlands!* And then of course there was the Devil. And he existed in all the dead cities of the "world" as a thing, a *personage* that had seduced and destroyed the *old ones,* the life before the *second* life (humanity), which the devil had almost destroyed, but not quite. Father Abram had fought a great battle with him, and with the help of Og and sundry other, lesser gods, had banished him forever to the underworld, reached through the catacombs of the dead cities. In essence, the devil, to Avalonians, was more a living adversary than any idiot embodiment of evil. Indeed, a man could be evil, do evil things, without ever being accused of such an affiliation. He had simply swerved from the paths of righteousness and needed but a good talking to by his vicar (a priest's true title), and a rereading of the *Twelve Commandments.*

So much for the religion of Avalon as explained by one, Hulok Terwydd. . . .

If I'd thought, however, to be able to call the shots myself in this developing montage, I had another think coming. A young court page, tow-headed, apple-cheeked and panting, came into our enclosure, spotted Hulok and ran over to whisper in his ear. He then ran off again.

Hulok, arising, said, "Well Warlord, let's to it. Lucky we have a friend in court. We've but minutes, sir, to retrieve our mounts and to lose ourselves in that town down there. . . ."

"Why?" I hadn't budged.

"The Baron has told Lord Finley that we're spies for the Sadans. You, with your green eyes, and me, because all dwarves have an overt proclivity for such liaisons. Finley's sending a squadron of swordsmen to arrest us for questioning."

"Nay. Hold!" I told him. "There's no point in running. Indeed, fortune may have favored us. Such a questioning is bound to happen sooner or later. Look at it this way: The Baron's wits have become somewhat addled by his hatred of you. He's also in the wrong. He cannot but lose in this matter, Hulok. We cannot but win."

"You forget one thing."

"Which is?"

"That I *am* a dwarf; that the laws are not quite the same for us—and that it's *my* ass he's after. If he gets you, too, well all the better for him, or so he figures, I'm sure."

I shook my head. "Trust me," I told him. . . . From the corner of an eye I'd seen the arresting squadron break through the crowd and head in our direction. I stood up to check my holstered weapons and loose my kuri-sword. Hulok did likewise with his three-fold shield and axe.

They came at us in a storm of dust and pounding paws. The leader, a husky young sergeant in chain hauberk, seemed prepared to drive us before him to Finley's viewing stand. One close look and he changed his mind. After shouting his charge he simply demanded that we accompany him.

At which I roared, "Afoot, sir? Are you mad? We'll go mounted, or not at all. Send to yon stable"—I pointed, then grinned—"then join us in a pint or two 'til they return. Ho! Mistress!" I called, gesturing to the entire squad and our own empty pots. She got the message. And thus, to Hulok's delight, we made twelve friends for the price of pennies while simultaneously showing that we two were a pair to respect, and *fear*.

The greater part of some twenty thousand Avalonians now swarmed around the tournament field, a majority of the fair-goers and an equal number from the town and villages around. Most stood or sat on the slope of the small hill that faced the field from the south. At either end were the color-ful pavilions of the contestents. On the north side was the viewing stand reserved for the nobility. It held perhaps two thousand and was awash with the colors, banners, gonfalons and pencils of this lord or that. Lord Finley's group of per-haps fifty lords and ladies sat, naturally, in the center front of it all.

And that's where we were taken, our accompanying squadron simply leaving us there and withdrawing to either end. We pranced our mounts, saluted Finley's great house-hold banner of some odd beast rampant on an azure field, and waited. . . . I'd advised Hulok to control his anger and to follow my lead.

All eyes were keenly upon us. And we were quite a pair: A beetle-browed, heavy-set, blue-eyed dwarf and a tall, space-burnt, green-eyed swordsman with red-gold hair and a surcoat of gold that literally gleamed with metallic points. A heavy man in his fifties, Cador Evans, seneschal to Finley, arose to halt the last jousting run until we'd been dealt with. The contestants informed, he then addressed us.

" 'Tis charged," he announced clearly, "that the two of you, sirs, are not what you seem to be. 'Tis suggested that you are here to spy upon this court and are in fact in league with the mad sadans of Lothellian. What say you to this?"

He'd said what he'd said in such a way that I knew immediately that his heart wasn't in it—which meant that Lord Oldus Finley's heart wasn't in it either. He'd had no choice, apparently but to extend the courtesy of a questioning and to thereby do what he could to assuage the baron's fears.

My reply was to begin a light laughter and to allow it to grow while nudging Hulok's thigh with my own so that he too began a hawking, roaring facsimile of my own now obviously uncontrolled mirth. We kept it up, both of us leaning to slap each other's back and wipe our eyes. Then, to the first small wave of responding titters from the stands (for laughter *is* contagious) we further grabbed our sides, convulsed, as it were, with the very idea of such an idiocy. More! For whatever reason, our kaoles, too, let loose with a braying series of honks so that all the court was shortly wiping its eyes and even clutching each other for support.

"My Lord," I called directly to Oldus Finley, and this between chokes and gurgles: "Would you—have—the—chaaarrgeesss—repeateeeddd—pleeeesssss." I then went off into another gale of laughter; and this with the kaoles literally howling like so many Terran dogs at the moon.

Smiling, for the seneschal couldn't help himself, he said, "When you've gotten ahold of yourself, sir. Still, I must say"—and he glanced back to the merry eyes of Lord Finley—"that this, so help me, is the first time in all my life that I've ever seen a dwarf to laugh."

At which Hulok deliberately honked all the more, so that spittal and snot dripped down his chin. Taking advantage, he called out, "With your permission, sir. . . . To call this young lord whom I found in the midst of Great Berween Forest whistling a gay ditty and without a care in the world; this, though he'd just lost his mount in a quite vicious battle with three great caaties, and along with the mount, all his luggage, and could *still* spit and whistle—to call *him* a sadan agent; he who barely knows what a sadan is, is beyond belief. Who brings this charge, my lord?"

"You know who brings it!" Dagar arose, roaring. "*I* bring it, dwarf. And I'll prove it on your body!"

"Like you did this morning, lord?" I called out, goading.

Dagar grew red then purple. "By the gods—" he turned to shout at the still-grinning Finley with a demanding wrath. "Will you allow me to be insulted in your own court?"

"I give no insults," I cried. "I but tell the truth; that this brave dwarf was *forced* to fight for himself and the honor of his people against a master-swordsman sent against him by this Lord of Weils. The swordsman was also a giant; this, against our dwarf's four-and-one-half feet and his one-hundred and thirty pounds. 'Twas an ungentlemanly, un-knightly act as all here will surely recognize. Well, the gods favoring the right, our brave Hulok soon shortened this *proxy* by a good four feet, then took his head—And even then, though doubly protected by the code, our Lord of Dagar would have had him slain were it not for the presence of the king's *vicar*, Loren Raddle, of Ellenrude Castle who rides with him."

All laughter had died with my words. I continued solemnly. " 'Tis asked that I tell from whence I came and who I am. I pray our Lord Finley's courtesy to do this." I looked directly at him, smiled—and put a deliberate twinkle into my left eye. He winked and nodded. I breathed a sigh. I'd chanced an unwarranted intimacy, and won. I then bowed to all of them, from left to right. "My name," I announced boldly, "is Jarn Tybalt. I am the appointed Warlord of a small fortress-town on an island off the southern coast of Sierwood. The town and fortress is called"—and I dared to say it, if for no other reason than to get them accustomed to hearing it—"*Eden Valley*! Hold!" I shouted instantly. "Know this: the town and fortress were named thus long before the *fall*, for then the name meant a place of beauty, peace, and where all animals and men, inclusive of those caaties who ate my mount and luggage"—I smiled—"could live together.

"For this very reason, and happy with our own world, the folk of the valley usually stay at home. Some trade with Lools and Coody-South, and that's about it.

"But I, as warlord, and this in a place that has never known war"—and again I smiled, forcing a smile or two in return from those who watched and listened—"felt a need to see the world as it really is, to journey abroad into Sierwood and to exchange ideas with others. In Lools I heard of a new massing of moodans for battle, the same in Coody-South. I swore then to go on to Weils and to offer my sword to King Tremaine so's to aid in this crusade.

"While coming north, however, I heard another tale. 'Tis that the king's been imprisoned and his chancellor murdered. What, I asked myself, should I do now? Well, sirs and my noble lords, the answer, it seems, now lies with our Lord of Dagar. For since he's been central to both the murder and the jailing, why, perhaps he can explain it all in such a way that I'll again be willing to offer my sword to Weils."

Most of the southern lords roared their appreciation at this. Indeed, I could only assume from all I saw that the new Weils minus its king, was by no means loved in Sierwood.

But Dagar, his red-purple turned to white, spoke out again. "One thing's at least been proven," he shouted. "Our warlord, from his mystery island has a silver tongue to seduce the very breath of Eostre. Mayhap he could have his way with the sadans, too. If that's true and if he's not playing their game, as he protests, why then I'll take his offer now, and gladly. For all must know"—and this time he spoke directly to the crowd, not just to Finley and me—"that the coming battle on the borders of Lothellian will not be easily won. Which is the real reason why I'm here, to seek your help in that battle—and *not* to play children's games with dwarves and green-eyed strangers.

"Weils, as you know, has suffered the burdens of the border wars alone and at great cost in blood and treasure. At no time have we ever asked for help. But now we do. And we expect to get it—For when the chips are truly down it is the duty of all humankind to protect their own. IS THIS NOT TRUE?" He'd suddenly raised his voice. . . .

He was answered with a chorus of enthusiastic ayes. "Moreover," he shouted, sensing that in this area at least the crowd was with him, "considering the forces being massed against us this time, it just could be the *last* time! Either we will destroy them—or they, us. 'Tis as simple as that. And if such is the case, and I swear it is, then what man who calls himself a man will stay at home in Sierwood when all that is best in humankind is off to defend its hearth and home against the horrors of Lothellian and the *Deadlands*?"

He'd pressed the right button. Shouts of support came from all directions. Swords were raised in pledge until they seemed to be a small forest. Seeing it all, he bowed, hands flat out, a supplicant who but humbly begged that they join with him in risking their lives to save their world. What indeed was the nonsense of dwarves and green-eyed strangers in the face of that?

But young Lord Finley was in no way taken in. When the

applause had died, he simply stood up and said, "Good friends, let us leave the problem of war and peace till later. I'm sure that at that time our Baron of Weils will be pleased with our answer. As to our dwarf and his young warlord companion—Well, Baron, are you satisfied now that they're not the devils you supposed?"

The baron wisely smiled and consigned us, magnanimously, to the heavens with a simple wave of his hands, and this to another round of applause and even a cheer or two.

I then bowed graciously to the court, kicking Hulok who, refusing, indeed, he stood ram-rod stiff and with a scowl to crack a mirror at fifty yards, was again endangering both of us. Growling, he nodded briefly.

But Lord Finley wasn't through. He said seriously, "Be of good cheer, Dwarf. It's not often that a moulder of stone has his way with so great a lord as our Baron of Weils, nor is it often that he has so good a friend as our 'Warlord' to speak for him.

"Sir Tybalt," he called to me. "Again, I beg your courtesy to sup with us tonight. It will be our pleasure to have you at our castle."

At which he waved a handkerchief in dismissal.

By the time we'd tied our animals off and climbed into the viewing stands, the last tilt of the lance had been run. That part of the harvest festival was over and there remained only the awarding of the prizes to the winners of the day.

Our seats, on a line with those of the Baron's party, allowed me to witness three interesting happenings. Climbing up into the stands, and reaching our tier, I'd chanced to look beyond the crowd toward the road we'd come down from the hills this morning. With eyes to spot a camouflaged Kartine warrior at a thousand yards, I saw a band of heavily armed men ride over the crest of the next to last military skyline. They flaunted no banners, not even a pennon. They held for but a few seconds, viewing what lay below. They then vanished, not making it to the next skyline. For whatever reason they'd remained in that intervening hollow.

Even then I'd have paid the incident no mind, except that turning to find my seat, I came face to face with the second happening. . . . My eyes fell full on the rapt expression of an almost unendurable joy as reflected on the face of the Princess Meagan Anne. It was but a fleeting thing, like morn-

ing lightning. But it *had* been there. She'd recognized someone. A warrior, lover? Whoever it was, it boded the Baron no
good. Her eyes shifted but slightly, and caught my own,
widened and held. She knew that I knew. I nodded courteously, and sat down.

That our line of seats was in the first row accounted for
the third phenomenon. The first prize of the day was awarded
to a strong and hardened veteran of the lists. He'd beaten all
who rode at him. The prize was a jeweled snuff box of solid
gold. The second prize was won by a bright young blade who
swore he'd have won the first had his cowardly kaole not
ducked at the wrong moment. The second prize was a great
and beautiful war-kaole from Lord Finley's own stables. The
third and last prize was a gorgeous saddle, tooled, leaded and
silvered. It went to the young man—he was announced as Sir
Percy Tarrent from a place called Histroot—who'd challenged Hulok earlier in the day for having bounced the rock
off his mount Primrose's parts. His tattered surcoat was now
more tattered still, his breastplate hanging loose from having
been turned halfway around from the last blow he'd received
and the fall he'd taken.

He beamed at Lord Finley's brief remarks, had a lackey
throw the new saddle to the rump of his mount, and then
made to go—and stopped. He'd spotted Hulok sitting next to
me.

"By the gods!" he exclaimed loudly. "So here's where
you've been hiding. *I* returned, you know, and you weren't
there. You promised, sir—and lied."

In his anger at Hulok, young Percy Tarrent had lowered
his great sixteen-foot lance and was tapping my dwarf's chest
with the dulled tip of it.

Hulok looked to me in utter disgust.

"Come out of there, sir!" young Percy shouted. "You upset
my Primrose and I'll have it out with you right here and
now."

Hulok shook his head—and stood up.

Percy's eyes bulged. "Why," he choked, "you're a dwarf."

Hulok said simply, "I'd be pleased, young sir, if you'd take
your lance from off my chest."

And Percy would have done so, I'm sure. But he'd only
seen Hulok both times as sitting down. He simply hadn't
known. He was stunned with both his error and the fact that

Lord Finley and the entire nobility of Sierwood was watching.

Hulok, who never asked any man twice for anything, then seized the great lance, jerked it from the curve of Percy's arm—and snapped it into three equal pieces with his bare hands.

Not stopping there, he dared to shout in Lord Finley's direction: "Your pardon, please, my lord. But dwarves are forbidden the use of lance and war-spear. I had no choice."

He bowed deeply while a roar of laughter swept the stands, even touched young Percy, who rode off foolishly with his beauteous new saddle. . . .

Five

Tag-Afran Castle had a plumbing system; this, to confound all my previous ideas as to the new Avalonian hygiene, or the lack of it. It would appear that every castle or large house was equipped with some sort of water tower and had a piping and heating system. Even the peasantry had a small log hut for steam or sauna baths. And, since they were usually located near running water, that, too, was no problem.

Thus Hulok and I were given a small room in the castle's great west wing, and with two rusk-filled mattresses and access to the communal baths. The setup adhered closely to the old Roman order. Bathing tubs for washing with strong lye soap, and rinsing—and then the communal pool for relaxing. The pool was kept at body temperature. When one left it he could plunge into a colder pool to close the pores and set the body to tingling.

Gifts arrived then, for myself, Hulok and the contrite Sir Percy who, guilt-laden and fearful—somewhere he'd gotten the misinformation that to harm a dwarf would bring the worst possible luck—had followed us into the tubs to beg Hulok's forgiveness . . . We received fresh underlinens, kilts, sporrans, cambric shirts and heavy black velvet jackets. There were also short boots, knee-socks and a feathered cap; all in the tartan of Lord Oldus Finley, Duke of Tag-Afran, our benefactor. *All* the nobility in Sierwood were dukes, for each held what amounted to a principality. And, since there was no king, there were no princes; nor anything else for that matter, excepting knights, and these by heredity and appointment.

The nobility of Weils, on the other hand was the usual, except reversed. The king was the sole ruler and arbiter. Instead of dukes, marquises and barons, there were barons, marquises and dukes—and knights.

A personal touch to my own gift consisted of a large badge sewn on the right breast of my jacket. The tailor had obviously had the aid of an heraldic artist, for the red dragon against its silver comet's tail was in exact proportion to the one on my tunic, though obviously smaller.

Sir Percy, too, had a badge. His erstwhile illegible blazonry was now revealed as an antiquated Terran bull's head against a flaming cape and sword. He explained solemnly that this blazonry had mystic qualities, being derived of that other world—before the great magic. He further explained that he was the seventh son of a thane with limited holdings in the western principality of Duke Ian Williams. Indeed, he'd been but recently knighted by the duke—who'd also given him the blazonry, created it, in fact—and had come to the tourney to gain prestige, honor and to follow in the footsteps of a famed warrior great-uncle whose existence, we later found, was questionable to say the least.

I congratulated him and wished him well.

And Hulok promised bleakly that he'd consider the apology in due time, explaining that dwarves were deep thinkers and seldom rushed into anything. To me Hulok said, "I'll be leaving you now for a bit, Warlord. I should be back before the night's out."

Irritated by his all-too-casual attitude, I snapped, "Is that the *way* to leave, sir, with never a hint as to where you're going?"

"Come with me. Then you'll know."

"My place is here, Hulok."

"Is it indeed? Look, my lord, though I'm your man in this peril of the northern beacon and have so pledged myself, I will say it now, just once, so you'll know: You, sir, are not my master either."

"Nor would I be," I grumbled. "Do what you will . . ." Duke Finley's remark about the insolence of dwarves had truly begun to reach me.

The somewhat dense Sir Percy then offered to go with him to wherever he was going—and was met with a glare to turn a *quoin*, a fierce meat-eating lizard, to stone. My wicked Hulok, from either a fine sense of black humor, or sheer nastiness, was destined to keep poor Percy on the hook for an indefinite length of time.

In the corridor paralleling the great hall my id demanded

that I preen a bit before one of its many full-length mirrors.
Finley's tartan, or plaid, akin to the original *Royal Stuart*,
was truly striking. Not taking any chances, I'd brought my
jeweled belt and weapons, hooking the sporran to it at front-
center. My kuri-sword was where it always was, across my
back with its gold and jeweled hilt all flashing in the light of
the corridor's candelabra.

The castle, like the great hall, was renaissance-feudal—a
massive pile of stones with walls, moat, great inner court-
yards, stables, dungeons, barracks and the like. It also had a
hundred or so rooms for guests, storage and whatever. The
hall, however, was the renaissance part. Instead of stone slabs
the floor was actually parqueted. The various arrases and
drapes were of a fine material, closely woven and with an
imaginative and artistic theme. The banners, flags, weapons,
shield-blazonry and general colors on all the walls, effective
and tasteful.

Even the lengthy tables, to right, left and center—Duke
Finley's "high table"—were laid in the whitest of linen, and
with proper chairs, too; no simple boards. Above it all a
number of quite interesting candelabra swung, and with perfumed candles; a contrast to the somewhat smoky light of the
tapers in their heavy sconces.

The one thing, however, that kept the scene in the feudal,
as opposed to the renaissance, were the swords slung over the
backs of all the noble warriors. For though Sierwood was not
constantly at war with the moodans, as was Weils, it did send
levies of stout swordsmen to the struggle. Moreover, the
dukes were in constant war with each other over the possession of this or that great forest, mighty river or great
mountain chain that divided their jurisdictions. Oddly
enough, according to Hulok, no principality had ever
changed hands. Indeed, at the slightest threat of such a happening the remainder of the nobility would instantly fly to the
rescue of whoever was losing. An understandable act, when
you think about it.

Properly announced, I was appropriately stared at by a few
of the more curious and then sent directly to the first table of
the beginning left "el" of the duke's lengthy "high table." A
full two thirds of it was occupied by the Baron Dagar and his
party, which caused me to think that Duke Finley could

match my dwarf in black humor—either that or he'd a rare perspicacity in that he's sensed my interest in the Princess Meagan Anne. No matter. I seated myself in the only space available, toward its far end and next to the "awed by it all" Sir Percy, who'd followed me in.

The Baron promptly ignored me, as did his knights. But both Meagan Anne and Jocydyn smiled and nodded so that I felt as a boy of twelve, being allowed *outside* for the first time to take my place in skimmer-floater practice as a fledgling warrior of Drusus Base.

The food was tasty, the wine, ale and beer plentiful. I ate heartily, but drank only a single glass of wine. Abstemiousness was the proper ticket, else I'd never get to the Deadlands.

We'd missed the piping for the general entry, but the young harpist who entertained us through most of the dinner played hauntingly familiar tunes. The dining over, a mutual visiting began. At the hall's far end a half-dozen musicians—harpists, flutists, one with something that resembled an oboe, plus two with large-bottomed lutes, were already tuning their instruments.

By the gods! We were going to dance!

To a man of the Colonies, dancing is on a level with breathing, eating and gymnastics. Forever confined to the closest of quarters, every movement for us is an aerobatic exercise. It almost has to be. For what else is there? Aside from its objective purpose, movement has long become something more than just getting from point "a" to point "b." It's a studied release from stress and tension; so much so that our bodies are now fleshly tuning forks to the silent music around us.

We, therefore, can dance to any music. I, for example, have but to watch a single measure of any formal or folk effort—and I can immediately adapt. Thus, I'm told, did Terra's ancient ballet artists adapt to any movement offered them.

And so, to the delight of the ladies, generally, and on occasion risking the black scowl of this lord or that, I danced jigs and graceful pavans along with stately minuets and wild "flings." More! They'd not forgotten the more heady waltz. I kept at it, delirious with the pleasure of it all, but deliberately dancing but a single dance with each solicited partner, *i.e.*, I sought no liaisons—at least not yet.

And then, after a heady reel of some sort with a red-haired vixen daughter of one of Finley's knights, I turned to leave her to her group and found my eyes staring directly into the blue-purple ones of Meagan Anne. She was with Jocydyn. They were returning to their table from wherever they'd been.

"My Lady." I stepped deliberately in front of her. "I'd be most pleased, as would the folk of all my southern Isle, if you'd partner me in just one turn to whatever those musicians choose now to play." I bowed slightly, raised my head and held her with my eyes.

"Why, now, Sir *Companion*," she replied merrily. "I've certainly no reason not to. Especially since you seem to have run out of partners. Or is it more accident than custom that you've not partnered the same lady twice this evening? Is it your intent to treat *me* thusly?"

I allowed the red to come beneath my tan, saying softly, "Nay. 'Tis no custom. I've simply taken the opportunity to practice, and to work up my courage the while for what I'm doing now."

"Courage?" A dainty eyebrow went up. "I'd say 'tis the last thing you lack." She then looked at me calmly, challengingly, put her hand on my forearm and nudged me forward to a line forming for a stately minuet.

I did my best. So did she. I kept her with me, or perhaps it was the other way around. The whole thing became ethereal, what with the music, the delight of her slim person in my arms, the flickering candles, the eerie smoking blaze of the great wall sconces—and the resultant, mocking dancing shadows.

Like myself, she, too, wore the kilt-skirt and the velvet jacket. There was a froth of white lace at her throat, too, with the plaid of her socks, cap and kilt in the Tremaine tartan of red ground with wide green crossings and a yellow overcheck, a stunning ensemble against the velvet.

She said once with her face close to mine, "I see, sir, that you wear Lord Finley's colors."

I shrugged. "A courtesy for the luggage I've lost." The dance was a waltz and her breath was hot upon my throat; so much so that I felt a weakening in my legs. But then I remembered the wild light in her eyes at the sight of that armed band. It was my heart's turn to feel somewhat leaden.

I'd returned her each time to Oldus Finley's group rather than to the Baron's table; this, between dances. I'd reasoned that in this way I could keep her with me and at the same time avoid any unpleasantness with Dagar.

But approaching the high table again, we heard the faintest winding of bagpipes to our rear. Meagan, recognizing the first faint notes, cried out, "Ah, ha! Here's a tune that's definitely for you and me, my lord. Do you know it? 'Tis the 'Sword Dance'! Finley! Do you dance this, sir? And if not, may I use your noble weapon to match this strange one of our green-eyed traveler of the dragon and shooting star?"

Finley, smiling—he hadn't danced at all—gave his fluted glass of wine to a page, snicked his court weapon from its jeweled scabbard and presented it. "For your father," he told her. "A man whom I've always loved."

This time she boldly seized my hand and like two teen-agers we ran together to where four sets of sword dancers had already placed their weapons, one across the other. I drew the kuri-sword. Its finely polished steel and haft gleamed and glittered. I placed it properly. She did likewise. We then assumed our positions—with me locking hard to her mind so that what I'd miss in reflex, I'd still see *there* before the fact.

Hands above our heads, sporrans and kilts bouncing as we toed in and out between the drawn blades to the skirling of the pipes, it became dreamlike. To add to it all a few birds flew in on the perfumed, harvest breezes; a salute, perhaps, to Finley's festival. The breezes guttered the candles. The skirl became wilder, the pace faster. Meagan's dancing was perfection. Mine was adequate. The dance being arduous in the extreme, sweat soon trickled from beneath my cap, beaded Meagan's forehead and glistened on the high-color of her cheeks. Seeing all that ebullience, that laughing, beauteous personification of perfect female health and joy, I could not help but reason that no one could be as arrogant as she—and *not* be healthy.

The skirling peaked, held, climaxed and died. She fell forward against me, so that I caught her beneath the arms. Gods! Daaammmmn that group of troublemakers on the road, whoever they were. She grabbed my hands and said, "My

Lord. By our Lady, sir, we've earned our pint and more. And that's a fact. Will you walk with me on the terrace?"

"My lady," I told her solemnly and with but the slightest twinkle in my eyes, "I would walk with you to hell and back!"

"Why, now," she answered quickly and just as solemnly, but without the twinkle, "you just may have to—if you love me."

Laughing at my startled look, she snatched two glasses of wine from offered trays, gave me one, and gaily pledged Lord Finley with the other. He pledged us in turn. Indeed, we'd even received a round of applause for our handling of the swords. Dodging a group of admirers and would-be hangers-on, she snatched two more glasses of wine and we left quickly for the length of hall on the west side, beyond which was the terrace.

More a raised balcony, it allowed for strolling couples plus an overall view of an extensive garden below. The air was redolent with the perfume of its late-blooming flowers. We'd walked but a short distance when Meagan stopped at a section of balustrade to lean on the rail and look down. I joined her, so close that our shoulders touched.

Suddenly serious, she asked, "Why are you really here, Jarn Tybalt?"

I laughed. "To save the world."

"Oh? From what?"

"From something out there." I waved a hand toward the stars. "—Imagine the loudest thunder you have ever heard, along with the greatest bolt of lightning; then multiply that ten thousand times ten billion, and you'll approximate it."

She'd turned to frown at me, a little angry. But then, when she saw the expression on my face, she said softly, "By the gods, I think you mean it." Her own expression became suddenly saddened, as if she'd irretrievably lost something. "Jarn?" she asked, "are you mad? Is that it?"

I smiled. "No. I am not. And why should I not, mean it?"

"Well, if you're truly a warlord, why then you're conversant with the affairs of lords, and their duplicities; seldom does one say what he truly means. . . ."

"Does this logic also apply to princesses?"

"Hey!" she said. "You are bold. But I think that we lie less than others, for the fact of our being already at the top."

I bowed, honoring her dissimulation.

In the hall the pipes had again been exchanged for strings and reeds and another minuet. The shadows of gracefully bowing twosomes extended to the flagstones of our terrace. Oriel, Avalon's first moon, already sat high on the horizon, silvering the night and the gardens with a wistful countenance. Meagan shivered suddenly and drew nearer to me.

"Why, my princess," I queried in turn, "have you *really* come south to Tag-Afran?"

"Don't you honestly know?"

"No, I do not. And I'm beginning to dislike the idea that I am, apparently, the only one who doesn't. I refer to your reference to the 'affairs of lords.' If it's all a game, why, tell me. For I've other things to do."

She withdrew, saying, "I know only what a man can see for himself."

"And the background?"

"Surely you know as much as I?"

"I do *not*, my lady. Why, for example, are you here in Sierwood and in the company of a man whom you obviously despise?"

"You dare to question *me*?"

"I dare. I must save the world, remember?"

A smile replaced her sudden anger. "All right. I betray no confidence when I tell you that the Baron would wed me to Duke Oldus Finley if he could; this with the full knowledge that Finley of Sierwood can never be queen's consort in Weils. Among the northern barons, Dagar's the first among equals. With me wed to Finley he'd be free of the threat that my very existence poses. Do you know, my lord, that if my imprisoned father dies, then 'tis I who'll be queen in Weils? If I'm wed to Finley, however, the throne goes to Jocydyn."

"Why then did he not marry you rather than your sister?"

"Gods!" she exclaimed, looking to the stars. "You *are* an oaf, sir. The man truly *loves* my sister; though 'tis from this love that all evil's come. And you know nought of it?"

I sighed heavily. "No, again! 'Tis oft' times the fate of world-savers that they begin with little knowledge and therefore mostly fail in their endeavors. . . ."

She laughed. She couldn't help herself. A warm hand reached out to seize my wrist, an act of contrition. "All right," she said. "So you are ignorant of these things. I'd not thought it possible, really. But not to know is to suggest an unworldliness on your part which makes things doubly difficult."

"So I'm still in the soup?"

"That's one way to put it, sir."

"And is it still true, what you said before—that if I was from another world, you'd turn from me?" My right hand had moved to cover the one holding my wrist . . .

At a slender five-foot-four, her tartaned cap barely touched the line of my chin. Odd how one notices things like that, conditioned preferences and the like. She was the exact size I'd choose, if I had a choice.

"Turn *against* you? Why to save Weils, sir, I'd link myself with the very devil."

"Or a sadan?"

She shrugged. "Lay no claims, sir, to what you can't prove, even in joke. No sadan's ever reached the age of three and twenty. And you, green-eyes, as any love-struck maid can plainly see, are over thirty."

"Are you such a maiden?"

"I am neither a maiden, nor love-struck, Warlord. Now have done with your stupid questions."

"So what of yourself and Lord Finley? He seems presentable. Would you wed him *if* you could still keep the throne of Weils?"

"Gods, you're the cool one. I'll choose my own mate, sir; just as I'll choose the one I'll bed with. As for our Finley, well, he's more for books and the freedom found in knowledge. Don't misunderstand me. The duke's no boy lover. But he has no desire for the marriage bed either."

I smiled inwardly. Oldus Finley had indeed had reasons to act as matchmaker between myself and Meagan, except that unless she'd agreed to the game, he'd still not have dared.

"What of you?" she asked suddenly. "Do you have a lady? Are you betrothed?—All this, of course, aside from barmaids."

"I am as free as you are, my lady. But what is it that you want of me? There must be something and I cannot imagine your seeking my company for my red hair and a steady leg at jigging."

"Don't underestimate yourself. You appeal to me strongly. But, yes. I want your help. I sense a rapport between us.

Indeed, there must be such, or I'll go no further. Tell me, am I right?"

"You are indeed so."

Gods! If she only knew. Perfume and body heat from her small breasts and throat touched my nostrils, made the very hair on the back of my neck stand up like a raging avack.

Sensing my feelings, she leaned ever so lightly against my chest. Her night-black hair brushed my chin. She knew exactly what she was doing. She said simply, "I guessed it to be so. . . ."

The barons, she then explained, had, at the instigation of Dagar, forced her sister's marriage so that both she and Meagan would then be hostage against any attempt to free her father. The missing Shan Duglass, she confided, had not been inactive. Indeed, he'd not only been successful in raising the countryside against the rebels, but had also planned her father's rescue. That he was here now, in Sierwood, meant that her father had been freed. She'd expected him at the dinner hour. As of now, he was due any second.

"What of protocol? Will the duke allow him to speak for your father. What of Dagar?"

"There are treaties. But these were made, sir, with my father, not the barons."

"Shan Duglass was with that group I saw on the road?"

"He was." She bit her lip.

The art of dissimulation being what it is in the interests of the power of kings, nobles, colonies and worlds, there was a small chance that she'd erred in confiding in me; therefore her fear. . . .

Mixed applause for the last pavan joined with a loud shouting from near the great hall's entrance. Her blue eyes narrowed. She asked directly: "Will you help us, Lord Jarn Tybalt, if in the end things go awry? As you may have guessed, though our Finley's both likable and affable, he's above all else a patriot—in Sierwood's interests, as he sees them."

The shouting in the hall had become an exchange of shouts, and listening, I could only conclude that the game was truly on. I said, smiling, "Your timing's perfect."

She'd turned to look at me. Two tears of anger welled in her eyes, coursed down her cheeks. My silence continuing overlong, she then coldly pointed her small nose to the star-splashed skies, released my hand, withdrew herself from my encircling arm and moved deliberately to leave.

"Hey, Princess!" I called. "Hold up. I've not said I wouldn't."

Well! So the young Shan Duglass had won and I had lost. So be it. The question now was which faction could best aid in my own priority—crossing that sixteen hundred miles to the blinker light. As for having lost to Duglass, well I could certainly understand why.

He'd entered the extensive anteroom with a dozen men, two young knights and ten tough sergeants, men-at-arms; all in helms, hauberks and with scabbarded greatswords. Their surcoats denoted their clans and houses. Only their shields had been left behind, at their kaoles' saddles, most likely. Just Duglass and his two knights had been allowed to advance. The others were held; indeed, were surrounded at the entry by the bared blades of Lord Finley's household warriors.

Finley was standing, hands on hips, while sternly admonishing Duglass. "You surely could have found a less dramatic way to announce yourselves, sir. We've had three enjoyable days of festivities and were experiencing a most pleasant last night—and now you! You are most welcome here, certainly. But not this way. Indeed, 'twould be safe to say, my lord, that had you done this in Tremaine's court, you'd be dungeoned for it."

But Shan Duglass stood his ground. "I beg your forbearance, cousin. One last word. Our problem is that the good king, Artorius, whom you've referred to as our 'imprisoned king,' is imprisoned no longer. *He's never been so!* For like my brave father, he was foully slain on the very day he was taken; and this, by yon bastard of Dagar who used the charade of imprisonment to force his marriage to the princess Jocydyn, so's to be one step closer to the crown of Weils. . . . And I council you, too"—and now Shan Duglass was shouting for all to hear—"that he's not here to petition aid against the moodans and sadans as he falsely claims. For the half-men are retreating from the frontiers for the first time in living memory. 'Twas this fact and this alone that tempted Dagar and his ilk to slay the king. And 'tis this fact, too, that now prompts his attempt to entrap you. For, sirs—if they can lure the best of yours to nonexistent battles in Lothellian, why then they can seize all Sierwood and the 'world.' 'Tis as simple as that!"

Finley's nobles had listened to all of this with an admixture of alarm, awe, deep concern—and some guilt. This last ensued from a large group who'd drawn apart from Duke Finley upon Shan Duglass's entry. They stood now between those who'd stayed with Finley and the small group of Weilsian knights surrounding the Baron Dagar. The festive tables had at no time been taken away. Dagar's people were on the far side of theirs, defensively, whereas the rest who'd been mingling, dancing and the like, were to the front of theirs. Shan Duglass and his knights were in the exact center of the parqueted floor.

Duglass, continuing in righteous anger, then asked bluntly that Baron Dagar be given into his keeping so that he could return him to Ellenrude Castle, the seat of the erstwhile king, for trial.

To which Finley called, "Sir Chancellor (the position was hereditary), all that you say may be true. But we'll judge no man, unless it be in a proper court and after a proper hearing. And this will certainly not be now. I beg you, therefore, to retire—if for no reason but that of simple courtesy to these gathered lords and their wives."

But Shan persisted. "My lord, I beg you to arrest this man now. And then hold your court. If you do not, I warrant you'll see him next time with an army at his back."

Shan Duglass knew the one thing that Finley'd overlooked. With the knowledge out that the king, too, had been murdered, the barons would unite more solidly than ever before in back of Dagar—for their own protection.

Finley said sternly, his anger mounting. "The answer's still no. Retire, sir!"

"Then give him to me! I repeat. To allow him to run free is to risk disaster for everyone."

Dagar had watched it all quite closely. Knowing full well that whatever Finley's hesitations now, there'd be none such when the facts were out as to what the moodans and sadans were really doing, he made his move. . . .

Greatsword in hand, he leaped the table, yelling boldly, "You speak of juries, Bastard Duglass. Well, by the gods, I'll take the one that all believers must respect. *Trial by battle,* sir. And may the devil take your evil soul for the lies you've told before this house!"

Red-haired Shan, no laggard shirker when the chips were down, tossed his cloak to the floor, bent beneath the first whistling shriek of Dagar's blade, and countered with a blow that, had it connected, would have split the first among Weils' new equals to the pelvis.

In the midst of the ensuing bedlam—Duke Finley yelling for more men-at-arms, shrieks from some of the ladies and curses from those who disliked having their pleasure interfered with in this way—Hulok returned!

With two facsimiles of himself, he came racing beneath the swords of the warriors around Shan's sergeants to seek my side and to immediately shout above the caterwaul: "My Lord. Do not involve yourself. Remember our quest. We've still sixteen hundred miles to go!"

But I'd spotted Dagar's knights, plus a dozen or so of his men moving stealthily to place themselves directly opposite the battlers. Moreover, that handful of potentially treacherous Sierwoodian knights were making ready to acclaim the winner—whichever he was. And lastly, Shan Duglass, despite his courage, seemed no match for the skilled and heavily muscled Baron.

The clang of steel on weighty steel was like the hammer to the anvil. If Duglass could hang on, I thought, Dagar would surely tire first—and lose his head. But Shan slipped in the midst of a particularly heavy exchange. His sword pommel hit the floor—and flew from his grasp.

Dagar's victory roar was sufficient to rock the rafters. He lifted his greatsword for the killing blow—But with the same fluid motion I'd used to impress Hulok, I swept the laser from its cradle and penciled Dagar's blade at the haft so that its length shot straight up in the air to bury its point in the wooden beam above. I quickly reholstered the weapon.

A medley of gasps circled the hall. Hulok shot out to neatly kick Shan's sword back into his hand. Shan grabbed it, staggered to his feet, looked round for Dagar, and that worthy yelled and fell back. Responding, his dozen or so men instantly leaped the table and fell on Duglass to make an end of him. But then Shan's two young knights entered the fray and the hall resounded to the clash of weapons.

Hulok—he'd had an eye on me every second since he'd come to my side—grabbed my arm, yelling, "Nay, My Lord!" But I wasn't about to listen. *This* was the chance I'd needed: to do a deed such as few could ever match, and to do it in a way that *none* could forget.

My kuri-sword drawn, and the meddling Hulok knocked ass-over-teakettle, as the Celts would say, I too moved to the center of the floor. I stopped just five paces from the howling melee. "HOLD!" I shouted with a studied, brazen voice. "LEST I KILL YOU ALL! . . . SHEATHE YOUR WEAPONS! NOW!"

Most turned in amazement, saw me standing, legs apart, my two hands on the haft of the kuri, which pointed straight at them. They'd never heard such a challenge, or seen such arrogance.

"You tell us to *hold*, with that?" The questioning knight had the build and muscles of Dagar.

"I do. And I'll not repeat it. I'll count to five. If your weapons are not sheathed by then—you are all dead men."

"By the gods, you sadan bastard!" The Weilsian knight roared, and did what I knew he'd do. He *charged*. So did the others. . . .

The ancient Samurai weapon, lengthened and made heavier, became, when in the hands of myself, Jarn Tybalt, *Warlord,* an incomparable killing wand. I was a true master of the blade and I killed seven men in as many seconds— then fought to control myself before those who had fallen back, gray-faced, in total terror; their limbs all trembling. Control at such a point is ever the problem. For when the urge is on, the killing, in all truth becomes what it is, an art form whose end product, unfortunately involves the taking of life. I confess this, though I do not consider myself a killer of men. At least I pray that I'm not. . . .

I remained on one knee before my last victim. I'd gone down that way to slash him with a double backhand cut through leather and steel to the very spine. I stayed, holding the tableau in the candle light for all to dwell on; the bright blade shining and bloodied; my eyes wide with the beaded sweat beginning to dampen my face and neck. I breathed deeply: Once. Twice. Three times. Not a man of them moved, friend or foe. I then arose to salute Lord Oldus Fin-

ley and Shan Duglass with the dripping kuri—and returned it
to its home across my back.

It was not that they'd never seen blood before; indeed, they
had—great gobs of it. It was the *way* that I'd done it! Duke
Finley, as pale as a man will ever get without collapsing,
called for all action to cease and courteously asked those to
leave who would not be a part of the council he was now
calling. Dagar and his men were disarmed and taken directly
to the dungeons.

Only the Lady Jocydyn, Meagan Anne and the Vicar remained.

To me, Finley said simply, "I honor you, Jarn Tybalt, for I
have never seen such sword work. Nor do I hope that I'll
ever see it again, at least against me and mine. . . . As for
you, Sir Duglass. If you'd listened, we might have handled
this in another way. But that's hindsight, and who is to know,
really? One thing I must ask"—and a tight smile touched his
face— "What now, Shan, would you have me do with our
Lord of Dagar's Lady?"

Shan Duglass smiled a beaming red Scots smile. "Why
cousin," he chided softly, " 'tis simple. *She's carried my child
for a full three months. Moreover, she was my betrothed before ever she was his.*"

And he advanced to take the tearfully happy "lady" in his
arms. . . .

Slightly stunned by the meaning of this last, I shook my
head to clear it. Someone handed me a tumbler of wine. It
was Meagan, sober-faced and wide-eyed. I think that at that
moment, even she was afraid of me. Not so the grinning Hulok and his two new dwarf companions. Wise in the ways of
men, he held them back for the moment, waiting for *me* to
acknowledge *him*.

Not so Megan Anne. She took my arm with trembling fingers and marched me to Duglass and her sister. The talk everywhere was subdued now, as it always is in such situations.
Shan Duglass, without the slightest equivocation, bowed low
before her and thus confirmed her new stature. For though
she had still to be crowned, with the known death of her father, she was now queen in Weils.

"My Lord Chancellor," Meagan said formally, "allow me
to present my *friend*, Lord Jarn Tybalt, *Warlord* of an island

called Eden Valley." She was watching me like a hawk, more curious as to what I'd do and say than she was of Shan's reaction.

"I'm deeply honored, sir," said Shan. "And I do believe that I'm somewhat in your debt." A grin touched the strength of his face and his eyes twinkled. He put out a hand and I shook it.

"I'm a friend, my lord," I said, "who just might ask a favor, to clear that debt."

"Ask it."

I laughed. "Would you believe that I'm in sore need of a guide and an escort to a certain place in your northlands?"

"You have it, sir. But 'tis a strange request, you'll admit. I'm tempted to ask: Where *is* your island?"

"Why, south of the world," I said instantly. And then; "It's also east of the sun and west of your moons. One might even say that it's up there—among those stars. Would you accept that, my lord?" The smile was still on my face and I'd even put a twinkle in my eyes.

"Why not?" He dared to play my game. "From a sunburned redhead with emerald eyes and a sword the like of which has scarce been seen before; from such a man who says he's my friend and who's not only saved my life, but has done the same for the House of Tremaine, itself—why *not*? Have you met my lady, Sir Tybalt?"

Shan Duglass was, without a doubt, a man after my own heart. I took Jocydyn's hand and put it to my lips . . . She smiled and thanked me prettily for my efforts on her behalf and Shan's. Beautiful she was, but without the spirit or the aggressive assertiveness of Meagan Anne. Some men prefer that. Duglass apparently did. I do not. I bowed deeply to Meagan Anne, albeit, with a straight face that had just the touch of *Cheshire*. We then joined in the march to the conference to be held on the terrace; this, to summarize briefly what had happened and to decide what steps to take preparatory to a larger conclave.

The meeting, short, was made shorter still by thunder, lightning, and a mass of clouds which doused us with a spate of rain along the full length of the terrace.

I'd been rewarded with the quarters of one of the Weilsian knights who'd been sent to the dungeons with Dagar. But I went first to the baths again, taking my dwarves with me. I've never particularly liked the smell of death. At the moment it was on me like a shroud. While the four of us were soaking—and we had the place more or less to ourselves—Hulok introduced his companions as Torgus Glendowr and Fergus McHeath. They would be going, he explained, with me and himself to find the blinker light. I shook my head. Then a thought occurred. "These names," I told him, "yours included, are from three different nations of the old world, Irish, Welsh and Scotch. Yet you are all dwarves. Should you not have sprung from a single tree at the time of the magic?"

"Why so?" Hulok countered. "The thing was simply an indiscriminate happening. The pure strain is ourselves, whatever our origins."

"And what do you do?" I asked of Torgus and Fergus, "besides splitting skulls and lopping off legs and arms with those axes of yours?"

"We work in stone, my lord."

"And having finished a contract, you are now heading north to your homes. . . ."

"Aye, lord."

I sighed.

Hulok said pontifically, "All dwarves, my lord, are stoneworkers."

"Except at home."

"Why do you say that?"

"Because someone has to plant your food, Hulok, as well as fish and hunt and make your artifacts and tools."

He shrugged. "Stonework is our trade. Moreover, my lord, I've something to tell you. It goes like this: Though dwarves are notably cleanly at all times, it is still *not* our custom to bathe twice in a single day. We hold, sir, that too much soap and water destroys the body oils, shrivels ones' skin and weakens ones' sexual proclivities."

"Hulok?" I asked, ignoring his nonsense, "where's the Whatzit?"

"Which one?" he stuttered. I'd actually caught him off balance.

"You mean you each have one?"

"I didn't say that."

"I think you did; which inclines me to believe that it is

those dwarves who travel, or who do jobs outside your country, who possess a Whatzit."

"You're fishing, my lord."

"May I see your Whatzit tomorrow?"

"Why?"

"Because there's a possibility that it can be helpful in our search for the beacon."

He shrugged. "All right."

"Where is it now?"

"Don't press your luck, Warlord."

Six

Baron Hardee Dagar, with three knights and over forty men-at-arms escaped Tag-Afran Castle two hours before dawn. They took with them their own kaoles and over two hundred castle mounts, inclusive of Sir Percy's Primrose.

I was shaken from my furs by Hulok's heavy hand. "Up! Up! Warlord!" he shouted. "We're beset!" He began throwing my clothes at me while I rubbed my eyes and staggered to the arrow slits overlooking the gardens. I saw only darkness and a fine rain. A rumble of voices grew, however, coming mostly from the courtyard. . . . Joining the infuriated Lord Finley, we found that the canny baron had fired the stables, too, hoping thusly to destroy the remaining animals so as to prevent pursuit. Many kaoles had been killed. The remainder, maddened by the smoke, were for the moment, useless.

In the great hall we were given strong tea laced with brandy. Meat and fruits were also carried to the single table where we'd gathered. Finley had been joined by as many as thirty lords and knights. A point to help understand our dilemma, however, was that a good half of those who'd stood aside the previous night as favoring the baron's "honest call to war" against the moodans and sadans, were no longer with us.

"They still believe they'll send their men against invading moodans," Finley explained. "They couldn't buy Sir Duglass' story of a moodan retreat. Note, for instance, that Davys Gwynedd of Coody-South is not with us. He confessed to me last night that he could not accept the story for the simple reason, as he put it, that the *Guardians* would never allow it; that they never have and never will! We'll have them back when they find they've been lied to—and *not* by Duglass. As for the others," he said darkly; "those who undoubtedly seek a personal gain from this, why they'll now ride direct to their holdings and call for a muster of warriors to either come down on Tag-Afran, or to join with the levies of Weils' barons against the forces of Shan Duglass and the Princess Meagan Anne."

Among these last were the four who'd clandestinely met with the baron at the inn. Indeed, it had been *their* warriors—on duty as part of the festive aid to Finley's guards—who'd slain a number of those loyal swordsmen to insure the success of the venture. Then, what with the portcullis being already up, and the moat bridge down—it had been that way all summer as a mark of the goodwill existent between the duke and his freemen—they had only to free the baron, seize the stables and open the gates. . . .

No one as yet had even so much as mentioned my use of the laser weapon. Indeed, the blade of Dagar's sword was still stuck in the beam above. An odd phenomenon. Of the lords and knights closest to Finley, I'd been introduced to Ross Gwynedd, uncle to the previously mentioned Davys of Coody-South. Ian Williams of Chuurns, a westerly holding. Tibbetts of Durin, also a westerly holding. Three feisty young brothers with lands bordering on Weils; they dearly hated all barons. Charlemont, of the northeast border, a duke almost as important as Finley, and the two brothers, Rex and Dorcis Thomaas, Warlord and Chancellor, respectively, of the Council—of which Finley was the nominal leader. These and perhaps a dozen others actually comprised the Sierwood Council; inclusive of those who had fled—Hargis of Tinellian, for one, and the Duke Mordid of Koors, a duchy near Vils. There were also a few still among us who were not necessarily in Finley's camp. . . . And Finley knew it.

"Whatever your conclusions, sirs—" Shan Duglass was speaking strongly— "One thing's for sure: what with Dagar freed and heading for Ellenrude Castle the civil war that will now break could be both long and bloody. It could be shortened, perhaps, *if* I could precede him into Weils and seize Ellenrude before his arrival. *I intend to do exactly that, sirs!* Which means"—and he spoke directly to Lord Finley—"that I'll need all your remaining kaoles, cousin. . . ."

"And you'll have them," Finley smiled—"if you'll just tell

us how you propose to do this. They already have an hour on you."

Shan Duglass grinned. "You've a hundred or so mounts still here. I have a dozen or so riders. We'll leave within the hour, and *all* the hundred mounts will be *saddled* so's to waste no time. We'll simply leap from kaole to kaole."

"You'll have them," said Finely. "And the saddles, too."

There was a round of applause at that, and Shan Duglass even bowed his head in thanks while the duke sent a lackey off to have the mounts prepared.

But then a voice called out, begging Finley's permission to speak. It was *Hulok*.

Finley, curious as we all were, nodded his acquiescence.

Hulok stepped out from our table. His two dwarf companions, Torgus and Fergus drew instantly closer to *me*.

"My Lord Duglass," Hulok began, "we know that they've taken two hundred kaoles with them—which means only that their speed can be increased by a switch from mount to mount. Four mounts as a matter of fact are all that a single rider can handle. Any number beyond that becomes counter productive. Indeed, *the* proper balance for 'God's speed,' as we dwarves would say—and I remind you that we are great travelers and know whereof we speak—is precisely that, four mounts . . . The distance from here to the border is one hundred and ninety miles. From the border to Ellenrude is another two hundred and sixty miles. Whatever the time gained in not having to change saddles each time you switch, you will *not* pass the baron between here and there."

Shan called out, "That's just your opinion, Dwarf."

"It is and I'm right. But there's another way—if you dare to take it."

"Control your impudence."

Hulok shrugged. "You know what I refer to."

"Who doesn't? You mean the 'Valley'—and *Hools!*"

"Quite right. The valley! Wherein, once entered, one has smooth sailing for its entire length of a hundred miles; except that he's also stuck in it; for the mountains to either side are passless. The valley's problem, as we know it, is that its northern exit is blocked by ruins of one of the greatest of the old cities. The farm thanes call it *Hools*, after the sounds the *whisperers* make. There are some who have passed through it in the daylight. Dwarves, too, have risked it and have suffered no harm; just as dwarves and men, together, have risked other, similar cities. It is only the night that we should fear. Now, sir, we can make that hundred miles in twelve hours, with a four-hour rest period—and *still* arrive two hours before sunset; if we leave in the next half-hour."

"*We?* Sir Dwarf?" Shan Duglass looked to Finley, then back to Hulok. "Since you include yourself in my troupe, may I ask why you wish to go with us—and does this include your master and good friend, Sir Tybalt?"

Reacting as he would to any inference that he served a master, Hulok scowled heavily, ground his teeth for a second or two, but then got a grip on himself. "The moodans and sadans are indeed retreating," he said in measured tones. "We dwarves have our own sources for such information. This being so, why then should I wait seven months for good sailing weather when I could be home, with a little luck, in two? I but seek the protection of your swords for the first leg of a journey which, in its last stages, will skirt the eastern borders of Lothellian and the Deadlands, and thence to Olgin-Dwarfland, our beauteous world of heavy forests and great stone mountains . . . As to our mutual *friend*, Lord Tybalt"—and he glanced at me in such a way that candlelight gleamed from off his square-cut teeth—"well know this, Sir Duglass: Since the question of Hools has just now been raised by me, I've had no chance to discuss it with anyone—he'll make his own decision. In effect, sir, he can most assuredly speak for himself. . . ."

Shan laughed, delighted with what he thought was a fine bit of dissimulation. The thirty lords watched intently.

"A last point, my lord," Hulok called.

"Which is?"

"Why to tell you that with me you'll be protected somewhat. We're dwarves, remember? We carry *Merlin's Eyes*."

"Hey, Tybalt!" Shan Duglass shot at me, ignoring Hulok's reference to the Whatzit. "Will you ride north with us—and risk Hools in the riding? Indeed, would you fight at my side against the barons? If so, why? You're not of Weils. And most certainly not of Sierwood. . . ."

"Why, indeed?" A clear feminine voice called out. It was Meagan Anne. "Allow me, Lord Duglass, for it is my army that you'll soon command, to speak for our Warlord of Eden Valley. *He* says that he *must* go north for to save our world and everything in it. Well, sirs"—and she grinned in sheer delight—"a quest like that is most certainly *not* to be denied; *nor should it be questioned!* A last point is that since, I, *too*, will ride with you to Ellenrude; this, though the path will lead through Hools or hell itself, why then I can think of no better sword to add to our small company, nor"—and this time her twinkling blue eyes sought out our Hulok—"the axes of his three brave stalwarts."

Oh, neat! I thought. She's bound my three to battle and not just as traveling onlookers. I then stepped out to hold up a hand. Duke Finley nodded. I said, "Princess. Sir Duke. Chancellor Duglass—and all you lords and knights of Sierwood. We have a saying on my 'Floating Isle.' It is that one should not look a gift-kaole in the mouth. I've a personal purpose, true, in going north. Perhaps we'll discuss it along the way. But not now, for time grows short. Allow me to just say simply that I intend no harm to any righteous man, or dwarf; indeed, I but ask for the chance to use my sword in your defense. . . ."

At that, Meagan Anne came over to take my hand and to lift it high. And she got a thumping round of applause for that and for her beauty *and* her commanding presence.

This, I thought—*this*—is what we of the colonies had truly lost. The mystery of it all; the sheer vibrancy of life's rock-hard assertiveness. We had become trained killers of necessity. Many, such as myself, were no strangers to history. But now, to be a living part of it, to participate freely, naturally, to walk naked, without a spacesuit at the very point of the decision-making process and with never a thought of the broken valve, the pin-prick tear—To just sleep and wake on the morrow to something new—rain, perhaps, sleet, great winds, snow, a brilliant sun—and a fair voyage. I felt suddenly as some newly awakened cryonic corpse; a neo-modern Methuselah, reborn for life—*outside* the laboratory!

What I'm saying, I guess, is that *not* to know and to feel all this, except from inside a suit, or from the cubicles of our living prisons, mobile or stationary—is to be truly already dead!

And now I was damn-well free of it all!

I even reveled in the fact that Hulok had known all along of Hools, but had told me nothing. Ah! Hulok, my friend, and the mystery of him. Duke Oldus Finley, reticent, knowledgeable; even intellectually interesting, as aside from not being afraid to commit himself when he'd finally made up his mind. Shan Duglass, fire-brand, a warrior after my own heart, who'd proven it, was proving it now. And my Celtic princess, an anachronism if there ever was one. . . . By the gods, I mused, as the council went about its job of mustering men to be sent to Duglass' aid, plus devising a means to check the question of just *why* the moodans and sadans were retreating, *if* this was true—If this was *all* of it, if the bloody CT warhead clobbered us all tomorrow, I'd not regret it. For I, among all the survivors of the colonies had already had the good fortune to have lived on Avalon for something like forty hours. Were I to be given forty more, I'd still thank the *whisperer* from my heart—even while he tore me to pieces for having made a mistake in the first place.

The thought that I might survive at all, and what that could mean, was sheer euphoria!

Seven

We were twenty, not a dozen, when we left the great stone-slabbed courtyard of Tag-Afran Castle. There was Shan Duglass with his two knights, Lors Aspin and Ward Turlock, plus his ten men-at-arms, all hefty sergeants and picked swordsmen. Then there was myself and Hulok, with the young Torgus Glendowr and the ever-glowering, Fergus McHeath. The Vicar-Priest, Loren Raddle, had demanded that he, too, be allowed to ride with us—as advisor and protector of the queen-to-be, and as the nonsecular voice of the realm.

I now sported a heavy shield to go with my own weapons, as well as a heavy war spear (not heavy to me). Considering the circumstances, our dwarves were offered spears, too. They declined them.

Meagan Anne, now in a close-fitting, silvered hauberk, and with a small Norman-style shield to her saddle's side, carried only a somewhat smaller scabbarded greatsword at her back. The fine link folds of her hauberk head-piece lay back upon her small shoulders and the tartaned, top-knotted Tremaine tam was tight on her streaming black hair.

"I'll ride with you, my lord," she told me boldly. "I'll be your shield-maiden, a guard to your left side—where the heart is," she quipped. She then pranced her little red-eyed court mare, Gucchi, causing my evil-tempered Huaclan to snort, spit, and attempt to bite her.

The rain had come again; indeed, had been with us since Dagar's escape. To a man, inclusive of my three dwarves, all wore fur cloaks reaching to below their knees. The fur, I was told, was like that of my own cloak, of the avaks, great wolves, running mostly in packs. Two avaks made a cloak, they were that big.

Shan was bidding a last good-bye to Jocydyn in her chambers, for there was no way that she could ride with us, considering. We awaited the saddling of the remaining animals. Duke Oldus Finley, plus most of the lords and the ladies of the castle were down to see us off. Muted pipes were being winded; drum-skins tightened. It had been an hour since the conference, two since Dagar's escape. We would gain at least six hours by the shortcut through Hools, and I, for one, looked forward to the experience.

"All *right*! Let's get to it!" Shan Duglass yelled to his sergeants as he came at almost a running clank through the main doors. "Go help our Lord Finley's ostlers and lackeys. I want those mounts saddled and in this courtyard in the next ten minutes, hear?"

Finley drifted unhurriedly to our little group to shake all our hands. He was accompanied by the two Thomaases, Ross Gwynedd, and the muscular, beefy, Lord Charlemont of Loors. They'd stopped by myself and Meagan. Finley asked softly of the princess, "Are things all right with you, my dear?" It was almost as if they shared a secret.

"Never better, cousin," Meagan replied in the vernacular of Avalon's nobility. "Especially since I'm content that our warlord here, though he may have other fish to fry, is still on our side with his sword *and* his magic. . . ."

Finley grinned at my startled expression. "I meant to ask you about that," he told me courteously. "But perhaps someday you'll tell me on your own."

"I'd tell you now if we had time," I said—and the rain and wind hit us hard then so that we were all pulling the hoods of our cloaks over our heads—"But, my lord, there's nothing worse than an interesting story that's lost on the wind."

"It was I," he leaned close, "in case you've wondered, who warned you that my warriors were on the way to arrest you. Allow me to say that I'm very glad you stayed."

He shook my hand then, and turned to Shan Duglass who was prancing his great war kaole to settle his hauberk. "And God's speed to you, cousin, through that damned dread city. I'll pray for you and for our queen to be. No mind. Whether you make it in time or not, I'll join you in two weeks' time with at least five thousand men."

"It may be twice that many," stout Rex Thomaas shouted. He seemed a solid man, one who did not give easily; a man we could depend upon.

"If we take Ellenrude, the war's won; if not, we'll need whatever you can muster. Whatever's done, it must be done before the snows." Shan Duglass had been forced to yell this last against a nightmare chorus of protesting, howling kaoles being driven into the courtyard from the stables.

"I'd come, even if you win without us." Finley's high-pitched voice cried above the bedlam. " 'Tis not just enough to know that the moodans are retreating. We must, and I mean *all* of us, discover the cause of the mystery. Anything that changes the balance of power between the beast-men and ourselves, *one way or the other,* is cause for concern. I, sirs, would prefer finding that reason while in the company of fifty thousand swords, than to send—as some have already suggested—a handful of good vicars and a cart of cleansing holy water. . . .

"And," he continued, turning to me, "that would certainly suit you, too, Lord Tybalt. Right? To go north, through the Deadlands—protected by fifty thousand warriors?"

"Why, yes, my lord." I answered with a straight face. "If I must indeed go north, that would surely be the way to do it."

Duke Finley burst out laughing, to be joined by Shan Duglass' bellow. But all that, including the howling of the maddened kaoles was put to shame by the raging, roaring tirade of one, Sir Percy Tarrent as he came running and hopping through the downpour to throw himself on his knees in front of us.

"My lords, all," he was yelling. "I'd thought my *Primrose* to be safe, but those bastards have taken him, too. I beg of you to let me go north with this brave Duglass. I'll earn my way, I promise. Moreover, Lord Finley, I ask you: What good's the bloody saddle you've given me without the mount to match it?"

Finley, his pale face now awash with rain, his red mop of watered hair all blowing in the gusts of wind, could only smile and shout against the elements. "Why not? We've a hundred mounts and nineteen riders. At four-to-one, we've enough for another. But give him a cloak, you." Finley called to a guard. "And he can leave that saddle here."

Percy's face, at being forced to part with his prize, so discomfitted the soft-hearted duke, that he then grabbed a war-spear flaunting his own household banner from another guard and tossed it to young Tarrent. " 'Tis my guarantee, sir knight," he called, "that your hard-won prize will be here when you return for it. Be off now. And mind you—hold my banner high."

Percy caught it from the mount into whose saddle he'd leaped. He had time only to blubber his thanks. For Percy, though ferociously courageous in battle, as time would prove, could also be an emotional disaster. . . .

Through the great gates we streamed, to the dull thumping of wet kettledrums and a skirl of weakened pipes. Five sergeants led off, then the eighty of our remaining mounts. After that, Shan and his two knights. Meagan Anne and myself. Sir Percy and the vicar-priest, Loren Raddle. Hulok and his two companions, and then the remaining five men-at-arms.

We were ghost riders in a storm the like of which I'd never read, heard, or even seen in all the video collections of our quite extensive library. There are fantastic windstorms on certain great gaseous planets; indeed, there are frozen particle storms on others; some strong enough to implode an errant starship. But a wind and water storm of this strength on a world sustaining humanoid life? No waaaay! But then, we'd known only Earth before, right. And this was Avalon. I now knew why no ship built by *this* society could withstand a winter's storm at sea. . . . We raced ahead and into what became almost at once, a veritable wall of wind and water!

And it kept up. And so did we. Perseus rose within the hour. But we knew this only by a sort of lightening of the wall of gray around us. We were kept to but half the speed we'd normally be making. Our five sergeants ahead clung to the original cart path, went farther east for four long miles, and then turned north on a better and wider road than any I'd seen to date.

I soon found the reason for the "Valley," though dead-ended by the ruins of Hools was, for all its hundred-mile length, a quite lush and productive farm and orchard area; this, between great forests and, in some places, narrowing canyons. After the first twenty miles the wind died somewhat and the rain lifted, became a steady driven sleet. Now we could see great fields where cattle, sheep and hottles grazed together. Kaoles, I noted, were kept separate from all of these. For, though not carnivorous, they could be omnivorous and would gobble up a hottle with great gusto if given the opportunity.

But there were still more forests than farms, great brooding stretches of heavy growth and giant trees. All forests are *virgin* on Avalon. In one of these wild stretches a monstrous pack of great avaks paralleled our strung-out kaole herd for as much as five miles, with here and there an avak dashing in and out to drag a kaole down. But our altogether vicious kaoles gave better than they got. The avaks, unable to cut one from the herd, would instead find one of their own lifted bodily by an enraged kaole who'd sunk his square teeth into a lean spine, shaken, tossed in the air to be caught by another kaole while still running, and, in short, *played with,* killed, and eaten. It was too much for the avaks. They faded back into the forest as silently as they'd come.

For six long hours we'd kept it up. Two hours longer than the usual four. It made the kaoles furious. Then they *had* to rest; ourselves, too. We'd changed mounts every hour, to no avail. We'd fallen behind in our schedule. We'd gone but fifty miles and had better than fifty more to go. In essence, we'd lost two precious hours of daylight. The margin now was nonexistent. With luck, after the next run, we'd have a half-hour to get through Hools *before total darkness took us!*

As Hulok put it, we couldn't have started out at a more inappropriate time. "But we've no choice now. We must chance it anyway."

"What, really, Hulok, can we expect? What is it that you fear?"

"Well that's the thing, my lord," he said blandly. "We don't know. Those who've survived a ruin at night have seen nothing, so there's nothing to tell. Those who haven't. Well they're just gone. . . ."

"But the whisperers? All of you know of them."

"Some have seen them from a distance—and heard them, too."

"It was a whisperer, Hulok, who brought my ship to Avalon. Moreover, you saw the one at the inn. I tossed a bottle through it. Both could have been but a mental projection. There's a form of misused power here, dwarf. We've no time now, true. But in the long run we should seek it out—and slay it if necessary."

"My lord," he said, "you are as stupid as you are smart.

Whatever the power of whisperers, there are other things in the ruins that I'd truly not like to meet up with; nor would you, if you knew what I know."

I shrugged. "As you say. We can't turn back."

He looked across at me, his great eyes burning in the half-light. "Nor would I, Warlord. Even if I could!"

And then I sensed it, the overt challenge. It was as if he wanted to see me; indeed, *needed* to see me in just such a situation—in a ruin, at night; with the whisperers all around us.

I said, "I've a few other things to ask you, Dwarf."

"In time," he replied. "In time." And he wandered off to join with Fergus and Torgus at their own fire.

During the rest, Shan's men had made hot hottle soup with sundry dried vegetables and spices. We had grainy bread, too, and heated wine. All this, while I sat with a large tree bole to my back, and against which I also rested my head, was still heaven to me as compared to *any* colony base. Meagan sat close to me, as did Shan, Percy and the others; indeed, Hulok and his two companions even deigned finally to join us, too. The continuing rain and the still sometimes howling wind depressed them. My ebullience, my very high spirits, depressed them further. They couldn't understand it. While Shan cursed the darkness and the storm, Percy, pumping wind into his waterlogged pipes, finally managed a sort of funereal dirge—to which I sang an approximation of the original lyrics, something about a young prince being forced to flee to a place called the Isle of Skye, wherever that was.

Shan Duglass, looking at me with a wide-eyed suspicion, asked hotly, "By the gods, sir, and where did you learn that?"

"Why, from the records—of the world before the magic. Not this one, but the one from which we all came in the long ago."

I'd thought it would be safe to say that, since I doubted they'd understand me. I was half right. For though mythology is born of religion, and vice versa, it still remains mythology, the blood and bones of any culture, and will usually live long after the religion's been disavowed.

"What?" Shan asked abruptly, "is the meaning of that wiggledy red lizard on your tunic?"

"It comes from a long-ago land"—and then I dared to say

it— "The birthplace of Merlin. He of the magic eyes. Its name, I think, was Wales."

"Weils?" His brows knit.

"Nay, sir. Wales! And there is a difference."

Meagan's small hand had reached out to rest gently on my arm; this, as her eyes sought his, for she meant without words to tell him something; to warn him? Seeing, he nodded silently. To me he said, "Well then, when there's time, we'll talk."

"That we will," I intoned. "I promise you."

They then drew in upon themselves, and the kaoles browsed and the rain fell and the wind blew. . . . Once I felt Meagan's lips against my cheek, my ear. "I take it, Jarn Tybalt," she whispered, "that we'll talk, too, you and I, and soon."

I dared to put an arm around her, risking, so I thought, a sword's point to my throat. But no. She simply snuggled up to me. Odd, I mused. Customs seemed strangely different. Somehow they'd known that she'd chosen me—at least for the moment.

"What," she asked once more against my ear, "is the meaning of that falling star behind the lizard?"

"Why, my princess," I whispered back, while brushing her cheek ever so lightly with my lips—" 'tis *me*, coming from Eden Isle to Tag-Afran. . . ."

She snuggled closer.

We drove hard again to make up the time—and failed. And we all knew then that we'd reach Hools only when the sun had set. And how right we were. Indeed, we passed through the town of Scardale—a center of as many as a thousand people—just as the faint light of great Persei sank ever lower behind the mountains to the west. They'd gathered to watch us pass. And seeing our faces and hearing our silence, they *knew* we'd be going on through Hools, a thing never done in living memory. And so they began a rhythmic prayer for us and crossed their breasts with the tau cross, over and over until we'd disappeared in the wall of mist.

Beyond Scardale, some twenty miles, the valley narrowed, became a gorge, all winding down to Hools, and then beyond Hools to something called the Great Plain of Birney Biern;

this last being split by a river of the same name to mark the border between Sierwood and Weils.

Would you believe that even as we reached the mouth of the gorge the skies cleared, the stars came out, and a strange glow from the yet to arise trio of moons began a silvering of the canyon walls?

At the end of the gorge—and its mouth had been like the fabled Terran pass of Roncesvalles—was that awful mound of tree-split granite blocks, ruined towers, amphitheaters, temples, squares and gargantuan buildings known as the dead city of Hools. The buildings, temples, *all* of it, was now but a monstrous labyrinth of moldering rooms-on-rooms and tortured, blasted corridors that led to nowhere.

Seconds before entering the first narrow break in what had once been the city's walls, I saw why no one could go around it. The cliffs, or escarpment to either side were sheer. Certainly there had been in its lifetime streets and alleyways to circumvent the center. But no more. Now there was but a single way: straight through and down!

We halted before the wall, calling everyone to the fore. We would ride together and *stay* together, whatever happened, Shan ordered. Small chance we wouldn't, considering.

Curious, I confess that my feelings were more a hopeful expectancy that *something* would appear. I would not have had it otherwise. Mythology, ghost stories and the like, were for the firesides of barbarians on lonely evenings; an escape, as it were, in a horror tale to set the red blood flowing. Whatever we'd meet with would be real, I knew. As real as the whisperer and the destroyed *Scot's Leap.*

The farther we rode on the sloping, twisting path, the closer the ruined walls drew in around us. Then the encircling clouds, first silvered by the light beyond, became suddenly like mirrors to the arrival of all three moons, Oriel, Pollo and Thisbe. They formed a perfect triangle. Everything sprang to life! The ruins became a steel-point etching in their starkness. Strange animals moaned and cried from yawning *thing*-made burrows. Small creatures shrieked and scurried. Others, huge and more indigenous to cave and forest, came out to watch our passing. But then, as we crossed the first plaza, the silence returned; pervasively mocking. Great ruined temples loomed on all sides, alike in the madness of their alien symmetry. Even the cut stone beneath our kaole's paws had once been polished ebon marble. . . .

I was the first to notice, or so I thought, that something was pacing us. The trail had taken us even lower; indeed, we'd crossed two more plazas before it happened. I alerted the others, and was told that the things were on both sides of us, for there was more than one. A glance back to Hulok, Fergus and Torgus revealed that their cloaks were off, their shields slung to their arms and their axes were out and gleaming. The others likewise now gripped their shields and war spears and guided their mounts with their knees as true warriors are trained to do.

And then, at a point where we'd emerged from a deep canyon of buildings which had not yet collapsed, we padded softly into the broad expanse of a last great plaza. It was similar to the others, except that here and there huge trees had thrust through to buckle the stone slabs as would a quake of monstrous proportions. At its very center there was an unbroken tableau of demonic pedestalled statuary. There were at least twelve figures, tall and barely humanoid. They stared down at us through awful eyes. Limbs writhed, twisted and seemed to reach for us, as the moonlight brought them all to frightful life.

I felt Meagan's thigh brush against my own, she was that close. I glanced down to wink. Her tight-lipped, ready-for-anything countenance broke then and she grinned, and even laughed—though silently.

And rightly so, for there was little to laugh at.

On the far side our exit road was seen to disappear between the heavily vined walls of two massive temples. Beneath the sheltering portico of the one to our left were a number of banked fires—and beyond them what appeared to be as many as sixty armed and mounted *men!*

Shan Duglass silently held up a hand. We halted. Across the way the kaoles yipped and snarled. Ours challenged accordingly. Shan said, "Well now. We expected ghosts, but instead we find something else. . . . What say you, Dwarf?" he demanded suddenly. "This was your idea. Can you explain that over there?"

And now the fires blazed up, deliberately fed by their tenders. The heightened blaze, together with the bright moonlight united to give us such a clear view of them all that we could not help but note the displayed gonfalons and pennons attached to their war spears.

Hulok—and his eyes, like mine, were such as to spot an ore seam on a rock-faced cliff at a thousand yards—said calmly, "They're sadans, Shan Duglass. Which means that we've something now to truly fear. For in all memory neither man nor dwarf has ever seen such south of Lothellian's border."

"Sadans indeed." Shan's anger was icy cold; made colder, if that could be, by the sure knowledge that whatever happened now, we'd most certainly lost the race to Ellenrude Castle. "Did you think I didn't know it, Dwarf? I've seen those idiot banners in more battles than you have teeth. . . . Hey, Seamus!" he called to a young sergeant. "Cut out thirty of those mounts. Hold them to our left. If they charge us before we decide what to do, drive the kaoles into them."

But now Hulok was angry. "By the gods," he roared. "Do you suggest—?"

"I suggest *nothing!* Dwarf-man! If I even thought such, I'd spit you now. And both your brothers. And yon green-eyes, too—for luck!"

I'd attracted his attention by deliberately moving Huaclan between Hulok and himself. My great kaole's pawed nails scratched sparks from off the granite.

"Shan Duglass, you bastard," Meagan then called in measured tones as cold and as icy as his had been. "You blithering Pictish idiot. Know that I love you, as I love my sister. But what would you now, sir, in your first command beneath my crown? Would you split even this small force when we're beset by three times our number? Do what you're capable of. You are a warrior and a leader of men. Now get us out of this!"

I then deliberately intruded, clapping on my helmet and smiling as if nothing had happened. I said simply, "Look there. I think they're coming."

And sure enough, ten riders from the sadan camp, refusing discipline as sadans always do, else they wouldn't be sadans, came storming at us through the moonlight, screaming maniacally, shields set, great war spears held aloft. Duglass, his head clearing, yelled for five sergeants to guard the princess—and Seamus to drive the thirty kaoles at the sadans.

The rest of us were to hit their flank and cut them down—the exact orders that I would have given.

Diverted by our kaoles, their momentum lost, we then slammed into them from all directions. I disdained the shield. The war spear came naturally to me, resembling as it did our colony exercise javelins. It had an eight-foot hardwood shaft and a two-foot heavy blade, razor sharp on each side of its length. Whirling it in my two hands, I dashed aside both the spear and shield of my first adversary—and took his head so that it flew screaming through the air. I ran my second man through to the haft; which was wrong, tactically. For I then had to take the time to shake him off it. In those brief seconds the remaining eight were slain. . . . But we'd lost two brave sergeants to their murderous fury.

"Well, now!" Duglass roared, pleased with this beginning. "We've lessened their numbers and gained ten mounts. We'll now ride at them," he cautioned, while holding up a hand. "But we'll stop just twenty yards of them—and challenge them singly. That way," he grinned with a certain elfish charm, "we should be able to take out another twenty before they realize they can't win in a one-on-one passage of arms."

"My lord!" I called, while fighting Huaclan's attempts to get a mouthful of one of the fallen sadans. "We need *prisoners*—at least two."

"Make prisoners of sadans?" Sir Turlock, Shan's knight called in horror. It was as if he thought the act unthinkable, akin to allowing giant, man-eating scorpions to live. . . .

I frowned, shouted stubbornly, "We must find out why they're here, sirs. *And how they got here.* I doubt that it has anything at all to do with Dagar. And for that very reason, we *must* know!"

Shan nodded thoughtfully. "We'll do it, Tybalt." He raised a hand: "Onnnnnnnn!"

And off we went, driving straight at them across the intervening hundred yards. They waited, yelling ferociously; hoping, we knew, that we'd foolishly come right in among them. They even began a withdrawal to either side in anticipation of the classic error. . . . But instead, Shan Duglass brought his great kaole, Gundart, to a skidding, spitting halt just forty feet from them, causing their jubilation to fade instantly.

Sadans were like that, as I was to find. Schizoid, incapable of truly rational thought, all reason forever succumbed to chaos at even the slightest change in their limited game plans. They were like brilliant children, playing at war—but with an almost nonexistent attention span.

Physically, there was simply no difference at all between us; a thing easily apparent even in the limited moonlight. They looked like us and that was that. A second departure from sanity, was in their apparel. The colors of their tunics were as varied as the rainbow. And I mean *each* tunic, or surcoat, was like that, a patchwork of mad striations and in-signia—for in their own minds they, too, were lords and knights, actually ruling over large dominions of beast-men.

But their blazonry, too, depicted only madness.

On each tunic-breast, shield-front and flaunted gonfalon, was a veritable caricature of a sadanic imagined reality. *Nothing* held true. Wavering scroll signs, meaningless half-words; for none could actually read or write; the internal and external organs of men and animals. A crazyness of propor-tion in all things. A madness of taste, or the complete lack of it. Anything went. Shields were adorned with giant phalluses, complete with vulvae, a plate of stew; a man's severed head as a child would draw it. And even the depiction, among a welter of bloodied arms and legs—of a baby's treasured rattle!

I was beset in those first few seconds with a sense of total horror, along with a bone-chilling sadness that this could be the summation of it all, the final dénouement. A wave of sickness churned my stomach so that I wanted to vomit.

But there was no time.

To prevent them from charging us, which was the last thing Shan wanted, he was holding them with his voice, shouting, "Hey, stinking sadans, beast-men! It's said that the only difference between yourselves and true men is that your brains are addled. I say that's a lie! I say that the magic took your guts out, too! OH! YOU DON'T BELIEVE IT?" he screamed to their answering shouts of rage and hate. "Then who among you will dare to face a single one of us in com-bat? Speak up, you cowardly bastards. . . . Or must I come and drag you out?"

Staring wildly at each other, they reared their war steeds. Some made as if to ride forward, but then fell back. The idea

of single combat was new to them and they were confused.
Seeing their reluctance, our eight sergeants jeered, made obscene gestures; to be joined by Shan's two knights. Then Sir
Percy, too, gave them the arm and finger and cursed them
loudest of all. My three dwarves spit to show their dislike of
what they thought was childish game's playing. But Meagan
Anne, understanding what Shan was attempting to do,
watched keenly.

When they could stand it no longer, a blond giant came
out, *sans* helmet but with a double-bladed axe at least twice
the size of Hulok's. His smile was so sweet in the moonlight
that he seemed more saint than devil. And, indeed, he hadn't
just "come out," he'd actually launched himself against Shan
like the missile from the catapult.

Our Lord Chancellor met him halfway, took the first terrible axe blow against the deliberate slant of his shield—and
plunged his spear's blade right through the smile so that the
blue eyes turned in, blood shot from nose and mouth and the
sadan collapsed and died. Shan's spearpoint, I swear, stood
out a forearm's length from the base of the mad thing's skull.

A wash of rain hit us then and two more rode forward. A
quick glance revealed the clouds to be coming in again from
the east. Our beetle-browed Sir Turlock simply *hurled* his
eleven-foot shaft with such accuracy and strength that it went
right through the first sadan's shield and hauberk; upon which
he darted his mount forward to seize it; to place an iron-shod
boot on the dead sadan's chest, and then, with a combination
jerk and kick, to send the floundering body to the flagstones.
Lors Aspin, Shan's second knight, a likable though uncom-
promising fellow, then exchanged sword blows with the sadan's companion, to neatly sever the thing's sword arm from
its shoulder. To the other sadans' wild laughter, and its own
howling, it then rode off to lose itself in the darkness of the
centered statues.

Poor Aspin however, overly curious as to where it was going, was himself cut down by a raging sadan who, seeing his
companion dealt with in this way, came flying out to drive
his spear point straight through Aspin's throat.

It was then my turn, for more were coming forward to
shake their spears and shout their threats. Sir Aspin's death
had given them heart. I chose his slayer first, and killed him
with my spear's butt. Actually, I'd missed with the blade

when I'd driven Huaclan against him. But, I had forced his shield down. So—I just came around with the butt to dash his brains out.

Sir Percy, answering a challenge on his own, killed two sadans in perhaps six seconds. The first with his shield's edge to its throat; the second, as Shan had done—by shoving his spear's point through the beard-ringed red mouth of a creature who seemed not to know where he was, or why. . . .

A trio of howlers rushed at me. Sir Percy cut one of them down just as I hurled my war-spear as Turlock had done. It pierced the first sadan's middle, but in no way silenced his screaming. I then drew my kuri-sword, tapped aside the second spear leveled at my chest with the spine of it, brought it around, as the thing went by me—and took its head from the back so that it hit the stone directly in front of Hulok where he and his two axemen guarded Meagan. Its eyes rolled horribly!

Riderless and uncontrolled kaoles were now all over the place. I looked for Shan. He'd just pierced a demon-visaged wild thing to the rib cage. Like me in my previous performance, he, too, was forced to shake the body loose—except he didn't. With the rage that had never really left him, at his finding the sadans here in the first place, he instead lifted his spitted, struggling victim from its saddle—*and drove spear and all through the shrieking torso of what seemed to be another godlike angel*.

To our combined cheers at the feat—I, frankly, had never seen anything like it; nor do I expect to again—he consigned the two of them to the now bloodied flagstones.

The fighting now was becoming dangerously general, though the sadans had still not grouped for a charge. We began to fall back, sensing simultaneously what could happen if we didn't.

To our right was the preferred exit between the two great temples. Between that exit and ourselves were the remaining sadans, thirty or forty of them. To our left, and at the far end of the extreme length of columns fronting the great temple stairs beneath their protective portico, was a second exit, a narrower street—stygian in its foreboding depths. That we'd chosen the right exit was simply because the light of the three moons had shown it to be free of fallen debris and, in the one glance I'd had down its immediate length, it seemed to be open and to lead down and through an area of ever-smaller ruins. It *was* the road out of Hools!

The more reason for the sadans to keep us from it.

As we withdrew they did what they should have done in the first place: They quickly formed an attack wedge, all spears to the front—and charged!

We were hit hard. The screaming was an instant bedlam. And this, with the crash of shields on shields and the ring of swords, spear-points and axes on helms, armor and the like, was sufficient to wake all the dead of the city, had they been ready for it. . . . Meagan was again to my left, with the aged vicar-priest just behind her. Our two dwarves, Fergus and Torgus were to *her* left, and Hulok to my *right*. An interesting arrangement, forged, I was sure, by Hulok himself.

Shan Duglass, to the right point, sought to lead us, spearing and chopping boldly toward the preferred exit. But we were met with a solid wall of swords, shields and biting kaoles. Again, our own mounts gave better than they got. Huaclan indeed bit through the throats of at least three great beasts that I can remember. But they swarmed around us, forcing us by sheer weight of numbers between the great columns of the portico and toward the steps (larger than human-size) leading upward to the great yawning doors of the temple entry.

And it was just then that they began to kill our kaoles; this, to the raging command of a maddened chieftain with small mirrors dangling from his helm. Half of our sergeants' mounts were quickly down, their necks hewn through. Percy's prancing mount took a spear thrust through the heart; Fegus' kaole, too. We'd already driven them up the first dozen or so of the broad flat steps and turned them to face our enemies. But it was too much. Then Meagan's mount was speared (fortunately it was a spare and not Gucchi). I leaped from Huaclan's saddle, whacked his rump hard to send him off, seized Meagan from her fallen, kicking mount, and with Percy, Fergus and the remaining sergeants as a shield-line, called on the others to dismount too.

"Shan Duglass!" I roared to where he fought two sword-swinging sadans. "Dismount and join us, sir. On these stairs they cannot take us!"

And he did, with the aid of Sir Turlock. Then, with the

vicar to our rear, myself, Shan, Turlock and Percy to the fore; with Hulok and his dwarves to my right and the five sergeants—we'd lost three more—to Turlock's left, we stood at bay before some thirty sadans, all shrieking victory!

And they were foolish enough to charge us—still mounted! We simply backed *up* a few more steps, then either speared or pulled their riders from their saddles and killed them then and there. But we lost Turlock. With the shaft of one giant sadan through his chest, the *thing* had pulled back, dragging poor Turlock with him. Then the others pounced on him and took him to between two columns where they killed him in such a way as to make all of us white with rage. . . . And we'd lost three more sergeants, too.

But they'd seen the light, as it were. And they were still *twenty* to our *eight* (not counting Meagan and the vicar). And so they dismounted, too; set up a wedged shield-front and came at us on an angle to flank us from *above!*

And my dwarves let as many as six of them do it; upon which, with a guttural chant in their throats and heavy shields lifted to protect their heads, they went straight up, *under* and through them. With broad sweeps of their humming axes they lopped off legs below the knees, split groins, chests and crushed spines. I, in the meantime, and with but a single swordsman to aid me, plunged into the midst of the six remaining sadan warriors on our right. Three, I slew immediately. A fourth, seeking to get above me, I slashed across the belly. The fifth sadan—he still held a spear—thrust at me from below, and missed. Turning, I slipped in the wet of the fourth sadan's entrails—and the fifth one tried again.

But my single swordsman cried in a clear but deadly voice, "I think not, you insane bastard!" and flew at him so that *her* sword's point stuck out a hand's breadth beyond the back of the creature's neck. The last of the six then flung his weapon from him and ran screaming down through the colonnades.

"Hey, now, my lord!" Meagan exclaimed, and her surcoat was bloodied with spindrift gore. "I think we've won!"

And we had. For of the eight remaining sadans on our left, seven were down, slain by Shan Duglass, Sir Percy and the two remaining sergeants. The eighth had fled to join the one who'd ran from me.

Shan, with a good presence of mind, then sent the sergeants after the sadans—"The prisoners that you wanted," he explained, grinning. We then began to round up the rest of the kaoles and found that we now had well over two hundred. As we drove them back toward the exit, I saw that it was now barred to us in another way. Something, unseen before in the half-light, had been boiling up and out of the temple across the way and to the right of the exit. Now it was *across* the exit and filling all the space in between.

Shan Duglass, returning to us with a present of Meagan's Gucchi, could not help but see the expressions on our faces. His eyes followed mine to the slowly advancing gray-white mass; saw the flowing, undulating front—pseudopods reaching, extending to cover all the space between ourselves and the exit. All bodies in its path, sadans and butchered kaoles alike were being simply devoured, or better, *absorbed*.

Our own dead had been almost immediately collected by Hulok and his two counterparts, thrown across the nearest saddled kaole and tied down; this, along with the two captured prisoners. The bodies would be properly buried beyond Hools—if we ever made it, that is.

"What is it, Tybalt?"

"It resembles," I told him pedantically, "an amoebalike life form about which I have only read and never seen; indeed, never expected to see in such a size as this."

He looked at me sharply, eyes slitted. "You know, of course, that I don't understand you. I'll ask you again: What is it?"

"Well then—it's a beast with the power to kill us all, if we stay here."

"And to whom does it belong? Who's sent it to do the job the others couldn't?"

"Again, you know as much as I."

"My Lord!" Sir Percy plucked Shan's sleeve in bug-eyed excitement. "Allow me to prick the damned thing. We'll see how it takes to steel."

Another wash of rain came. And now but two moons were visible with the clouds closing in.

"Stay where you are, sir." Shan said.

"But, my lord—"

"Nay, Sir Percy," Hulok said harshly. "Do not be fooled by the slowness that you see. A part of it could reach and take you, just like that"—and he snapped his fingers. "And I

must warn you, too, that the luck of our presence does not
extend to trifling with such a beast."

"He's probably right," Shan sighed. "Well what do you
suggest, Greeneyes? You know at least what it can do."

But a keening had begun all around us, and the great plaza
darkened, though the moons were still there. Large shadows
seemed to writhe among the statues, to join with them in
some obscene, demonic pavane. . . . Meagan drew close, put
out a hand to take my arm. The keening was like before,
above, around and *in* the *Scot's Leap*—and in the woodsy
inn. Hulok, too, drew close to stare me in the eyes. He knew
quite well what it was, and so did I.

It formed, took shape to the rear of us, huge, twice again
as large as the statues or of the shape in the inn. It was wavering, shroudlike, ectoplasmic. And as before, the agonized
keening drew in upon itself as would a coalescing gas. The
sound tightened, resolved itself to *my* name. . . . "Ohhhhhh,
Jaaarrrnnn! Heeeeeeerrrrrr—Leeeaaaaavvvveeee, Jaaa-
aarrrrrnnnnnn! Ohhhhhhh, Leeeeeeaaaaavvvvvee. . . ."
And a blasphemous phantom arm, jointless, with ghostly ten-
dril fingers pointed directly to the black and yawning pit of
the second exit which, I thought, could quite easily be the
very gate to hell.

"Jaaaaarrrrrnnnnn!" it said again. "Coooooommmmmm-
mmmmmmm, Jaaaaarrrrrnnnnn!"

And did I mention that the sadan's banked fires till glowed,
lending to the whole scene a Dantean touch. . . . Even the
kaoles—and we now had over two hundred of them—were
silent, waiting, actually trembling in their fear. All their eyes
were riveted on the encroaching horror, and I knew that
within seconds they'd be running in all directions.

"My Princess, and all the rest of you," I said as calmly as I
could, "hear me out, for we've little time. I do not know
what that thing is that calls my name, though I must confess
to a previous visit by it. Nor do I know what the other thing
is which will kill us all in the next few minutes if we do not
follow the suggestion of the thing that cries my name. We
can, of course, retreat. The decision's yours. I'll follow you,
wherever."

"My Lord," Meagan asked harshly, deliberately, "for my
love: What of your magic?"

I shrugged. "It's not enough. I can stop it for but a few minutes. Watch!"

I whipped the laser out and penciled the beam all along the front of the advancing wave of pseudopodal flesh. It recoiled horribly, turned in upon itself—and came on again. The stink of destroyed flesh mingled with the over-strong perfumes of the sadan dead to assail our nostrils. I did the same with the blaster, firing five energy bolts; each one tearing great livid holes in the blanket of it—only to see them flow together while the thing continued on.

I held out the two weapons. "There's not much 'power' left in them," I explained. "As you've seen, that *thing*," and I gestured toward the gray-white horror—"I cannot kill. Whatever awaits us in the passage—well, we'll just have to take our chances."

Meagan reached to take both my hands and to look me squarely in my eyes. "My lord," she asked, "if you commanded here, what would you do?"

I shrugged and nodded toward the second exit. "Better that than to retreat."

"Better the thing we don't know, than the one we do," Shan Duglass quoted. He'd reversed the meaning. "Let's to it then, Tybalt. Hey, Percy! Hulok! Drive the damned kaoles ahead of us. If we're to be eaten, sirs, we just might be able to sate the eaters' appetite before we get there!" Then he winked. "You and I, warlord, will bring up the rear."

The two dwarves with the sergeants immediately herded the kaoles so that they streamed toward the narrow alleyway of the second exit. Sir Percy and Hulok followed with the two prisoners and our ten dead strapped across the saddles of their mounts. Meagan and the vicar were next. She rode quite close to him, for he'd ceased to be really with it since the beginning of the last battle for the steps. His eyes were staring, his face was a pasty white, while a clammy sweat shone on all his flesh.

The advancing gray horror was within forty feet of us now, the flow of it seeming to accelerate. But Shan called and I wheeled Huaclan, caused him to rear one last time—and swept the advancing front of grasping pseudopods with one last laser beat. Again the recoil and the stink. I then joined with Duglass in a mad race down the length of the colonnade in the wake of the princess.

The whisperer vanished just seconds before we plunged into the blackness—which we instantly found to be not all that black. Indeed, moonlight, what there was left of it, filtered through rents, tears and great gaping holes all along its length.

An errant thought touched my mind. Had the many who'd disappeared—at least in this particular ruin—simply taken the wrong exit? Stupid! Stupid! My subconscious replied. The blanket-beast could more or less do what it pleased. But then, not necessarily. Motivated it was. But was it also *manipulated*? And if so by whom, or what? If we'd had time, we might have learned the secret. But we had none.

The kaoles to the fore brayed back to our mounts, and these brayed and honked in return. The honks and brays, Shan said, suggested no danger anywhere. As we plunged ahead, we passed what seemed to be side streets or alleys, leading to more openness and moonlight. But we continued on in what now was an arcaded street, with the collapsed buildings forming a roof overhead. Then we reached a flat open space—not a plaza or square, but rather what appeared to be the site of an ancient games *playing field*. Beyond the far side we saw only moldering rubble. Our road meandered through it to tie into the original main road we'd started out on.

We were free of Hools!

But there was no elation, no shouts of joy. Just a tiredness in all our bones. True, we were still alive, but we'd lost the bigger battle. Just before midnight, we halted to bury our comrades in the lee of a hill's slope and covered them with a cairn of stones to mark the site of their courage and to protect them from avaks and other beasts. Vicar Raddle, somewhat recovered, even found strength to say a few words; all this, in the wet which had returned as a gently falling rain.

Some twenty miles farther on, we freed the complaining kaoles for rest and grazing—and slept.

Eight

Driving hard, we reached the border ford of the Bierny River in the early hours of the following day. The signs were as expected. Baron Hordee Dagar had spent the rest and grazing hours on the far side and had broken camp just three hours before.

"Damn the bastards!" Shan Duglass shouted at the banked embers. But we'd still been right in risking Hools, he told us. For Hulok had been right. We could never have caught them the other way. As it was, Dagar had had two rain and storm-free hours on us before ever we'd crossed Tag-Afran's bridge. We'd lost three hours on the valley road to Dagar's two. The bloody battle in Hools had cost us another three— For what can be described in minutes, oft' times takes but seconds in reality—or, conversely, a day or two. To bury our dead took another hour. But neither Meagan nor Duglass would have had it any other way.

Shortly before noon—and the sun in this capricious latitude was again shining brightly—we were led by Shan down a side road to a small village in the meadowed lee of a bend in a white-water river. We were met by eighty newly arrived, husky, bright-eyed young swordsmen. All wore the Tremaine colors. At news of Meagan's presence, they instantly gathered to go down on one knee, doff their caps, extend their bare blades and to swear fealty to her as Weil's rightful queen to be. It was an inspiring sight, with muted drums and pipes in the background and our Vicar reading the oath aloud.

Their leader, a young knight and friend of Shan, Sir Roggs Quigley, told us that lookouts on the main road had brought him the news of Dagar's passing. He could have attempted to run him down, he confessed, and with luck, could have captured him. But he'd been given no orders to that effect. Moreover, excepting for our presence now, he'd been completely

112

in the dark as to what had happened and whether Shan and the princess were even alive. . . .

Shan Duglass, the new *Lord Chancellor*, was not exactly happy with that report. Still, there'd been no guarantee that if Roggs had pursued the baron, he'd have caught him. So much for those small bits of luck that if taken advantage of immediately can oft' times change the course of history.

Meagan Anne, as a princess soon to be queen, had immediately been taken in tow by young Quigley's equally young wife, Margaret, her two sisters, and a few village girls eager to serve. We bathed in the racing river, relaxed naked on its banks in the noonday sun, dozed until dinner, retired after small talk, and that was it. . . . At least that's what I did.

Shan Duglass, not sparing himself, had gone to work the first moment he'd left the river's bank. A full half of Quigley's swordsmen were sent in all directions with the news of the king's murder at the hands of Dagar and the barons; of the ascendancy of the Princess Meagan Anne Tremaine to royal power prior to coronation—with this last to take place after victory, and with orders from the new Chancellor, Shan Duglass, for all levies and musters loyal to the House of Tremaine to gather in Duglass' duchy, and specifically in the small town and castle of Kilellen on the Wys River. . . . A full report, inclusive of our battle against the *sadans* in Hools, and of our escape from the great *thing* which sought our lives, was also written up by Vicar Lors Raddle and forwarded to Duke Oldus Finley at Tag-Afran. As if by an unspoken agreement, no mention was made of the *whisperer*, or of its use of *my* name!

"We must leave tomorrow for Kilellen," Shan told me at dinner. "The 'race' has never stopped, sir. Indeed, we must gather sufficient men in sufficient time so as to keep him from marching on our duchy. With luck, we'll also be mustering around Ellenrude so that when *we* march—and it must be before the snows—the chances of taking the 'king's seat' will be good. And cheer up, Greeneyes," he'd noted the noncommittal expression on my face, "at Kilellen, you'll be a hundred miles closer to the north—and at Ellenrude, another two."

I sought to speak to Meagan before wandering off to sleep. Hulok, Fergus and Torgus had made camp at the river's bank and had even made me a small tent in case it should rain again; which, Hulok said with a straight face, was quite possible in these times. But Meagan, too, was tired. I'd only to remember that she'd been in the saddle every day, from Ellenrude to Tag-Afran, with the baron—and to here, a distance, altogether, of almost eight hundred miles.

She did, however, pat my arm, look at me sleepy-eyed—or was it *sloe-eyed*?—and say something to the effect that though I indeed had a nice body, that it was downright indecent for me to go cavorting about in the nude before the village maids. She then sighed and dismissed me, for after all, she *was* the queen.

And that was precisely what we did, go to Kilellen, that is, and on the following day. And when I think on it now, that two-hundred mile forced march was as difficult in its own way as was the mad dash through the storm to that evil plaza in Hools.

In the process of the march, I found that Shan Duglass, other than being a skilled and resolute swordsman, was also a damned good administrator-organizer (his father had trained him well), and an excellent commander—and I mean a commander of armies, not just of men.

The difference, I think, between the feudalism of ancient Terra and the new, quasi-feudalism of this single continent of Avalon's vast land mass, was that Terra's had come of age, sociologically, in areas of Europe already used and worn by countless centuries of barbarism. Its forests were already depleted, its animals slain and much of its arable earth ruined. The forests of Avalon were endless and virgin. Animals, beasts of all kinds roamed these forests in profusion; so much so that no man rode through them without company of some sort and knew how to wield a sword or spear. Each village, too, was an independent entity. It paid taxes, yes. But its farmers, its peasantry were *not* serfs, but freemen; and this in Weils *and* Sierwood. Moreover, in such a bounteous land and with such a limited population: I doubted much if there was more than two million all told, and this on a single continent of some *six* million square miles—no one could go hungry; and, from the cottage industry potential, a little work and no one would lack for any reasonable thing.

And so the road to Kilellen, though it passed through a number of villages, was still more often than not in the center

of great brooding forests, scrabbling in the stone-cold passes
of great mountains and fording an endless array of white-
water rivers. It resembled the Terran land of America in the
sixteenth century. And, too, the forests, though brooding,
were anything but silent. The howlings and the roarings and
the general hullabaloo of the myriad carnivores, as well as
those who were being attacked or eaten by same, made oft
times a constant bedlam all around us. Great winds blew after the first day, accompanied by lashing rains and, at higher
altitudes, driving sleet. The march to Kilellen was indeed, as
young Quigley would put it, a corker. . . .

Princess Meagan Anne became ill on the second day. And
on that same night, Shan chose to question our two sadan
captives. We'd been joined by at least two hundred warriors
and as many as five knights; all being a part of those who'd
answered the first call to rise against the barons. The five
being duly informed of all that had taken place in Hools;
again, excepting the *whisperer's* aid and the like, they sat in
on the interrogation.

The two were naturally young, eighteen or so; this, since
no sadan lives beyond the age of twenty-two. They had been
given into the keeping of Fergus and Torgus, since these two
were more stable and less inclined to kill them on the spot as
a reply to their constant flood of scathing insults. With the
dwarves, they were quiet; indeed, silent. For they had a
strange dread of them, insisting to us that all dwarves were
liegemen to the *Guardians*.

Hulok's reply to this, when asked, was to state cryptically
that all sadans are insane and he'd not dignify the question.

To which Shan Duglass said, laughing, "You will, you insolent bastard, if I string you up for a while to the nearest
limb."

"Don't press me, my lord." Hulok ground his teeth. "Your
humor is sometimes offensive."

"As is your attitude, Dwarf!"

They had a strange rapport, a mutual respect that lead
sometimes to an odd sort of baiting.

At the time of the questioning we'd taken over the inn of a
small village named Persifalls, causing our own Sir Percy to
check its lineage with two of the elders against the background of his own questionable roots—and this despite the

fact that Percy was *not* his surname. . . . There were the five knights, Sir Percy, Sir Quigley, Shan, myself and Hulok. The vicar was taking notes.

"We will do this in an organized way," Shan Duglass led off. "I've prepared a number of questions. Allow me, therefore to ask them first. Then, if any of you have more, feel free to ask them. . . ." Everyone muttered assent, or kept his silence.

The two sadans were blond, blue-eyed look-alikes, even to the visible fact that their hair was falling out, that they had ulcerous sores on their faces, and that the palsied trembling that had seized on both their bodies at the hour of their capture had never left them. Their filthy clothes were the gaudiest of rough weaves; their boots and belts of untanned leather and poor workmanship. Small mirrors dangled from their earlobes; each had a double necklace of uncut stones, some obviously precious, others, just stones. Their hauberks (taken from them), were of the simplest kind, metal rings sewn to leather as opposed to the human well-knit links. They were slender, muscular, and *terminal*. This last in the sense that their very nervousness suggested a physical deterioration which, if not taken in hand, would bring their deaths in months, if not weeks.

I'd asked before about their open sores; found that they were apparently something new. But disease in Lothellian was simply taken for granted, with one plague following another; with whole communities of moodans wiped out, rebuilt—and hit again by some loathsome new epidemic. The moodans were immune to nothing; nor were the sadans. Under normal circumstances, I'd be inclined to check things out further, to aid them if I could. But now was not the time. . . .

Shan began a calm, almost friendly interrogation. A thing unheard of to the others, for according to the new scriptures, reflecting the thoughts and commands of Father Abram, his son, Og, and his wife, the Lady Eostre, one "should not allow a sadan or moodan to *live!*" Indeed, the very phrase *was* the Twelfth Commandment!

"Where in Lothellian do you come from?" he asked, pointing to first one and then the other.

They were two knights of Jarkbund Castle, they replied between curses, hissings and attempts to spit in the faces of their captors. A knife-prick to the throat of each by Hulok calmed them somewhat. They served the Lord Wulsping, whom we'd killed at Hools.

"Where is Jarkbund?"

"On the Kiel River to the east of the Dark Mountains."

"What of the sixty sadans we slew? Where did they come from?"

"Also from Jarkbund."

"How then," Shan probed softly, "did your company traverse the almost eight hundred miles from Jarkbund to Hools, in Sierwood? More! Why Hools? Why did your Lord Wulsping take you to Hools?"

Their answer was to laugh maniacally and to tell us that they had traveled in *dream* through great caverns below the earth, and sometimes on the quick-flowing breast of stygian rivers. Many times great monsters had sought to kill and eat them, but they were always protected. Then suddenly they had awakened—and the dream was true. They had found themselves in Hools.

"How long," Shan asked, "were you there before we came?"

"A week, ten days."

"What did you eat on your dream journey—and in Hools?"

"For the journey, we'd brought our own. In Hools, we had—Temple food."

"What's that?"

But they would only look at each other and grin and smack their lips.

"What," Shan persisted, "did your Lord Wulsping tell you of Hools and your reason for being there?"

Again they but looked at each other, eyes blazing with what seemed to be an ecstatic secret quite difficult to retain—"That *we* would live when all else died!" the first sadan finally shouted; "That we had only to serve the Master!"

"Why would all the others die?"

But they could contain themselves no longer. "WHY?" the first sadan continued: "WHY? YOU STINKING, PUKING HUMAN SCUM. YOU ASK US WHY? 'TIS YOU WHO'VE KILLED US," he screamed. " 'TIS YOU WHO'VE ALWAYS KILLED US, DENIED US THE RIGHT TO LIVE. WHY? LOOK ON THIS. 'TIS YOUR WORK!" And he tore open his shirt to reveal a chest covered with the scabrous, ulcerous, running sores that covered his face. . . . "ASK HIM!" he raged, pointing directly at Hulok. "ASK YOUR TRAITOR TO THE WORLD, THE *GUARDIAN* LAP-DOG—THE KEEPER OF THE KEYS! ASK *HIM!*"

The second of the duo, caught up completely in the volatile frenzy of his comrade's accusation, and its evident—to him—truths, began to howl and scream: "KILL THEM, GODS! KILL THEM, NOW!" so that his face, already dangerously flushed, grew suddenly purple so that he fell to the floor, with his eyes straining from his head and awash with blood. His feet then beat a fast tattoo on the wooden floor and he hemorrhaged massively and died.

Upon which the first sadan grew deathly pale and would say no more. Hulok, at a gesture from Shan, took him away; anxious, or so I sensed, to get away himself, considering the accusation.

In the ensuing silence we were served with a hot mulled wine, ale or beer if we wished it and an Avalonian herb drink, also hot and served with spices; it was a tea of some sort. Grainy bread and cheese, a standard staple with everything, was also brought in, along with some cold slices of roasted hottle. . . . Shan Duglass again got down to business, asking us all what we'd gotten from the sadan's answers to his questions.

"I have heard," the huge Sir Tideman said; he was a baron loyal to the dead Tremaine who'd just come to us from his holding of Trypstyle on the western seacoast, "that there's a great ruin near where the Kiel River leaves the Dark Mountains in Lothellian. There are others, too, of course. But that one, supposedly, is the largest. If Jarkbund castle's also there. . . ." He shrugged.

"We must learn more of what they actually did in Hools," Vicar Raddle arose to say, "and about their trip there. As for this new sickness the things spoke of, well there has always been sickness and plague in Lothellian. 'Tis a part of being accursed. So say the scriptures. Who among us who have wandered the border in peace and war have not seen moodans and sadans, the half of which were dying even as one looked. The curse is forever. And I adjure you: In the eyes of Abram, there can be no pity!"

"Still," Sir Quigley said, ignoring the lecture, "the thing is that when they left Lothellian, they went only to Hools, which can certainly pose no peril to us. I ask you, who, except for reasons of dire necessity"—and he nodded toward Shan—"goes to Hools? Whatever the mystery, I deem it to have little importance for us at this moment. The fish we fry, sirs, are much closer to hand."

Shan, listening, nodded an acquiesence. "What of you, Sir Tybalt?" he then asked suddenly of me. "What do you see in this phenomenon of sadans being in Hools?"

"Why, sirs," I replied slowly, "like Sir Quigley, here, I deem it as being apart from anything pertaining to the differences between Weils' barons and the House of Tremaine. But their fantasy of caverns and dark rivers, as being the road to Hools, bespeaks a method of travel *and* communication which we've known nothing about 'til now—if it *truly* exists! Moreover, it would seem that another force is involved here, a thing that would seek to use the sadans to an end we know not of. . . ."

I simply left it at that, and Shan nodded, saying, "Well put, Sir Tybalt. I would agree. I would also strongly agree that the question of sadans in Hools is not our immediate problem. The priority, sirs, is the throne of Weils. Let us deal with that first—now!"

And they agreed, refilled their tankards and began to talk of the proper use of this group of warriors or that, and of the sending of this levy or that to which peripheral village around Kilellen—and Great Ellenrude!

After sup I visited Meagan briefly in her tent and with the gift of a small vial of scent, pressurized and concentrated so as to last at least two years. She asked me gravely of the questioning. I told her. I also confessed that I was slowly becoming aware of the existence of a dark tragedy in the land of Lothellian that no true human could dismiss with a simple sword's edge, or a flight of arrows.

She regarded me strangely from where she was propped up on her pillows, and put a hand out to touch my arm. Her way of establishing rapport.

I then showed her the tiny button to press on the vial to release a measured mist of scent. She was delighted. I also, and with her permission, took her *four* active pulse beats, surreptitiously took her temperature by a simple ring contact and gave her a small antibiotic candy—a magic potion, I told her, again, to her delight.

Holding to my hand as I rose to go, she pressed it to her lips; this, in full view of the Lady Margaret and two serving girls, peeped up at me with one slightly feverish blue eye and asked softly, "Who are you, really, Jarn Tybalt?"

"We'll talk in Kilellen," I told her. "I promise you."

She said simply, "Indeed, we will."

She appeared at breakfast the next morning, bright-eyed, cheerful, and with a merry word for everyone and a big bold hug for me. She called me her "Doctor," and swore to Shan Duglass, who'd begun to watch us with a jaundiced eye, that I knew more of physik than all of Weils' chirurgeons.

For the next four days we rode as madly as ever we'd ridden on the nightmare road to Hools. We had, so I found, to cross a mountain chain which, though small, was exceedingly rugged. Our fourth night, therefore, was spent on a hewn-out cliff's edge extending for as much as a thousand yards. Below us, at some three thousand feet, a great river churned and boiled its way through a white granite defile. On the ledge where we'd camped, its muted thunder was in no way conducive to sleep.

The following night, the fifth, was spent in a village at the head of the lengthy Valley of Kilellen, where we joined with a muster of eight knights and three hundred warriors, all to be added to the two hundred we'd already collected along the way. Shan Duglass, though he'd expected them to be waiting there, was still pleased as punch that they were; the reality of things oft' times not measuring up to one's plans, as he put it.

For—as I was to learn immediately and for the first time, though he swore he'd explained it to me before—Kilellen castle and town were in the hands of an old rebelling warhorse of a baron, who'd seized it for his group on the very day of Shan's father's murder.

Before we could use it, or even sleep in it, therefore, we first had to take it.

Which we did the next night, the sixth, in a stunning, driving coup that once unleashed took all of forty-five minutes to complete. . . . One must remember that Kilellen was Shan's home. He knew every street and byway of the town and every stone and passage of the picturesque castle. *He also knew the first name of every male capable of wielding a sword.*

Moreover, the three hundred were but a part of those who'd prepared in minute detail for the recapture of Castle Kilellen.

At precisely midnight and favored by the soft luminescence of Oriel, Pollo and Thisbe, the town was abruptly cut off from the castle in one quick rush. All four gates were seized; all roads immediately posted. Simultaneously with this, a hundred swordsmen, led by Shan Duglass and his knights, stormed up from a series of secret labyrinthine passages to seize the great courtyard, lower the moat-bridge, hoist up the portcullis—and open the iron-bound gates—across which myself, Sir Percy (he carried Oldus Finley's Household Banner) and the loyal Baron, Sir Hugh Tideman, came charging to flood the courtyard with swords—and end it!

Scarce two dozen men had been killed; and these, because of their stubborn resistance. True, the following morning, Shan Duglass did hang the swearing and bravely stupid, Baron Angus Cready, for his participation in the murders of the king and Shan's father, plus the unlawful seizure of the Chancellor's castle in the absence of his son—but that was it!

The grizzly, unrepentant baron, damned Shan and all his kin to the hell of the Deadlands, spit in the faces of the two stout men-at-arms who led him, bound, to the castle wall and placed the noose around his neck. To confound Shan's justice, he then broke free and himself jumped from the wall to snap his own neck at the rope's end.

All those who'd gathered to watch, inclusive of all of us who'd ridden with the Duglass and the queen-to-be, applauded his courage. His hundred or so men who'd surrendered were fairly treated. They were given the choice of either pledging themselves right then and there to the Royal House, or to freely return to the holdings of their slain baron—which now were automatically forfeit to the crown. If they chose the latter, and if at any future date they were still found to be in rebellion, they would be taken and instantly slain. . . .

Half joined us then and there. The others left for home and fireside beneath the scowls and glares of our victorious swordsmen. I hardly need point out that, under the circumstances, they would have had no choice at all had not their disciplined but grasping old baron not kept them under a tight reign during his tenure. Had there been any pillage, any maltreatment of the folk—any *rape*—they would all have gone to the wall to join their lord.

The following night all guild leaders, town officials and the like, inclusive of all the nobility of the extensive valley-duchy who were not in rebellion, converged on Castle Kilellen to pledge themselves to Duglass and to do honor to the queen-to-be.

It was a gala occasion. As stated, Shan Duglass had been well trained, as the bastard son of his father, the Lord Chancellor of Weils. And, too, and without a doubt, this training had extended to a mastery of all the conceptual laws of power, plus the art of the manipulation of both events and people so as to maintain the continuity of a given status quo!

I, for example, despite our closeness of the last ten days or so, was *not* seated at the high table, nor even at one of the two tables in a line with it to either side. In fact, both Sir Percy (as a lesser knight of Sierwood) and I found ourselves at the first right-angled table to the *left* of the high tables, a position with which Sir Percy Tarrent was quite satisfied— despite the overlooked fact that he bore the banner of Tag-Afran's Lord Finley. I was not satisfied. For I'd sought the company of kings and dukes for reasons other than a participation in the feudal idiocy of the "pecking-order." I had a job to do! I needed the center of power for no other reason but to aid me in that job. The one thing I had no time at all for, was Shan Duglass' obvious game-playing!

The single enjoyable event of the evening, other than the fact that I could sense, telepathically, the presense of Meagan in my mind—a kind of rapport that even she was unaware of—was that a portion of the nonsecular service, as performed by priest-vicar, Lors Raddle, with the aid of some thirty other priest-vicars, both men *and* women, contained certain Druid rites as well as age-old paens to Father Abram and the Trinity. A dew-dappled length of mistletoe, for example, was brought in, as well as a black-iron pot in whose crystal water one can supposedly see his past, present and future. The priest-vicars, their formal robes of purest white, trimmed with red, and Druid colors, then passed down the length of the connecting high tables to cut single leaves from the mistletoe with a small golden sickle. One leaf would be given to but a single person who would put it between his or her teeth, break the skin, but barely—it has the power to kill—and then toss it in the pot.

The rite completed, they would then be asked to look, one by one. What they saw, I do not know. Most likely they saw nothing. But there was a noticeable stirring here and there.

After, I had a last cup of wine and moved to retire early. Protocol demanded, however, that I approach the high table before leaving. I did, smiling and bowing my head ever so slightly. Shan, his eyes laughing at my stiffness, looked to Meagan. Upon which she frowned, bit her lips, and nodded her acquiescence. I'd known that other things had been planned for the occasion. Music, dancing, perhaps—and introductions. The setting for such was certainly at its best. The hardwood was polished. The woven tapestries had been cleaned, as well as all the banners; the armor and weapons polished to a high lustre. Our erstwhile baron had been a spit-and-polish martinet in his own right, and he'd certainly kept the castle up. Had I been Shan, I'd have freed him for that reason alone. A last point was that each and everyone of the guests was wearing his best—as were Shan and Meagan Anne.

I'd been given a double apartment in the castle's west wing, right next to that of Sir Percy Tarrent. The second half of my double—and this was most certainly a courtesy of Shan's—was specifically for my three dwarves. They were there now, and occupied in some weird rite of their own. They'd made a ring of pine boughs on the floor, placed red candles at the cardinal points, set up an incense pot of some kind—the stuff in it was sufficient to fly one right out the window—and were dancing around it. I watched for a while. They were fantastically graceful despite their disproportion. Then Hulok broke off to join me for a moment in my own large room.

We moved to the stone balcony overlooking the river and seated ourselves on the hard bench against the tower wall. Hulok had brought a large jar of ale and two stone cups. We drank silently, allowing ourselves to become immersed in the beauty of the night black sky and the myriad jeweled stars. The constellations, to me, were strange and different.

Out of curiosity, I asked, "What is that one there called,

the sort of four-starred crescent bordering on those other three?"

"Well what does it look like?"

"Your axe blade?"

He shook his head in disdain. "And you say *you* come from up there?"

"Well one has a different perspective from different points. Why do you smoke that stuff?" He'd hauled out his pipe, a stubby piece of limb-joint, holed neatly on its long end and with a carved out bowl on the short. He ignored me, stuffing the bowl section with a dark-colored weed. He then lit it and began studiously puffing away. He smoked, I'd noted, but infrequently. The weed he had now smelled of the stable and wet hay.

Sighing contentedly, he finally deigned to answer my question in his usual way: with another question. "Why?" he queried, "was our sadan prisoner slain?"

"We've discussed this before," I groaned. "My answer now is the same as then: I don't know why you killed him."

"*I* didn't, Warlord."

"So you say."

"It was Duglass."

"Why Duglass?"

"Why were you not at the high table tonight?"

"No" I said, and laughed. "You go too far. He may have had sufficient reason—from his point of view—to kill the sadan. But Shan's not a fool."

"Indeed, he's not. But he will protect the crown—from both the barons *and* you."

I got up, walked to the balcony, spit over it and returned to say flatly, "Relieve me, Dwarf, of your tedious mystique. Get to the point. What are you trying to tell me?"

He grinned a nasty grin. "Why that I, sir, and my fellows are not with you to play the games of the castle-lords. You've convinced me that you speak the truth and that the 'world' is in danger. Indeed, I've *promised* to help you, as have my Fergus and Torgus. They both fought well at Hools, remember? My point, sir, is that we do not serve our cause by playing vassal to Shan Duglass' chancellorship of the Tremaine heraldry."

"And?"

"That you should cooperate with Duglass *only* to the extent that he gets us to the north in safety—and in *time*."

"Which is precisely what I've been doing."

"Perhaps, lord. But when you get right down to it the killing of the sadan, though a small thing, means that Shan Duglass' priority—the recapture of Weils and the reestablishment of the crown—will allow for no other parallel responsibilities."

"Such as the north *and* a possible future tie-in of the sadans with the thing in Hools."

"Aye, lord. Shan Duglass knows of the potential peril. And he knows, too, that whatever's happening, is happening now. Yet he'll put it all aside to guarantee his own priority."

I grinned. "There speaks the statesman."

Hulok's great eyes blazed. "Do you mock me, sir?"

I glared right back. "Don't be so thin-skinned." I refilled my cup from his weighty jug. "You are right in everything you suggest, friend Hulok—except one."

"Which is?"

"That I, sir, am a pawn in all of this."

His eyes narrowed, sensing the possible intrigue that he dearly loved. "Oh, no? You're not?"

"Nay, friend. I'm not. 'Tis the Princess Meagan Anne who'll command here. She needs but a few days to feel her strength—which will come, I might add, from the very crown that Duglass fights for. . . . No, Hulok. We've but one task, and that is to seize Ellenrude before the month is out—*and then drive north!*"

He grimaced; a true devil's advocate. "And if we don't?"

"Why then we'll know in sufficient time *before* the fact—and act accordingly."

"Which means," he concluded sarcastically, "that it will then be up to the four of us to make it through Lothellian and the Deadlands on our own, to the blinker light?"

"Exactly."

"By the gods," he mumbled, "You do disappoint me." He then looked away and began puffing and drawing on his pipe so as to put a wreath of smoke almost completely around our tower. Indeed, I feared that the lackeys below would see it and cry FIRE!

He finally said, "They are dying, you know."

"The moodans and sadans?"

"Aye."

"I guessed as much."

"Oh, did you now?"

I changed the subject just as the first moon, Oriel, swung around our tower's northwest curvature to peek at us. "What's your celebration about, old friend—the candles and the dancing?"

He looked me over calmly, liked what he saw again and said, "Today is the most sacred day of dwarves. 'Tis All Saints' Day; All Hallows' Eve; the day of renewal, of *rebirth!* It's known, but it's not celebrated by our vicar-priests. But we who honor all gods, the ones who were as well as the ones who will be, give special thanks to all of them for having saved us from the ultimate curse of the great magic."

I absorbed that quietly, then asked suddenly for the simple reason that I was "suddenly" curious: "Are you a married man, Hulok? Do you have children?"

He grunted. "Yes I am married, but I am a dwarf and not a man. And, yes, I have children. I've a wonderful missus who makes a meat pie to make your legs to weaken and your mouth to drool. I have three sons who are already skilled craftsmen. And I've also a daughter who I'd not trade for even your Meagan Anne."

"*My* Meagan Anne?"

"Aye. For she's yours if you wish— And that, Warlord, is what you're really counting on, right? That *she'll* have the power and that *you'll* have her."

I stiffened. "Though you are right, friend, know this, too: For whatever reasons, I feel strongly about our princess—and I am not a gamesplayer."

Hulok first scratched his nose, then his left armpit. He was actually gurgling his pleasure. He'd reached me at last and he knew it. "Hey, now!" he exclaimed. "Whoever said you were, *Greeneyes?*" Then he chuckled. "But don't let your heart control your head," he advised heavily. "We've a date to keep, you know. A final thing you must know. Though I and mine have a certain skill with the axe and shield, we, sir, take no delight in unending stupid battles. Therefore, let us do what we have to do as quickly as possible—and be done with it!"

Again we sat in silence to watch Pollo, the second moon, come timidly around the tower's curve and blink at us. I asked softly, "Would you ride out with me tomorrow, Hulok? I've a desire to be apart from all this for a few hours...."

"I'll do that."

"—and leave Fergus and Torgus here."

"Why not?" He blew a great blue cloud of smoke toward poor, timid Pollo.

"—and bring the Whatzit."

He burst into hoarse laughter, beating a heavy thigh and gasping, "I fear me, Warlord, that I'll never survive your company; even if *we* survive that thing that's coming at us."

He arose then to knock his pipe against the balustrade so that a stream of small bright coals fell to the Wys river a hundred feet below....

"Come," he gestured.

"To where?"

"Why to honor us at our dance, of course. Your skill should add a new element to our worship."

And that's what we did—for the next four hours.

Quick zephyr-like gusts of wind had almost stripped the gorgeous budry tree of its featherlike blue and purple leaves. And they'd fallen mostly on me, where I lay flat on my belly beneath it, and eye-to-eye with the Whatzit, though this could as easily have been eye-to-fanny. For the Whatzit's position—it was again in the form of a leather purse with drawstrings—could not be known.

I'd tried word imagery, pleas, simple questions, direct commands—everything. Nothing worked. No picture images; no reflex communication. Then, at a point where I was even singing a song to it, I'd felt a sudden sense of warmth, of a pleasantness; even of a loving *goodness!* Then again, when I'd finally given up to turn on my back and gaze up through the budry tree's denuded branches to the blue skies and fleecy clouds, I literally felt a sunburst inside my head—the sound, as it were, of a thousand angelic voices. By the gods! I thought. The thing's seeing the sky through my eyes. It's letting me know its sentiments.

I felt good all over; especially since this was proof-positive, too, that my dour Hulok hadn't just set me up to stare at an empty purse for two solid hours.

I dozed then. I couldn't help it. The sun was median warm, the purple leaves a downy blanket, the autumnal grass a yel-

low wheaten-gold beneath me. The humming of late insects,
together with the gurgling stream below and the measured,
relaxed chomping of our two kaoles as they ate their breakfast, lunch and dinner was also a quite natural sedative.

Hulok was fishing. At least I think he was. The last time
I'd looked, he'd been sitting with his back against a large
rock, a pole held slackly in his hands and with his cap tipped
over his face.

A flash-pic interrupted my dozing reverie. It was of Meagan Anne glaring down at me. Beautiful, I mused. Right out
of a museum. A portrait of the young Mary, Queen of Scots.
I thanked my subconscious, for it was a fantasy I could go
with. I stretched, sighed and pulled my own cap down over
my now tightly closed eyes. . . . And then the toe of a small
boot actually kicked me hard, in the ribs, and an imperative
female voice called, "Wake up, Sir Lout. Night's for sleeping,
and I'd have a word with *you* right now."

My eyes flew open. It *was* Meagan. Blue eyes flashing,
booted legs wide-spread, her left hand rested solidly, a fist on
a slim hip while her right flicked a riding crop against her
thigh in a series of impatient slaps. She'd caught me off balance, to say the least and was now in no mood to accept my
idolatrous stare.

A quick glance revealed a party of knights and ladies on
the road a short distance away. Her mount, Gucchi, was
moving to join my Huaclan and Hulok's Kaars, but Meagan
whistled her back.

I sighed and sat up. "Well, now," I said, "it's not often that
a man's daydream takes on a solid form." I'd reached my
feet, so I bowed. "I'm at your service, my lady."

"Really?" She looked me over. "I'm minded, sir, that you
ran off last night with never so much as a thought for me."

By the gods, she's guileless, I told myself; either that, or a
master of the art of manipulation. I said contritely, "I ask
your forgiveness, my lady. But I did have work to do."

"Oh? More of your plans to save the world?"

"Yes."

She raised an eyebrow. "The way you were saving it a few
minutes ago?"

"Meagan, please. I was attempting to communicate with
Merlin's Eyes, with the Whatzit."

"Indeed? Where is it?"

"Right there." I pointed to the leather purse.

The raised eyebrow turned to a black frown. "Do you really think me such a fool, Jarn?"

"No. Nor should you think me such." I picked up the purse. "This *is* Hulok's Whatzit."

Her lips tightened. She took the purse from my hands and examined it. "And did you communicate?" she asked, with just the right touch of sarcasm.

"In a way. But not as I'd hoped."

"Jarn," she said, and a tear had brimmed one eye, "This is ridiculous."

I shrugged, reached out and stroked the purse—and flashed a mental pic of the Whatzit in its true form. *And,* miracle of miracles, it immediately became that. Meagan gasped and almost dropped it, but it clung to her left hand, a small yellow puffball with pseudopodal feet, a tiny pink nose and ears, and big blue eyes. It looked at us soulfully. I reached to stroke it again. More. I glanced at Meagan so that she stroked it too. It actually purred then, and was quite suddenly a purse with drawstrings. . . .

She said, "Oh, my!" and returned it to me.

"Cheer up," I grinned. "You're forgiven."

"Well, you're not. We were to talk, remember?"

"How could I forget?"

"Well, you've certainly done nothing about it."

"I am not the Princess, Meagan. You are. It is you who commands here."

"Except that my authority, apparently, does not extend to you."

"Not completely true. You command far more than you know."

"Oh? And just what does that mean?"

"My lady," I said softly as I seized a small hand and brought it to my lips. "Try me and see."

"All right, I will. You will visit me in my quarters tonight, Jarn Tybalt—after dinner."

I smiled. "And what of our Lord Chancellor?"

"Ah," she said. "So that's it."

"It is, indeed, my lady. For I have a job to do beyond the offering of my sword to you and Shan for the taking of El-lenrude. The problem is, Meagan Anne, that I can help neither you nor me, if I'm imprisoned in Kilellen's dungeons. Do you understand me, my lady?"

"I damn well do."

"For the sake of our two ventures then, I think it best that both you *and* Shan Duglass know who I am, and at the earliest possible moment."

"Agreed. But not tonight. . . ."

"Well, now——" I began. But her other hand reached out to silence my lips with her fingers. . . . "Tonight!" she said, and swung gracefully up into little red-eyed Gucchi's saddle. Cameo perfect, her dimpled knees gripped her kaole's middle as she sat stiff-spined and graceful in that split second before leaving. The breeze had returned to toss her black tresses and to lift the whitest-of-cambric collars from off the velvet jacket so as to daintily pat her cheek. I swear, if she'd remained one minute longer, I'd have displayed a weakness that was more of will than of body—and therefore the more dangerous!

But she didn't. And a short time after that Shan Duglass came trotting by with a dozen or so swordsmen. He was returning to Kilellen—he'd been scouting, so he said—so we mounted up and joined him for the quick trip back.

After the baths, and having made a choice of clothes from those given me by the new Lord Chancellor, I dressed for dinner. I'd told Hulok of my decision to inform Meagan and Shan as to who I was and what I was doing here. He'd disagreed strongly. "My lord," he'd said, " 'tis well known that even among the best of leaders there are still those who deeply fear the things they cannot understand. . . ."

"Is that your real reason for disagreeing?"

"All right, Warlord. Just what do you mean by *that*?"

"That I damn well know that you've not told me all the truth about yourself. The accusation by the sadan, for example: that you are the guardian's 'keeper of the keys.' It may be, sir, that for them to know of me will automatically open the door to *you*—and that you're not ready for it."

"All right!" he said suddenly, bluntly. "What you've said is true. There are things that I know, that all dwarves know. But believe me, now is not the time."

"It is for me, old friend."

"Then I warn you. Do not include me in any part of your disclosure."

"I can tell nothing of you that I do not know."

He grunted his displeasure.

I said, "Hulok. It has to be this way."

"I am not convinced," he said, and left me to join his companions.

The festivities of the preceding night had drained the energies of most to a certain extent, and the great hall after dinner was emptied quickly. Even Sir Percy, who sat longer at sup than most people, had gone off with Hulok, Fergus and Torgus to play at cards. Since all four of them were born gamblers, I would have been tempted to join them if for no other reason than to see how it worked out. . . . But not on this night.

I enjoined a lackey to guide me to the princess' quarters, asked the sergeant of the guard to announce me, and waited in an antechamber. I didn't have long to wait. The doors opened and one of the ladies in waiting beckoned for me to come forward. Inside, I waited in another antechamber until a serving maid came to take me into a small sitting room with a brace of candelabra, pleasant furnishings, drapes, sofas and the like, and a most interesting oriole window-seat; more bed than seat, really, in that it was sufficiently large for a double occupancy if the need arose. It was also raised so that one could look down to the court below. Its luxurious softness caused me to think that it would be a most pleasant place to die, too—a thought quite indigenous to the mind of a colony person. It was now covered with a great fur robe.

It was only then that I noted that the maid had, for whatever reason, taken my furred cloak and my Tremaine tartaned cap with the red feather. . . .

Time went by. Nothing. Below, I watched various lords call for their mounts and then, with their ladies and a covey of personal men-at-arms, take their leave of the castle for the ride to either the town below, or to other holdings in the great valley.

Then Mcagan came, and with a plate of small sweet cakes and a jar of liquor distilled, I swear, from oranges. It was true ambrosia. She'd quick poured me a small glass of the stuff, and seeing my expression of utter bliss, she could not help but kiss me. At which I instantly fell back against the cushions of the window seat, holding her close.

She'd changed from dinner attire to a simple knee-length shirt, and this of the thinnest stuff that one could imagine. She wore nothing else. After holding me tight so that I could feel the heat of her breath against my throat, she then pulled away to stare into my eyes. Moonlight touched all her face and upper body. Indeed, I'm inclined to think, in retrospect, that the three moons, Oriel, Pollo and Thisbe had actually set themselves to watch over Meagan and me during those few short weeks before the blood-bath of Ellenrude. They seemed a trio of inquisitive, avuncular voyeurs. Two of them were out there now, peeping in: Pollo and Thisbe; a truly weird effect. It was like two great round eyes, staring at us—but friendly.

Meagan pulled back to ask bluntly, "Do you believe in destiny, Jarn?"

"I believe that we, in part, make our own; just as, in part, others make it for us."

"Do you love me?"

She was indeed, guileless! The question, so straightforward, so fiercely put, startled me into giving the true, subconscious answer about which even I was unaware. "By the gods, Meagan," I told her frankly, "I think I do!"

"You think?"

"Nay. I know it."

"That's better. Would you believe, Jarn Tybalt, that I sensed that I loved you the very moment I laid eyes on you at the inn? And that I *knew* it when you fought for Shan and me, though you were sure, then, that I was the prize for another. . . ."

At this disclosure, and being what I am, a male and a somewhat demanding one at that, I could not help but reach for her again, but she fended me off, saying, "Wait. Disrobe, sir; as I shall. For I would see and hold you naked—and likewise be held."

And who among humans could argue with that?

Naked, she was the Aphrodite of the Terran Greeks; except that her body was more slender, more youthful, akin to the clean-limbed Spartan girls, or to those dark-haired, blue-eyed Druid priestesses who, with the Derwyd and Fillyd masters of that ancient art, could charm the whole world with their magic. Pale white she was, but with a glow of vibrant health in cheek and breast, to mock the immortals, if such

things be—outside the ruins of places like *Hools*, that is. . . .
Naked myself, and watching her, I could not help but believe
that in *this* area at least, we were well matched.

Straddling me and with her eyes drinking in what she saw,
she asked curiously, "Why so brown, Jarn? Do warlords of
Eden Valley work their own fields?"

"Do you dislike this touch of sun?"

"To the contrary, I love it. Were it not for Father Abram
and Mother Eostre, I'd worship the sun alone—as do you,
apparently. If you were brown all over, I'd think you different. But since the part of you upon which I sit is as white as
me"—and she jiggled up and down and smiled wickedly to
make her point—"why then 'tis the sun alone that does it.
And I love you the more for it."

I rolled her gently and easily beneath me then, legs wide,
arms spread, her dark hair cupped by my hands and with my
arms thrust beneath her shoulders. I murmured, "There's a
thing I would ask you, Meagan Anne. . . ."

But she shook her head, muttering, "No. After." And she
came up beneath me so that her wet tongue traced a zig-zag
line from my chest to my belly. Her mouth became instantly
a searching, finding facsimile of her love. I tensed for seconds
beneath her demands until I could stand it no longer. I then
bent to draw her mouth and her entire body to mine. I even
whispered a ribald pleasantry into a small ear so that she
laughed gleefully as we settled to a wild and wonderful kaleidoscope of flesh and warmth and demands and the fantastic
oneness of the true "unity of opposites."

During a brief moment of satiety, I swung open the center
panel of the oriole window. Rain-washed zephyrs from off the
fields and forests immediately entered to cool us. . . . One
would have thought that that would be the end of it. Not so.
The freshness of it all simply reminded me again of Meagan,
and of her quite singular perfume. I reached for her among
the furs—and found her reaching for me. The passion remained, though now it was more a thing of love than simple
coupling. Should I confess that I took my cues from her? It
was better that way—more relaxed. By this time, too, Oriel,
the third and last moon, had come to join the others so that,
with all the candles cupped, the silvered light inside our
chamber resembled somewhat the light of our own Arian, as

reflected from Drusus—and into our cold dead crater world of Eden Valley.

We dozed for a few hours in each other's arms. Awakening, I reached for the orange liquor and drank deeply. Meagan shook a sleepy head, rejecting an offered glass. I stared down at the half-awake eyes, the finely molded features, the faint dew upon brow and lips, the sweaty film of lust upon her small breasts and white belly. So, I mused, remembering all the ancient film-clips and books that I'd perused: This is what a queen looks like. And a Celtic Scots Queen at that. In my mind's eye I again saw the dark-haired *Mary.* They looked so much alike. I'd time to wonder before she pulled me down to her, if I'd end up like the laggard 'Boswell,' whose aid had been much too little, and too late!

Later, when she chose to send me from her, I found a double surprise awaiting me. The first was that I was to leave through a panel in the oriole room so as to make my way by a secret passage to my own quarters. The second was that Hulok was already in the passage, heavy axe at the ready and his three-fold shield at his back. "I had him posted to warn us, should anyone else come prowling," Meagan told me. "Though to my knowledge only Shan, myself and our Vicar still know of *all* the passageways. We discovered them as children."

I asked, curious, "What of Jocydyn?"

"Oh, yes. But I doubt that she remembers."

"What of the guards? They'll know I never left."

She grinned an elvish grin. "Nay, Warlord. Those who were on duty when you came were given a simple courtesy drink. It's always done; except that this time it made them a little more sleepy and a little less aware, enough so that our good Lors Raddle could leave hurriedly in your cap and cloak. In effect, it was *you,* my lord, who left. Believe me!"

"As for our Hulok," and she nodded toward the stoically staring dwarf, "well, sir, he's loyal to you for whatever reasons. And so I trusted him, too."

"A final point then. . . ."

"The meeting?"

"Aye. With you, Shan and myself. It must take place at the earliest."

"Or the world will die?" Meagan smiled.

"Exactly. It most surely will, my lady."

"Better, my lord, that *you* ask for it, tomorrow morning at breakfast and in my presence. If Shan opposes, I'll back you—all the way."

Breakfast at Castle Kilellen was in the tradition of Terra's English aristocracy, i.e., it was an open-air smorgasbord on the east terrace to catch the first sun. It offered fish, fowl, beef, hottle-steaks and whatever fruit was available—plus three kinds of Avalonian tea plus scones, crumpets and various kinds of hotcakes. To simply sample it all was to doom one's self to a lifetime of obesity and an early grave.

I'd invited Hulok along to assuage any fears he might have that he was being used, and hopefully to prod him into being more open himself. The question broached, Shan instantly agreed, saying that he would have had to pin me down sooner or later anyway—so why not now?

The four of us then retired to a table and chairs at the south end of the terrace, with Shan Duglass setting polite pages to shooing everyone else away.

"So, Warlord," he said lightly while popping a well-buttered scone into his mouth (we'd all brought our platters, well-filled or otherwise). "You will now tell us who you are and just what sort of games you have up your sleeve."

"No games, my lord," I countered briefly and instantly. "But I think it proper that you know who and what I am, for you've a right to the information."

And so I told them—all of it!

I went into far greater detail, too, than I had done with Hulok. "So that's it," I concluded. "As things stand now, we have a little less than two months to get me to the blinker-light, where, hopefully, there'll be some indication of how this thing can be handled before it enters our skies. I do not know," I told them slowly, "how much of this you've understood. But what I've said is the truth. In the final analysis, therefore, you have no choice but to help me."

"And we shall, Sir Tybalt!" Shan said heatedly. "Just as soon as we take Ellenrude Castle. And in this last respect, the sooner the better; not just for you, Warlord, but for our cause, too. As a matter of fact, since, as you put it, you are not of this 'world'—and you'll forgive me if I find that still difficult to accept—the very nature of our winters, sir, demands that we take Ellenrude Castle within the month. If we do not, or if we fail—why then, we must wait till spring."

"And how will it be in the north, two months from now?"

"Hasn't our stone-carving friend told you?"

"He has. But I needed to hear it from you, too."

"Well, sir, it's pretty damned awful."

"And yet it's there that we must go."

"Warlord. I cannot help you until we've taken Ellenrude. After that, well I'll ride with you myself, sir. And so will every knight and lord of Weils."

I had to say it. And I had to say it in a certain way so as to bring its meaning home: "And if I'm killed, Sir Duglass, at Ellenrude?"

His eyes flashed fire. "But you're released right now, *this minute*, from any pledge to me. . . ."

Meagan's face had blanched at my suggestion. "My Lord Duglass," she ventured harshly. "Our Warlord's meaning is clear. If he's to die with our three dwarves, why it should be in the quest for the blinker light. That, if you believe him, should be the priority. I'll ask you now: How many men, sir, do we need to invade the north before it's too late?"

Shan shrugged. "You heard Duke Finley, my lady. Fifty thousand, he said."

"And we have—?"

"We'll have but twenty thousand at best, for Ellenrude; to be joined, hopefully, by another five thousand from Sierwood. My lord," he said directly to me, "there simply is no way. Weils' barons command a full half or more of our swordsmen. We must first *win*. And if we do so in the next three weeks, we'll have the men *and* the time."

"My lord," Hulok spoke up gravely. "There is this to say: Both the moodans and sadans are dying. The job, therefore could as easily be done with *five* thousand men. . . ."

"How do you know this, Sir Dwarf?"

"I cannot tell you. But I do *not* lie."

"Good. I accept your word that you do not lie. But I will not accept your statement that you cannot tell me how you know. The *code* protects you, Hulok. But I swear that if it didn't; and this, despite our friendship, I'd have you up by the heels until you *did* tell me."

"But think on it, my lord. If our Warlord's right, and *I* think he is, then all that we've become since the evil of the magic and the hell of the Deadlands will have been for naught. We will just—cease to be!"

He'd said the wrong thing. Shan Duglass' face was suddenly a coronary red. "By the bloody gods," he roared, "I will not be threatened with unproven rumor—" He'd arisen to his feet and was thumping the table with his two fists. "Do not lay your fears on me, Dwarf—or your hopes—or your ill-conceived plans. Five thousand men? For what? Why not ten? They're as easily asked for. Why not one thousand? That's truly all you'd need if the moodans and sadans are really dying, as you say. But even if you were right, Sir Dwarf—and you've still shown me no proof, you have not defined the *conditions* for the need of ten, five, or one—or none at all!"

Hulok's eyes went stony, his expression flat. Without explanations, he had no answers to Shan Duglass' truth. And he knew it.

Shan sat down again, poured a huge mug of steaming tea and drank half of it. Meagan Anne was watching me closely. Shan said, exhaling, "Nay, Warlord, Hulok—and you, too, my princess who will be queen—until I'm given solid proof as to how and why this task, this *quest*, if you will, should take precedence over the way that I myself have suggested, why then I'm forced to turn you down."

Meagan said calmly, "All right. But our centerpiece, which is our warlord, here, has yet to have his say. And before he does, I'll tell the three of you right now that I believe he has not lied and that the purpose of his quest is real. It follows then, to me, that we may well indeed lose all our world if we act wrongly here—for whatever reasons. I'll therefore seriously consider his conclusions."

And how was *that* for taking the decision-making power right out of Shan Duglass' hands? Neat! Oh so, neat! And I would now return that power to him in such a way as to gain his undying friendship *and* support in the task that lay ahead. For I, too, was a believer in what I *knew* as opposed to the 'worlds of if' . . . Ellenrude would be taken whether I fought there or not. And, since I believed the truth of Duglass' pledge—that he would then escort me north with all the swords he could command—well why not the "bird in hand"?

"My Princess," I said, "and you, Hulok, and my lord

Duglass." I'd covered them all. "I believe essentially that our dwarf is right; this, though he does lack the particulars. I also believe that our Lord Chancellor is right, within the concrete realities of the situation. Therefore the priority remains, to first capture Ellenrude. I accept it with this proviso—" and I grinned a merry grin and winked at the three of them. "It is, that should we be driven back from those stout walls, that *we then retreat immediately in the direction of the blinker-light!*"

And how could our Lord Chancellor disagree with that?

Again his face grew red, then purple. Then he burst out laughing. "By the gods, Jarn Tybalt," he exclaimed. "I can see that I've a lot to learn in terms of options, and I now know where to learn it!" He turned to Meagan Anne, saw the tears brimming her eyes. "I accept the charge, my Princess— in *every* way. . . ."

I knew then that in his eyes we'd also won another point, i.e., if she wanted me as queen's consort in Weils, he'd support that, too, and fully.

Hulok was shaking his head. Pleased with this unforeseen turn in our fortunes, he had an idiot grin on his square face to make a toggle-bird laugh. But I'd something else to say, too; a thing, as it were, to bring them back to the total scene—and its peripheral aspects.

"There's one last thing," I told them, "that should worry us all. It goes like this: I believe with Hulok that the moodans and sadans are dying. I do not have to know the reasons to believe this, nor will I question him as to the source of his knowledge now. But in this respect, I am reminded of Hools, of the scabrous, dying condition of our two sadan captives, and of a certain remark made by our Lord Tideman. Put them all together and we have the following. . . . The sadans are dying, true. But they've been approached at Jarkbund Castle by the *thing* of Hools. It has promised them life, if they will serve it. *They* have agreed! Will this mean just the sadans of Jarkbund? I don't know, but I doubt it, for power in motion seldom leaves loopholes. I think the offer has been made to all the sadans *everywhere*. This being possible, it stands to reason that just as Hools is the probable center of the *thing's* control in the south, so could that great ruin, described by Lord Tideman as being 'near where the Kiel River leaves the Dark Mountains;' which, again, and according to our Hulok, is quite close to Jarkbund *and on the old road*, be the center of control in the north; a mustering point for fleeing sadans, as it were.

"One can only imagine what could happen eventually in the south were all sadans cured, allowed to breed—and then unleashed upon humankind by the *thing* of Hools, and others like it, for there must be more than one. I therefore strongly suggest that three units of three each of your most trusted, courageous and intelligent young warriors—more than that would only be cumbersome—be sent immediately and directly to the area of Jarkbund Castle and the area of the ruins; this, to find if sadans are really mustering from all Lothellian for the purpose I've described. If we find this to be true, and if, as a consequence, the sadans do escape, why then, so help me, comrades, all humankind will pay in blood for our lack of diligence."

That very night, at three hours after sunset—two after sup—we met again; this time in the chamber set aside as a receiving room for the queen-to-be. There was myself, Meagan, Hulok, Shan Duglass and ten lords and knights of Weils, inclusive of Lord Tideman. They had been thoroughly briefed and had participated in a discussion of the matter.

Nine young men were ushered in, three of them warrior-priests, or vicars. They were told again and in detail of their mission, and that they were to risk no contact with either sadans or moodans, for *whatever* reasons, and that they were to studiously avoid even the slightest danger. Their job was intelligence. If forced to fight, however, they were to do so, either to the death, or until they'd broken free to return to us with the proof, or the lack of it, of sadans mustering near Jarkbund and the ruins!

Their faces shining, they kneeled before the slim figure of their princess to take the double oath of fealty. I swear that watching, I actually envied them their youth and enthusiasm. We saw them to the courtyard, Shan and I, and thence to the drawbridge where we shook hands, wished them god's speed and watched them melt silently into the darkness.

The road they would travel would take them into the very heart of Lothellian, Shan told me; indeed, they would penetrate deeper into that country than any humans since the time of the great magic. He added soberly, "I'd not envy them, Warlord, if I were you." He'd seen the light in my eyes. "In case you've not been told, both moodans and sadans are cannibals. They sometimes eat human captives."

Nine

The war for Ellenrude and Weils truly began the next morning. We now had two deadlines to meet. Indeed, given the facts of Ellenrude and the CT-Nova, we'd no choice now, timewise, but to commit ourselves immediately. And there could be no turning back. . . .

Ellenrude, at a hundred miles to the north of Kilellen and a road paralleling the "great road" to the east of the mountain we'd just crossed, was *the* junction where these roads met. As fast as new volunteers and levies arrived they'd be sent forward along these roads under the command of this young lord or that knight; all loyal to the queen-to-be. Posted messengers fanned out from Kilellen as sparks from a wheel. Often, in the beginning, they met their opposites from the baron's forces on the same purpose and even in the same villages. The orders for heralds, however, was to avoid all fighting unless attacked. Indeed, many villages and towns would have their locals pipe assembly so that the people could first hear the words of first one herald and then the other, depending only on who had preceded the other. The elders could then stand aside and absolve themselves of responsibility by letting the would-be-warriors make up their own minds. . . .

But that was in the beginning. As the days flew by it began to appear that all to the north of Ellenrude was more or less for Dagar and the barons, and all to the south, for the queen-to-be. Shan Duglass, Tideman, Tristansson, Jones, Lewellyn and a half-dozen others who now made up the new Privy Council, therefore ordered a general advance throughout the south, toward Ellenrude.

With but a few skirmishes on the road to slow us, we arrived to within halloooooing distance of the great eyrie and its town below at the end of the first week. Our rear was safe, provisions secure. We had only to await sufficient strength to attempt the single decisive battle.

Envision the area if you will: Ellenrude was so situated as to be at the juncture of two north-south roads and the confluence of two north-south rivers. Following the Wys down the Valley of Kilellen, we'd mounted the west bluff just short of the castle and positioned ourselves precisely at its tip, where both the road and the Sert river swept round it to join but a mile or so beyond the town. The road juncture was achieved by a large stone bridge erected, so Hulok told me, by dwarves some two hundred years previously. On the promontory's flat surface to our rear and at perhaps a mile was a village. Through it passed another road, or cartpath, coming up from the parallel valley of the Sert, then across the now narrow valley of the Wys, to finally mount the eastern hills and so come to Ellenrude from that southernly direction. . . . In essence, our position was that of a flat-topped, fortress-like abutment, protected by two rivers and thrusting sharply into the very breathing space of Ellenrude. It was the one spot in all the square miles around the castle that should have been fortified. I marveled that it was not!

For Dagar to destroy us now, before we could mount our attack, he'd first have to cross the Wys and Sert Rivers and then storm the bluffs to get at us. We, on the other hand, had only to cross the Wys and to climb the hills to the plateau before Ellenrude—For there were no bluffs, except at one small point, to the east of the Wys.

On the second day of the occupation of this position, we were greeted at high-noon by trumpet blasts, a skirling of massed pipes and a rattling of drums like spring hail, to announce the arrival of the Lord Oldus Finley, together with sundry knights, inclusive of his Warlord and Chancellor, the dukes Rex and Dorcis Thomaas, respectively—*and five thousand swordsmen*! The main road along the banks of the Sert was a miles-long twisting, colorful snake of banners, gonfalons and glittering steel. He had two hundred pipers and half again as many drums. Finley had class, no doubt about it!

Indeed, he himself, and joined by all the chivalry of Weils, under Shan Duglass' banner of the Royal House of Tremaine, advanced to the very edge of the bluff facing mighty Ellenrude; whereupon, and with all his pipes and drums to make his point, he waved the great household banner of Sier-wood's Tag-Afran (two sword-swinging caatis against a forest glade) for all to see. A mighty cheer went up from ten thousand fighting men (our number at that moment). From across the way, and from all the ramparts of Ellenrude, we heard the faint but sneering defiance of the barons' contingents. . . .

Amused and somewhat *high* on it all, I fought my way through the press of armor to put my mount next to Meagan's. Seeing me, she seized my hand exuberantly. Her eyes shone. "By the gods, my lord," she bubbled. " 'Tis like we've won already."

I brought her hand quite naturally to my lips. "Would that we had," I murmured. "Where's Duglass?" He'd disappeared.

She smiled. And then I knew. For a palanquin of sorts had accompanied the five thousand. A marvelous contraption of springs, freely suspended carriage and with four graceful, wire-spoked wheels with a kind of changeable hard-rubber tire on each one.

"Jocydyn?"

She nodded happily.

Across the way Dagars pipes and drums were answering, too, and as the bedlam grew so did the enthusiasm on both sides. Indeed, I was in no way surprised when a party of Dagar's knights came bursting down the hill to the very banks of the Wys to shout insults and to toss their swords in the air and then clash them against their shields.

But the grim Lord Tidesman, a disciplinarian of the old school, sensing what could happen and having no desire for an uncontrolled spate of individual duels, asked quickly that I take a force down the narrow cliff-path to prevent any on our side from answering this first challenge. He was one of those who'd been informed of the CT-Nova. He also knew that I had a cool head.

I nodded, squeezed Meagan's hand, beckoned to Sir Percy, Sir Quigley and to one other knight, yelled to a platoon of warriors under a grizzled sergeant and led them all in a mad dash down the cliff face. At the bottom, I was pleased to find no one at all. Apparently, at the first sound of the massed pipes on the road, they'd all come up to see what was happening.

We rode to the river's edge anyway to silently have a look

at Dagar's covey of shouting stalwarts. . . . A maneuver which prompted one of the oddest—weird is more the word—confrontations that I, for one, have ever seen. Sir Percy, staring keenly, as did we all, suddenly rose high in his stirrups, his eyeballs literally popping from his head. He then shook himself, muttering to no one in particular—"By bloody Og, that bastard has my Primrose!"

Without so much as a fare-thee-well he then dashed off through the Wys shallow waters—in spring's spate it could easily be six feet deep—arrived at the other bank, rode up to the rider in question, and then, without ever freeing his weapon, called the man to one side.

The fellow, curious, sheathed his sword and went with him. A discussion then ensued with both men raising their voices and arguing vehemently. The two armies watched in amazement. Sir Percy was then seen to withdraw slightly and to shout something. Upon which his adversary's mount kneeled and rolled over so that the man had to quickly jump off or else be crushed by a twelve-hundred pound kaole. Still on his feet, and safe, he was then seen to scratch his head and nod agreement. Percy then dismounted, shook his adversary's hand, handed him the reins of his own mount, whistled the other one to its feet, leaped into the saddle and rode him at a leisurely pace back to us. . . .

Whether the viewers of this small vignette knew or didn't know what had happened was essentially beside the point. Whatever it was, it looked funny; a most unusual departure from the norm. A ripple of laughter, beginning in both armies, grew to become a roar so that finally the two riders involved, Sir Percy and his adversary, simply waved and saluted their particular colors and retired to a great round of applause.

"All right," I asked, when he'd rejoined us, "What happened?"

Percy, his face still puffed with righteous anger, said, "Why, 'twas simple. I told him, 'Sir! That's my mount you're riding; stolen from me by that dastard, Dagar. I must ask that you give him back right now.' "

"But the knight told me, 'By god, I shan't. You'll have to prove it, sir!' "

"And so I did. You saw it. He even agreed with me that it

was surely mine, for in all his life he'd never seen a kaole trained to do a thing like that. . . ."

Duke Finley remarked later that he deeply regretted not having brought the beauteous saddle Sir Percy had won, for if a kaole ever deserved to wear it, it was certainly Sir Percy's Primrose.

War councils, general assemblies and festive dinners; all of it within a bugle's blast of Great Ellenrude. Hardly a day went by without a skirmish on this or that road; some of them quite bloody. Each side was attempting to cut the lines of new recruits and provisions. I was involved in at least three. I'd been given a scouting troupe of a hundred swordsmen and both Sir Percy and Sir Quigley had asked to ride with me, for different reasons. Sir Quigley, I think, was Shan's man. He'd come along both to keep an eye on me and to keep me *safe*. Percy's reason? Well, for one thing, he stood in awe of me *and* the kuri-sword. Moreover, he swore that his ascendency to the good graces of the three dwarves had, luck-wise, changed his life forever.

As for the dwarves, well they were no longer three, but *four*! The fourth, introduced by Hulok as Colin ap Werliggan, had supposedly come to us through the lines from Ellenrude City. What had he been doing there? I supplied the answer for him, and he agreed as to the correctness of it: He'd been under contract to the city fathers for some stonework and was now sitting it out awaiting the return of summer and a fair wind to take him home again. He'd heard about Hulok—and me; gossip will travel. I, he told me, now had a nickname; this, from Dagar's swordsmen who'd seen my skill at Tag- Afran. *Death Blade*, they called me, and *The Wizard!* Hulok had also been given a name for his slaying of the giant, Horvil. *Loki*, they called Hulok now, after that sly Norse god of ancient Terra—and *Axe-bearer*. As to this last, the connotation was that though many men and dwarves carried axes into battle, there was still but one bearer and it was *Hulok!*

On the afternoon of our last skirmish, when we'd returned to the kaole compound with six of our saddles emptied, we were met by Shan and a half-dozen swordsmen.

"Well, now," he said, observing our condition of cut links

and stove in shields, "I do hope that you gave as much as you seem to have taken. . . ."

"We did," I answered tersely.

"Since I've taken you seriously, Warlord, I must believe that to lose you is to lose the world. I will therefore strongly urge, sir, that you not ride out again."

"Do not fear for me, my lord," I responded, half angry. "What you see is the exception. Indeed, I'm well protected by all of these—" I gestured to Percy, Quigley, and the four dwarves. "Moreover, I'm a man, sir. I cannot be caged. 'Tis said that more 'heroes' die from swilling ale, or choke on plum pits, than ever die in bed."

"I cannot command you," he then said harshly. "But I tell you now that what you do is wrong." To Hulok he raged, "Guard him well, dwarf. For if he falls, your head will follow!"

To which Hulok ground his teeth for all to hear and roared, "You know my feelings on all of this, my lord. So I say to *you* that if he dies—you'll not survive him by a single hour. And that's a fact!"

Shan Duglass' mouth fell open, and he roared with laughter until his eyes teared—but my Hulok's expression never changed. Still, I did think better of what I was doing and turned to other things.

As the camp grew, for instance, and with the arrival of that fortunate hiatus of balmy days between the end of summer and the beginning of winter's snows, I began to studiously practice my *colony* exercises; this, in a selected area of the great grassy field whereon we organized for bloody mayhem . . . After the first day, I had a crowd in attendance. On the second day I had a dozen followers attempting to ape my every move. On the third day there were *two hundred!* By the end of the week, with permission from Shan and the Council to form a *Special Forces Unit,* I'd chosen a hundred from the ever-growing mass of enthusiasts for a particular task.

I began with simple exercises designed for flexibility and a high degree of muscular coordination. To this I added our colony improvements on the centuries-old Terran arts of Karate and Judo. I insisted that a knowledge of what I would teach them would allow a man armed only with a five-inch blade to slay the finest swordsman—and proved it by challenging the boldest knights among them to come at me with everything he had. Three or four were foolish enough to try it. Holding back at first, then finding that they could come nowhere near me under the best of circumstances, they then settled to the effort of deliberately trying to kill me. I evaded every charge and every swing of the blade; each time just touching them here and there so as to use their very momentum, their strength against them; pulling and pushing them off balance so that floundering, staggering this way and that, they inevitably ended flat on their back or on their stomach—and with the point of my blade at their throats.

But! Though I continued to be applauded by my neophytes, not so the gallant swordsmen. They'd begun to shun me like the proverbial plague. Indeed, I was summoned to a meeting of the privy council and told in no uncertain terms that what I had done was injurious to our cause in that far from disclosing a new and more capable road to those who would follow the martial arts, I had demeaned their prowess, insulted their class and instilled *doubt* as to their true potential in every breast that had fought or even watched me. I was to therefore, Shan told me bluntly, cease and desist immediately in such displays and to attend to my own business and nothing else—Either that, or stay confined to my quarters until Ellenrude had been taken.

They were right. Anything that would detract in any way from the elan of our most courageous cadres, and this on the very eve of battle, was indeed a deleterious and foolish act. I apologized to them all, asking only that I be allowed to continue the training of my hundred, explaining that that at least might be of some service.

The following day, to assuage the feelings of certain knights and lords who'd remained true to Tremaine, I entered the tourney lists and allowed myself to be un-kaoled three times in a row—the last being tumbled straight over my Huaclan's fat rear end to lie flat on my back and feigning unconsciousness.

Hulok, the first to reach me, growled harshly, "Don't overdo it, Warlord. They're not that stupid." Upon which, I staggered to my feet and was led off to my pavilion.

The following day, and this time in the sword lists where one practiced with dulled blades, I further won them back to me by standing in full armor, hauberk, helm, plates and three-fold shield, to battle a champion who was indeed a *champion* of the art, for a full forty-five minutes of cut and parry. Having established my willingness to stand up to him that long with his own weapons, I could then down my sword and honestly beg his forbearance; thus admitting my defeat, but without losing face. Indeed, I even took his hand and gave him the age-old warriors' *abrazo*—a recognition of his prowess.

And have I said that Meagan Anne in a single piece of close-fitting stuff had been joining us in all the initial warm-ups? She was a natural: a lithe and muscular body, beautiful coordination and a fantastic will to succeed. She was absolutely fearless. . . . My students looked on her with an awe beyond the fact that she would be their queen.

Then came the morning we had dreaded, hoping to stave it off just one more day, and then another. Even I knew immediately that *it* had happened, *i.e.,* we'd awakened to a bite in the air that was totally different than anything that had gone before. Hulok eyed me keenly as we hurried off to breakfast.

"By the gods," I'd said, drawing my great furred cloak tightly around me. "The bloody temperature's gone down twenty degrees, at least."

" 'Tis dread winter, my lord," he said morosely. "It's here."

"Just like that?"

"So it has always been."

"And it'll stay like this till summer?"

He laughed, his blue eyes snapping. "Not so. It'll get colder—*much* colder."

The War Council remained in session all that day. The change in the weather demanding that whatever plans we had should be immediately readied, honed to a razor's edge of perfection. They were not bad plans, considering. They were just not all that good—too many complexities.

But still we waited, honing and organizing. More bright-eyed young swordsmen arrived with their heavy spears and bucklers. I continued to train my hundred for the one thing I was sure we could do, if we had to.

And then time—as it will eventually do to all living things—caught up with us. That morning there was just that extra bite in the air, and a certain stillness. On all the horizons there was a grayness. Not clouds; at least not yet. But our priest-vicars pronounced that *snow* was coming; that we'd be faced with a storm in the next three days ... The assault must be launched, *now*!

That very night we began to move into position, according to the plan. ... As at Kilellen, Shan Duglass and Meagan Anne knew every passage of Ellenrude. But so did Dagar and the Castle Senaschal who'd gone over to him. Nevertheless, a part of the plan included two units of two-hundred-and-fifty swordsmen each who were to position themselves against the cliff base of Ellenrude, just north of the town and across the Wys River. They would attack through two hopefully unguarded secret tunnels which led direct to the main courtyard. This would be done on signal, at the height of the battle. Control of the gates and of the two bridge towers would herald their success.

Ellenrude's claim to impregnability lay in a monstrous ravine which began as a cleft in the hills above the town and extended for as much as five miles to the west of Ellenrude, while passing directly in front of it. Thus the two towers in support of the hundred-foot bridge which alone could span the gulf.

With the ravine, the bridge, the stout walls and the castle's very position in mind, there would be little point in attempting to seize it by storm. To lure Dagar's army outside those walls, however, and *then* defeat him, was something else ... And why would he come out? Well, if he didn't, he stood to lose all his holdings as the winter progressed—which meant he'd eventually lose Ellenrude too, for lack of provisions. Still, in the last analysis, Dagar himself would be the one to determine what he'd do—unless, as suggested, he could be lured out by some trick.

And Shan Duglass had devised exactly that!

Indeed, great Persei had hardly slipped behind the hills to the west when his entire army stirred to implement that devious game. ...

Careful so as to reveal no movement to our enemy, the gathered units waited the last few minutes for dusk to become darkness. Then, at two miles to the south of us, an engineer-warrior corps of some five thousand men, aided by an equal number of requisitioned peasants, took the secondary road down into the narrowed Wys valley, followed it across the ford, up into the hills and to the very edge of the flat plain before Ellenrude's gates. This process took all night, for they had with them a number of interlocking sections for a new bridge, as well as some pre-constructed units for the raising of two siege towers; all of it on gigantic wheeled platforms. At the plain's edge the peasants were released and sent back to our promontory.

The remaining fifteen thousand of Shan's army, plus Duke Oldus Finley's five thousand, had in the meantime occupied all the valleys and ravines of the hills opposite our bluff; remaining just below the crest and out of sight of the keen eyes on Ellenrude's walls.

By the time of the false dawn all was ready. Indeed, so as not to tire our five thousand unnecessarily, the period between the false and the true dawn was used by levies from below the hillcrests to drag the great siege weapons to within a quarter mile of the gates; upon which they then scurried back to their positions.

And so, with the first pearling of the skies the scene, from Ellenrude's walls, was that of a contingent of five thousand mounted warrior-engineers, laboriously converging on the ravine and the castle; this, along the castle road from the south. As to the parallel ravines and valleys, nothing was visible. But! On our promontory across the Wys, and therefore in full view, was the glittering sight (supposedly), of ten to fifteen thousand of the Duglass' finest. . . . We'd depleted the kaole herds to mount every peasant, cook, lackey, ostler, provisioner and what have you to create precisely this illusion. More! The great banners, flags and blazonry of the houses of Tremaine, Duglass, Tideman, and all the loyal nobility of Weils were there—as well as the blazonry of Duke Finley and the great lords of Sierwood. My own was there, too, a golden banner given to me by Meagan Anne herself, and flaunting my red dragon against the silvered comet's tail. In a sense this last deserved to be there. For excepting myself, Duglass, Finley and a half-dozen of their personal knights, *I* was the only other lord of any stature on that promontory. All else, to a man, were across the way, hidden below the hillcrests and awaiting Shan Duglass' orders.

What was the bait, exactly? Well, Dagar would know of a certainty that other contingents would be hidden below the hillcrests. But he wouldn't know how many. In essence, as he'd see it, he'd been given the chance to destroy all the massed siege equipment, *plus* our five thousand men in one foray of sufficient strength!

He'd almost *have* to try it. For to sit idly and to allow that much equipment to, in effect, be raised against the most important section of his keep could be perilous indeed!

Shan and the Council figured Dagar to hit our five thousand hard and to simultaneously prepare for whatever might come at them from the ravines and valleys. And therein lay the true problem, for us. Everything would rest on the ability of our first five thousand to *hold;* and this, through at least two heavy assaults and with but few reenforcements to come to their aid.

What Shan and the Council wanted was for Dagar to commit at least ten to fifteen thousand men to the battle—at which point they would then strike; *i.e.*, come roaring up out of those valleys and ravines to force the issue, *one way or the other!*

At which point, too, Dagar would have no choice but to then commit his full army. The clincher, of course, was that the barons had at least thirty thousand to our twenty-five. It would therefore be a toss-up under the best of circumstances as to who would win.

I am one who has always believed in miracles—the kind that inevitably come to the bold and the daring. I, therefore, had had nothing but praise for Shan's ability and insight.

Ah, yes! There'd been one last thing to insure Dagar's risking his all. . . . Each day since her arrival, our devious but happy master of manipulation, Shan Duglass, had ridden the full length of our promontory *with the Lady Jocydyn his side,* and accompanied by myself, Meagan Anne, Duke Finley and as many as fifty others of the nobility of Weils and Sierwood. Within minutes of the first kaole promenade, Dagar had appeared on the walls to watch. And he'd watched again on each succeeding day.

I'd been reminded of Meagan's words: "Why, sir," she'd told me, "the man truly *loves* my sister, though 'tis from that love that all our evil's come . . ."

At the faroff windblown shout of defiance from Dagar's walls, now thronging with a show of steel and men, Shan Duglass encouraged our mob of mounted lackeys to flaunt

their flags and banners and to shout back. But it was time
now for him and Duke Finley to leave. Dagar would be making a decision, one way or the other in the next few minutes.
They pranced their mounts and waved their weapons; so did
our peasants.

In the odd privacy that one often finds in crowds, Shan
took the weeping Jocydyn in his arms one last time. She
clung to him, desperately, so that he was forced to hand her
over to her ladies who took her hurriedly in the direction of
the village some two miles to our rear. A special guard of
hardy swordsmen rode with her, cursing their luck, Shan
Duglass and each other, that they'd come so far and were
now forbidden battle.

"As for you, sister!" Shan yelled to Meagan Anne from the
cliff's edge. "Yon Warlord with his four dwarves and his
hundred new-fledged acrobats will keep you from all harm. *I*
trust them. So *you* trust me!"

She laughed and waved a small salute from the depths of
her belted cloak of avak fur. The salute included Finley,
who'd just given me his handshake and abrazo. They were
then over the edge and on the downward path.

I'd noted that Meagan was armed again. A buckler hung
from her saddle horn. The haft of a blade stuck from the
scabbard across her back. Her mount wasn't Gucchi either. It
was a great gray stallion who dared to roll its red eyes at my
Huaclan and gnash its teeth and spit at him.

"Well, my love?" she asked; sidling up so that our thighs
touched as we watched them reach the bottom and trot
toward the river. "What do you think?"

"It goes well, so far."

But her eyes had shifted to the horizon, and she shuddered.
"Damn me, Jarn. It's that I *feel* it! Those blasted clouds!"

Following her eyes, the clouds seemed far away. But still
they were there, ominous—encroaching! "You *feel* it?" I
asked.

"Hey!" she exclaimed. "I keep forgetting. 'Tis a thing one
knows, if you've lived with it: the feel and the very *smell* of
snow and storm. I'll warrant, sir, there's not a man of us
who, if you asked him, wouldn't bet for snow by nightfall."
She turned to the heavily robed Lors Raddle. "What say you,
Vicar?"

"That you're right, my lady," he answered morosely. "But

soon; before nightfall. 'Twould be better that we prayed for those on yonder hill than all this idiot jumping and shouting."

A great sound of trumpets burst then from inside Ellenrude, to be echoed by a second blast from off the walls. We watched sharply. The bridge began to shiver and rattle to the shriek of turning wheels and released chains; these last moved forward in their slots to drop the bridge, foot by ponderous foot, until it finally berthed at the far end. Simultaneously with this the equally monstrous portcullis had slowly risen . . .

The final act came quickly. With the hundred-foot span down and seated and the steel-toothed port now dangling at twenty feet, the iron-bound gates were flung suddenly open to reveal exactly what we'd expected—the steel-shod spearhead of the first mass of Dagar's warriors who, like our own, were some of the finest in all of Weils, if not the "world." With hearty *huuurraaahhhsss* they streamed out across that yawning abyss, heading directly for our five thousand warrior-engineers. . . .

Prepared for exactly such an eventuality, they fell instantly into their mounted echelons and drove hard to right and left, hoping, I think, to split the massive front of Dagar's unleashed armor. At fifteen hundred yards and with the air so crisp and clear (and wasn't that a shadow overhead?) the maneuver was a beautiful thing to witness. Failing to split the front, they did the next best thing. Each mass of separate squadrons smashed into Dagar's flank on either side. At least two thousand castle riders were instantly cut off; upon which, Shan's swordsmen drove in on them from all sides to slay a full half of them before they themselves were driven back upon their siege weapons.

And time passed and the fighting continued—a dull shouting and screaming amid the wild shrill cries of wounded kaoles. More contingents crossed the bridge, and still more. They formed on either side and waited. It grew somewhat darker then. But the clouds that were coming, had *come,* were unlike rain clouds. Indeed, their very whiteness held a seeming luminescence so that everything was still clearly visible. . . . To the southeast then, and this to the skirling of a hundred pipes, as many as another three thousand of Shan's bravest, burst out of the larger valleys and drove at breakneck speed to arrive just in time to smash into the flank of Dagar's main body as it, in turn, rolled thunderously into the front of the already wearied remnants of our original five thousand.

Just three thousand? From our promontory our *ten thousand* or more lackeys and peasants set up a cheering and a howling, as of a million banshees freed from hell! They waved their banners and tossed them in the air. They pranced their great war kaoles. I think we were quite effective in our deception. Indeed, I know now that we were.

Dagar, from Ellenrude's walls, could not help but see *and* believe. The clincher came for him, however, when Shan Duglass then launched but a paltry half-hearted *thousand* swordsmen to the aid of the eight thousand he'd already committed.

That did it!

Within but a few minutes, if not seconds, there surged through the castle gates at least five thousand additional warriors to join with the ten thousand now fighting beneath the banners of the barons of Weils. They quick dressed their mounts in a line of squadrons from left to right and hurled themselves toward the great melee of swinging swords, axes and spears around the now burning remnants of the siege equipment.

Shan Duglass had won!

Hordee Dagar, having brought out half his force, would have no choice in the face of what was about to happen but to commit the remainder, too, to bloody battle.

Again the pipes—a hundred, two hundred; a mighty skirling to mix with the staccato beat of an equal number of drums, the like of which few men had ever heard, or would hear again. And fifteen thousand belted warriors rode their screaming kaoles up from every ravine and valley. And they flaunted the real banners of all the chivalry of Weils and Sierwood. Duglass commanded the Center. Duke Finley, the left, and Lord Tideman the right. Knowing exactly what they would do—they'd planned it long enough—Duglass and Finley hit the great vortex of the already existing carnage, while Lord Tideman rode on to strike the flank of the fresh thousands streaming across the bridge to the matching staccato beat of the drums and pipes upon the walls.

I will never forget that sight as long as I live. In all my thirty-eight years I had never seen more than six hundred people at any one time. And there before my very eyes was a collage of living, quasi-dark-ages battle the like of which has inspired tapastries and songs, and epic poems. There is no way to describe either the horror or the beauty of it. I simply sat frozen, literally, in my saddle, unable to draw my eyes away.

But then I blinked to clear them of the white spots. But the white spots stayed, drifting across my vision; more and more of them, until suddenly the very scene itself was blurred, as if seen through a fog, a mist. I blinked rapidly and frowned, turning to Meagan.

Tears coursed down her cheeks. And I saw the white spots on all the fur of her cloak, on my own—and saw some of them touch her face, to instantly melt and to join their moisture with her tears. . . .

"Gods!" I said. "Is it snow?"

She nodded, buried her face in her hands.

"Is it snow?" a voice asked mockingly to my rear. It was Hulok. He thrust his kaole forward on my left. "All right, my lord," he shouted. "Enough of childishness. We've twelve hundred miles to go. And by your own listing, we've less than four weeks to do it. I advise you now not to parley when they come back. They'll be demoralized and placing blame in all directions. Don't hold the Duglass to his promise. Ask for but two hundred men and a kaole herd of five hundred; each to be laden with provender for the march, for we'll find damned little as we go . . . I beg you, sir. Play no more games."

His broad face was so solemn-serious, so downright honest that I could not help but feel a qualm of guilt. Still, straining to see across to the castle plain—the roar of battle had never lessened—I said reflectively, deliberately, "So you've really believed me all this time—And I'd thought it was you who played the games."

A shadow of true guilt touched his eyes. He shook his head. "My lord," he said tersely. "Whatever the games from either of us, the fact of the *thing* is true. Let's to it then. We must prepare now, Warlord!"

I but stared at him and said nothing. I then turned to Meagan who'd been listening intently. "One can still scale a wall in such a snow, if one can but find it; one hardly needs eyes. For a wall is flat, straight up and down, and it has a top. Moreover, the far side is exactly like the front. But my lady, in this case, we've another problem. You've told me that the ravine is two hundred feet deep, a veritable chasm. Yet to climb that wall so's to seize the gates and the bridge, one must first go down into the ravine and come up the other side. In essence, we must first span the ravine with a sturdy rope so that my men can cross, hand-over-hand. . . ."

"Hulok!" I yelled suddenly. "What of the Whatzit? Would it allow me to see the ravine's perils through its eyes?"

His face drained, grew instantly white. Then the red rushed back to bulge his eyes. In his anger, he could scarcely speak. When he did, the resonance rattled the stones of Dagar's walls. "May the gods damn you to bloody hell, you bastard!" he roared. "Daammmm your stupidity! Daaammmm your sickening arrogance—" The eyes of his companions grew wide, then narrowed; their callused hands moved quickly to their axe hafts—"Daammm all human souls to the darkest pits!" he swore. "You're not fit, I say, to rule a world wherein all life that is not yours has never done you harm, but for your evil must now die with you should you err in this one last thing.

"YES! You idiot bastard! The Whatzit *can* show the way. But not to you! Oh, not to you. For you've not studied it. You've had the *power*, but wasted all your hours in other ways." His glare touched on my now steely-eyed Meagan, while he spit in absolute disgust and returned to me. . . . "I curse the day I ever met you, Warlord," he went on. "For 'tis *I*, yes, ME, who am now stuck with *your* damned fantasy. Yes! I, Hulok Terwydd, will do it. I'll personally take the rope into the ravine and across the chasm; this, with the aid of *Merlin's Eyes!* But I swear my oath right here and now that if on the seizure of castle and town, that you, Jarn Tybalt, do not hie instantly with me and mine and all that we can muster to the site of the original EDEN; for that, sir, is where the blinker-light is—Why then I'll kill you myself with my own two hands!"

And who could argue with that?

I didn't try. "Old friend," I said calmly and with a straight face, "know that I deeply appreciate your efforts on our behalf. I shall, however, accompany you across the ravine. For it may be, since as you say, I *do* have the power, that the eyes of the Whatzit *and* yourself, will act as windows for my own. Besides, I'd see you safely down and up. That chasm's not for stubby legs, and that's a fact. . . ."

At which Hulok choked and gasped for water, and then became silent.

Ten

The fighting, once enjoined, couldn't be broken off that easily. Still, the coming of the snow had destroyed all possibilities of the *coup de main*. The brilliant maneuver, the cunning use of wheeling and charging units to cut the body of the foe to ribbons; to roll up his flanks; to circle and drive into his rear, and so destroy him—all that was gone!

The storm became dead white, an all-encompassing shroud to blanket the myriad bodies of the dead and dying. But even then, in the very midst of an insane and screaming chaos of swinging swords and clashing shields, Shan Duglass managed the retreat. Lines of men, ten feet apart and anchored on the major ravines leading to the Wys became the escape paths.

The last battle broke off at perhaps four that afternoon; this, with whole units still lost and wandering aimlessly. . . . I'd reached him just an hour before that—and had been forced to wait my turn in the face of the disaster all around us.

In a hastily constructed tent—he'd refused to leave until the greater part of what was left of his army had been led to safety—I told him what I and my hundred were prepared to do. He refused, angrily, to even listen, saying that his best cadres were scattered, dead. The wounded were just now being collected. Most were already frozen. And, too, he'd collected as many of Dagar's men as he had his own. He swore that if by nightfall he'd found ten thousand men still willing and able, he'd be damned lucky—And Dagar had twice that many. Even the five hundred he'd sent to the two secret tunnels had been betrayed, ambushed and put to the sword. Moreover Dagar's twenty thousand were now sheltered, warm—and eating great bowls of hot soup, no doubt, while pledging their "victory" with all the broached casks the cellars could provide.

"Why, by all the gods, Tybalt!" he shouted at me. "Given the slightest letup in this devil-spawned storm and they'd be out among us now, slaughtering the wounded and chasing the rest of us to yon hill beyond the Wys. Let's face it, we've failed for now." He smiled bitterly. "Either the gods or the eternal dice of Og were against us."

But Duke Oldus Finley, who seemed strangely strong in the face of duress, sided with me, saying, "Hey? What difference now? 'Tis as our Warlord says: We must either flee or fight—for you're quite right, Cuz, in that when the snow quits, he'll be on us with everything he has. And his swordsmen will *truly* be rested and fed."

"*Which!*" Meagan Anne announced loudly, in interruption, "will be your luck, too, and shortly. There's stew, bread and ale for *twenty-thousand*, sirs. It's on its way here now, thanks to our own Lors Raddle and his vicar-neophytes, and to all those peasants whom we've finally put to a proper use. It'll be cold, however, sirs," and she grinned wryly, "so light your fires for to warm it when it gets here—now!"

They gave her a heavy round of applause and even cheered her and rightly so—for she'd been the true organizer of it all.

Finley spoke up again when the cheers had died, saying bluntly, "What of your magic, Tybalt? Could you not just cut those chains and drop that bridge; even knock open those gates?"

He was only half serious, but Shan's eyes still glittered briefly. "Yes," I began, to the surprise of everyone. "But considering its weight, it would only smash itself to pieces and wind up in the gorge. Nay, sirs. My magic, as you call it, is limited. What we need here is a movement of swift dispatch and in absolute silence. If yon Duglass says yes, I promise you this: We, me and my men, will cross that ravine. We will scale that wall. We will kill all in the courtyard and in the gate towers. And we will open those gates and drop that bridge. . . . With a bit of luck," I smiled, "there'll not even be an alarm."

"Moreover," I continued quickly, "if even a thousand men were available to seal those barracks, filled right now with drunken warriors boasting of their deeds, I daresay we'd have their surrender, or burn them out—one way or the other!"

"By the gods!" Tideman chuckled. "You're a ruthless man, Lord Tybalt."

"Not at all," I said shortly. "At least I'd give them a choice. Dagar wouldn't." I turned to Shan Duglass. "My lord, given but one brief hour free of snow and the castle would be yours now. For we saw it all, the princess and I, and believe me, I do not lie to cheer you up. Witnessing, I had no doubt of it. And I said as much to Meagan. Now hear me again, sir. For what I say is true: Allow us, me and my good comrade, Hulok, here, and my hundred 'acrobats,' to give you all the second chance that you deserve. Say yes to this venture."

Smiling, Shan shook his head. He said, "By the gods, Jarn Tybalt, I do love to hear you talk." He stood up in the make-shift tent to shout to a dozen young knights crowding the entrance. "Send to every captain at every campfire," he told them. "They are to warm their men, feed them well with the food that's coming—for which they can thank their queen-to-be—and see to it that each man gets his pint of ale. And mind you, no more than a single pint. For you can tell them, too, that tonight we're taking Ellenrude—and that we've some scores to settle."

The hurrahs that instantly swelled their throats were contagious, reaching shortly to the farthest ravine so that it seemed that the very dead had joined us. And the snow continued to fall. It had been our enemy. It was now our friend. And Shan's men dried and warmed themselves in the lee of the hills and ate steaming hottle stew with great chunks of grainy bread—and nursed their single pot of heated ale.

My own stalwarts, commanded by four sergeants named Ras Murphy, Dirk Benson, Pat Rifkin and Lars Kiber, stayed close to their own fire. They'd already changed to their absorbent undergarments of cotton I'd ordered for them, plus the double-thick tight-woven body suit which would be their only outer garment. They wore rough moccasins, too, with sand glued to the soles for purchase—and gloves whose palms had been treated in the same way.

A broad belt at their waist held three six-inch knives, honed razor sharp, a half-dozen feathered darts dipped in a substance with the power to freeze a man's scream in his very throat; a light rope for casting, and two garroting nooses made of the thinnest of wire. Over it all—but for the moment only—they wore great fur and woolen cloaks. These would be cast aside at the ravine's edge.

Two new lines of men were posted as guides all the way to the now silent castle. Our kick-off would be some hundred yards to the west of the bridge. Shan's first thousand were to advance silently, their kaole's feet all padded, to within a hundred yards of the bridge, and wait. At the first sound of its being lowered they would advance.

"The whole operation," I told Shan's captains, and with a wink to give them courage, "will be a piece of molly-brittle."

Going *into* the ravine was not at all difficult. Hulok and I simply slid down the two-hundred-foot length of rope that was supplied to each of us. Climbing the tricky opposite face was something else. In this respect, we tied a length of heavy cord to our rope's end, left the rope there and simply unwound our cord as we climbed. To carry the weight of *four hundred feet of one-inch rope* would have been impossible. The problems were jagged rock outcroppings that we had to work our way around, and heavy, growing brush through which we had, literally, to tunnel our way. The precious *Whatzit*—it had disguised itself as Hulok's scarf—was fantastic. Throwing my mind open to Hulok, I could actually *see* through his eyes, or, since I at times saw him, too—*and* the Whatzit, I was seeing through my own eyes, but with little lenses. Doesn't make sense, does it? I've yet to figure it out. Still, Hulok was the one who could turn the Whatzit on, or "tune in" to what it was seeing. Wrong again. That last won't work, because the Whatzit wasn't seeing anything. It just *knew* what lay directly ahead and it showed this to us.

Through my eyes it was as if no snow were falling and a faint light shone just above my head to clearly reveal each nook and cranny, each handhold and each ledge. I'd been right about Hulok's stubby legs. But I'd forgot the strength and surety of his arms. He literally swarmed up that almost precipitous face like a Terran ape.

Once on the small ledge beneath the wall, my dwarf, skillfully and silently; this, with a leather-padded mallet, drove in four eye-holed iron spikes to a depth of three feet each. I, in the meantime, had pulled the rope ends up, threaded them properly—and doubly tied them off, each to two spikes. . . . A jerk on the ropes and seconds later we each felt the tension of it being tied off on that side. In scarcely five minutes from the time we'd achieved the ledge, we were hoisting our first two *assassins*, sergeants, Benson and Rivkin, from the rope juncture.

The crossing was easy and fast. A short chain was attached to a hook at their belt: the other end clip-leashed to the rope. Their sturdy arms did the rest. Three men on the ropes at one time; two minutes to cross. We had them all within a half-hour. And still no time had been lost because I, in the meantime, had settled the four padded, two-foot, four-pronged sets of hooks to the top of the castle wall; this, at a distance of but ten feet apart, and brought over by my four sergeants.

And the friendly snow still fell, softly, silently. Moreover, since we'd given Dagar's men plenty of time for wine and wassail, it was now at least five hours *after* sunset, so that the castle, too, was now silent, sleeping—a steel-point etching, gripped in the shroud of storm. My four hooks, I might add, had made but the dullest of clanks. . . .

On the wall, we'd climbed through each crenelated section to jump to the inner walk beyond, I directed forty men to the two gate towers, dropped the four ropes to the inner courtyard, and sent the rest down them. . . . It was indeed a piece of molly-brittle. The courtyard was as barren as the ice-gripped fields. Only at the top of the steps to the hall before Ellenrude's main room did we see any sign of life. Six guards in a sleepy stupor and bundled together for warmth. I sent ten men under Benson to flit wraithlike and to settle on them like so many bats. Only one of the six even managed a groan. Six of mine then seized their weapons, hauled the bodies to the dark lee of the wall and took their places.

My forty, already attacking the top sections of the gate towers, had been advised to descend the inner circular stairs with extreme caution, and to wait 'til we ourselves had taken the lower, guardroom floor—or had signaled for aid. Keeping ten men with me, I directed twenty each of the remaining forty to seize the lower guardroom floors of each tower. They did. This time the cries were louder, but what fighting there was was brief. We lost four men. We slew *sixty*. Within seconds there was only the cold again and the sibilant whisper of the snow.

In the meantime I'd set the winches to moving on the

bridge and portcullis. The creak and clatter wasn't all that loud, still the alarm eventually sounded. My eighty assassins, for that's exactly what they were, since I'd trained them as colony-warriors were trained, but without lasers or blasters, then seized the swords and bucklers of the dead and set up a defensive wedge to my rear so's to fend off the expected charge from all points of the courtyard.

At that very moment, however, the great bridge seated itself and the first squads of sleepy, charging spearmen were hit by Shan Duglass, Finley, Tideman, our own Sir Percy Tarrant and all the chivalry of Weils and Sierwood who'd come storming across the bridge. . . .

Meagan Anne was in the forefront, glittering sword in her right hand, the reins of her stallion between her teeth and the reins of Huaclan in her left hand. My stalwarts, afoot, had fallen back to make way for Shan. She spotted me in the press and fought toward me. I grabbed her screaming, protesting mount by its nostrils and pulled it and Huaclan to the protection of the gatehouse. Then, because I was strangely angry that she'd come—there'd been no knowing what those who charged would find—I yelled, "Why, Miss? Couldn't you have waited?" Indeed, I was so irrational in my sudden fear for her that I walloped her bottom and shook her till her teeth rattled.

In the midst of these altogether bizarre administrations, she dropped her puzzled wonderment at what I was doing, frowned deeply—and kneed me square in the groin.

I grabbed myself, threw my head back—and howled!

Not a bit nonplused by this, she stood spraddle-legged, hands on hips and yelled, "Shut up, great baby. I didn't kick you *that* hard. . . ."

My stalwarts who'd seen it all set up a roar of laughter, to be joined by all those knights and swordsmen still streaming across the bridge, though few knew what they were laughing at. Ahead, those of ours who'd swept the courtyard clean of foes and were now pursuing them through every warren, also heard it, and were cheered. At the gatehouse, I fell to one knee, swept the black hood off my head so that my red hair streamed, and said, "My lady. I ask your forgiveness. 'Tis that 'twas dangerous here and I feared for you."

She bent down to stare into my eyes, her blue ones blinking. "Well now, and here's a proper sight—at last. I confess, I never thought I'd see it. Up, up, my own true lord, we've work to." And she kissed me soundly before the "world," put a hand under my right elbow and helped me to do just that.

Again the laughter. Would that the taking of Ellenrude Castle had been the same for all. . . .

Most of the ensuing fighting was in the corridors and halls of the castle proper—and all through the barracks, warehouses and great stables to the rear.

Fortunately for Shan, and thanks to his own skill, he was able to surround all exits from the barracks; upon which flaming, oil-soaked bales of fodder were literally catapulted into the inner chambers. A large number of the enemy were asphyxiated. The rest, considering the nature of the monstrous trap, chose the better part of valor, and surrendered. Half were immediately marched down the one connecting link to the town below, a lengthy sunken road, waist-deep in snow.

In this last respect, I'd stove in the great southern gates of Ellenrude town with two blaster bolts at fifteen hundred yards; this, from the gate towers. The deed done, another two thousand of Shan's men had stormed in and took it. They met the prisoners coming down.

The vicious, no-quarter fighting, as stated, was in the corridors and living quarters of the castle proper. There, and this with but a single important exception, each baron and lord in rebellion against the crown, fought to the death. Forcing our way through a body-strewn corridor that had already been fought over twice, Meagan, myself, Hulok—he'd taken the time to enjoy a quick smoke on the outside ledge until his three companions and Sir Percy had come storming in with Shan—and the remnants of my hundred, advanced ever closer to what had been the royal chambers. Shan, fighting along these same halls before, had hoped to catch Dagar there. He didn't. Meagan, as I shortly found, wanted only a hot bath and a change of clothes, for she expected her original wardrobe to be intact. Such is the arrogance of royalty. And she was right!

But still we had to fight for the quarters. The swordsmen and knights of one great baron: Finsterre, I think his name was, driven from his own area, had fallen back on the royal quarters hoping to align with Dagar. But, as stated, Dagar had fled.

Our small battle was short and brutal. What with the yells and outright commands from Meagan that I hold back; not risk myself; take no part in it and the like—this, while she herself managed somehow to be in the midst of every tight melee—I had finally to take a hand. Baron Finsterre, a huge, bluff fellow, had just killed my brave sergeant Rivkin, breaking his head with his shield's edge. He would no doubt have killed a few more had I not intervened.

Without boasting, I gave both my swordsmen and his a repeat of the lessons I'd taught in my classes. The Baron, sensing he was up against something extraordinary, was wily—but not wily enough. At one last point, for him, that is, wherein he stood at bay, panting from his efforts to both catch and evade me, I made a feint to the left, faked a stumble, and came up beneath his whistling sword to kick him square against the side of his right knee joint upon which he'd placed all his weight. Twisting and off balance, he fell flat on his back.

With my six-inch blade at his throat, I yelled to his men: "Throw down your weapons, now! Else your lord will be crow's bait for the walls." But Baron Finsterre, and he was either exceptionally brave, or abysmally stupid, would have none of it. He actually thrust himself up and *against* my point—and fell back, awash in his own fountaining blood!

Sir Percy and as many as half my acrobats then marched the hundred or more prisoners to join the others below. My remaining men, along with Hulok and his companions—they'd found a half-eaten feast, still warm, upon the tables in the erstwhile King's Privy-Reception Chamber—requested my permission to finish it. Permission granted; they damn-well deserved it as far as I was concerned, they ostentatiously distributed napkins and fell to the task of feeding their faces.

In Meagan Anne's quarters—and with a handful of my own to guard our door—she went immediately to the bath chamber. The boilers were working. The water was at least warm, if not hot. And why not? Dagar had won a great victory, right? And he was ever the one to take full advantage of the creature comforts of privilege.

A bit of a sybarite myself, I'd looked for wines or liquors

and found them—with a little help from Meagan. . . . I stood idly drinking, glass in one hand, bottle in the other, while Meagan ran a bath, glanced at herself appraisingly in a full-length mirror as she disrobed, saw me peering over her shoulder, and said, "Hey! Come join me, love. We have but an hour or so, for I must go soon to Jocydyn with the news. . . ."

I did, surprised to learn that the bath, though small, was still large enough to hold both of us. Later; indeed, an hour or so later when we lay back against the scented pillows of her very own bedroom, wherein she'd slept all the twenty-two years of her life, she told me stories of her childhood. Her head was on my left shoulder, the warmth of her breath was against my throat. It was a storybook tale of a well-ordered kingdom where all the knights were brave and courteous, the free-farmers hard-working and orderly, the guildsmen and merchants honest and considerate, and life for the two little princesses, Meagan Anne and Jocydyne, was just one wonderful party after another.

Now that she was an adult, she confessed, she knew that things were not really like that. Still, this didn't mean that they couldn't be. She and I, she swore, and this while straddling me naked and with a happy smile on her face, could make it that way, together. I hadn't the heart to disabuse her of her fantasy. Instead, I agreed and praised her concern and devotion to the "people," as she put it, and to that glorious tomorrow that we would share when we'd returned from the north where I would slay the thing that was about to destroy the world.

"When we return?" I queried. "Meagan. There's no reason at all for you to make that arduous trip. Stay. Rest yourself. Take a bath every day and think of me. All will go well, I promise you."

"My lord," she exclaimed sternly, while looking me squarely in the eyes. "I am the queen and I will *not* be told of things second-hand. What affects the 'world,' I must know from the source. I would see with my own eyes this thing that's coming. And I would see just what kind of magic the gods will give you so as to slay it. I must see and know all there is to know. . . . Surely you understand?" She asked this last with brimming eyes and the voice of a very young woman who desperately needs help and who is seeking it from the one source where she most prefers to get it—from her lover, *me!*

"Well then," and I began to tell her exactly what she wanted to hear. "You'll come with me. We'll play it safe; stay alive so's to reach our destination, finish the job, and come safely home to an Ellenrude free of all this—" A wave of my hand indicated the castle with its bloodstained corridors, the barracks and donjons with their mounds of corpses; the cold stones; the driven snow and the white fields now seeded with as many as ten thousand winter dead.

She thought about it, then shook her head to free it of the memories of these last months, the rising of the barons and the murder of her father . . . And, since she had the ability to switch from the unpleasant to the pleasant, she suddenly wiggled her soft bottom in the lewdest possible way, bent her head so that a small ear was against my chest and listened to my heart. She peeped up at me and winked. "By the gods," she said, and she wore the foxiest of looks. "You do excite easily."

"Be flattered then, for you're the catalyst."

"La! I'd like to believe that, sir. Indeed. . . ." and she put on a ferocious frown. "I'll have that quite interesting hide of yours flayed from toenails to hairy ears—if it should fail to happen. . . ." Upon which we grabbed each other tight and continued our love play for the short time left to us.

An hour or so later I stood with her in the courtyard, holding the stirrup of her mount while she munched the last of a noxious slice of meat-pie. Shan Duglass had come, and the Lord Finley too, his left arm all bandaged and bloodied from a sword's stroke. He was very proud of himself, I could see. I'd say that half the potential court was there in a salute for their queen-to-be, who'd been with them from the first to the last. However, she was only going the three or so miles to the village to tell Jocydyn of the victory and to bring her back tomorrow morning. Moreover, Shan told me on the side, he'd feel more comfortable with her safely away, for there was still work to be done. Dagar had not been taken.

"Fear not, my lord," she yelled to Shan as she pranced her mount and made to join her escort of fifty strong swords. "I'll have her here in time tomorrow—And after, sir; *why then we're off with our Warlord to Lothellian, right?*"

He laughed and nodded. We gave her a last *hurrah* as she galloped through the gates.

More luck. The storm had broken. It was all going our way. Indeed, there wasn't a one of us who didn't feel as Meagan did, that we'd won, and that the end of it all was near. Shan, glowing with pride, had kissed her soundly; the kiss, he shouted for all to hear—to be given to his Jocydyn.

But someone else had arrived in the village before her. Dagar, with a hundred knights and warriors. He'd fled earlier through the single exit tunnel large enough for kaoles. It came out from beneath the west wall, exiting on the farm lands that occupied that side. Shan, aware of the tunnel's existence, had sent men to guard it at once. But Dagar had already fled—*and* the still falling snow had obliterated his prints. In fact and deed the guard had been set after the barn was empty. Thus Shan's reason for believing Hordee Dagar to still be somewhere in the labyrinthine depths of Ellenrude. He simply couldn't believe that Dagar would choose to run while he still had a fighting chance to hold the place.

But Dagar didn't have it where it counted. He wasn't descended from a thousand years of lord chancellors; indeed, the only thing that Dagar believed in was *Dagar*. Why stay and take the chance of dying when he could run and be free. There were other castles, other duchys. And the barons would always be willing to lend themselves to a bit of skulduggery. He'd also been appraised by prisoners from Shan's camp of the mystery of sadans in the Sierwoodian ruin of Hools. Sadarns from Jarkbund Castle, so they said, near the Keil River in Lothellian. They'd told a strange tale before they died. Dagar had found it compellingly interesting.

The ambush was a complete success. It had not been intended to capture Meagan Anne, for Dagar had had no way of knowing she was with the fifty swordsmen. He'd simply thought they were in pursuit of him and he wanted no one left alive who could tell where he was going. That he was still here at all was because to travel the west tunnel route from Ellenrude meant that one had also to go the full six-mile length of the ravine and double back. That would mean thirteen miles to the village as opposed to the fifty swordsmen's three. . . . Luck that Meagan Anne, the queen-to-be of Weils was with the fifty. Luck, too, that the one thing he loved in all the world, Jocydyn, was in the village.

Losing as few as thirty men in both the ambush and the village fighting, he took all the kaoles available, plus all the ready provisions—*and* the two princesses, and was thirty miles from Ellenrude by dawn's light.

Eleven

And that's when I heard that my Meagan had been taken, with Jocydyn—at dawn's light!

For the first two hours after the knowledge reached us, Shan Duglass was insane, raving mad. By mid-morning he'd calmed somewhat. By noon he was icy-cold and moving fast. He'd loosed a hundred hard-riding scouts on the east, west and south roads to pick up Dagar's trail. Three flying squadrons of two hundred men each were to follow to bring the Baron to bay and to hold him for the arrival of Shan Duglass.

By *mid-afternoon*, two riders, the sole survivors of the nine we'd sent north to the sadan castle of Jarkbund some three weeks before, drove hard into Ellenrude town. Their mounts were on their last legs. The heart of one of them burst and it fell and died in the first plaza; upon which the young riders begged to be taken at once to the Lord Chancellor and the Queen.

Their message was: Yes, the moodans and sadans are dying. Yes, the sadans are mustering at Jarkbund Castle. And, Yes, there *is* traffic between Jarkbund and the evil ruins of Cloos near the Kiel River. All these things were true. More! And this was perhaps the most important truth—while breaking camp in the early dawn, and this in a grove of trees which had protected them from the storm, they saw on the road as many as seventy knights and warriors led by Baron Dagar. He'd had with him some two hundred kaoles, most being loaded with provisions and bales of fodder. At the center of the train and clearly visible from the grove, so that there could be no mistake, were the two princesses, Meagan Anne and Jocydyn. The queen-to-be's hands were strapped to her saddle horn.

It was the judgment of our two young heroes, the first a priest-vicar neophyte, the second a simple knight, that for whatever reasons the baron was driving the entire lot in a desperate run *for the Lothellian border*.

We heard it all a second time after dinner; this, in the fought-over shambles of Ellenrude Hall. In the storm's aftermath the temperature had dropped considerably and was not to be allayed by either our warm furs or the roaring fires at each end of the hall. Indeed, the cold was everywhere—the *winter* that Hulok had spoken of was truly on us. And, too, our mood was one of solemn silence; there'd been no joy in victory. For both myself and the Duglass, and all of Weils for that matter, had been robbed of those whom we held most dear.

"We will leave at dawn's light," Shan told the assembled three hundred knights and lords. "But in all conscience," he announced gravely, "I must now inform you that it is not just for our two princesses that we take this evil journey, though I and mine would still do it if that were the only reason. But, as stated, it is not. And you have the right to know the whole of it. Hear now a tale of 'world death' from our Warlord Tybalt. His story's true. I therefore beg your courtesy, sirs, to hear it without interruption from his own lips."

And so I told them, omitting nothing. They listened, enrapt, of their lost true homeland, Earth; of the two-thousand-year hell of the colonies, and of our loss of all contact with themselves—the single world in all the galaxy to rival beauteous Terra. I then confessed what the Colony Council had done in its agony; that they had deliberately chosen to destroy great Avalon. Their flawed reasoning? That Avalon's very existence—without access to it—was totally destructive to our own efforts to survive.

The coming of the *Whisperer* had changed all that, I said. I then described the incident, my world of Drusus II; the ship, the *Scot's Leap* that the Whisperer had somehow managed to send across the void to find *me*, so that I could return here to destroy the monstrous thing that was coming to blow their 'world' to hell. I'd led up to the current events, the crash of the ship, my meeting with Hulok and our journey to Tag-Afran and the good will of our courageous Duke Oldus Finley. And finally I spelled it out: that in just a few days beyond three weeks, if I had not found the northern blinker-light, and with it the means to destroy the *thing*, they could then but pray for their world, for all would truly be lost. . . .

I'd confessed, too, that I had the voice of the Whisperer on tape, and that the means to translate the significance of those words also lay in the north. I then, belatedly, explained what a tape *was*.

Hulok had come alive at that particular disclosure. Indeed, when I'd finished, he hastily got to his feet and asked Shan Duglass for permission to speak. It was as if he'd made a sudden and quite important decision. . . . Shan Duglass nodded.

Hulok, less pale than most, since he already knew the story, went to the nearest wall, ripped aside the torn and half-burnt banners, and with the blackened stub of a torch drew a large rough map of the Deadlands beyond Lothellian and drew in the site of the original *Eden* exactly, so he said, where he'd been told it was.

"And now," he announced strongly, "I will tell you that which we dwarves have known for all these years, and you have not. I do this because the 'world' has indeed come full circle and the time for cold hard facts has arrived.

"To begin with, the 'great magic,' as pointed out by our Warlord, was a man-made thing; an accident of total destruction. The men who caused it were like yourselves, men of Earth. Because of that magic, all humans within the area of what is now called Lothellian and the Deadlands, sickened and *changed*. We dwarves, too, were a result of the magic. But our strain proved true, so much so, that the Guardians—and they, too, were men who'd survived as men"—and he looked me square in the eyes when he said this—"then allowed us to go to a new land. That is the land of Olfin, as you know. And it too is free of the sickness, like Weils and Sierwood. The simple condition was: that we as a nation should never bear arms against any country, kingdom, or populace.

"The ruined lands, the Guardians told us, would stay that way until the poison had run its course. Only then could true humans return. For the moodans and sadans, however, the end of the poison could bring only death. Indeed"—and he lowered his voice to impress his spellbound audience with the importance of his words—"their lives, from the very beginning, were but a gift from the Guardians. For the plague that destroyed the *Old Ones* still lives in this world. The new humans from Earth were and are immune to it, as are we dwarves. The sickened moodans and sadans are not. And now you will know a startling and terrible truth. . . . The Guardians have deliberately kept the moodans and sadans alive for the single purpose of preventing humans from reentering the Deadlands. To achieve this, they put a medicine in the very air (a different form of radiation?), so as to stay the effects of the plague.

"The truth, therefore, is that the half-men have *never* threatened the South. *They have but obeyed the Guardians in preventing humans from invading, and therefore advancing to their death!*

"It has been told to us," Hulok continued, "that *this* year would be the one wherein the 'world' would be free, finally, of the poison. It was also told us that simultaneously with this, the medicine protecting the sadans and moodans would be withdrawn; thus they would be allowed to die naturally.

"And so it has happened. The 'world' is cleansed and the half-men are dying. Is it not strange then"—and he stared hard in my direction—"that with this gift of renewed life, we are given the new peril of 'world death' from another source— a human source, I might add, who, as we now know, destroyed the birthplace of all mankind and gave two thousand years of death and horror?"

How much the nobility of the world had gathered from all this, I don't know. They did, however, recognize a threat or a condemnation when they heard one. There was a rustling and a reaching for sword hafts until Shan Duglass himself called, "Hold! We'll not be provoked by insolence; especially, since in some ways our dwarf does have a point. What say you all to this? You, Finley? Tomaas? Charlemont? And you, my Lord Tideman? 'Tis clear to me, sirs, that the job will be the last one—and in the doing, we'll finish it, once and for all!"

They cheered him for they generally believed as he did, and though they but barely understood it all, they still staunchly pledged their lives to the venture—even if it meant that they'd now be sword-to-sword with the mysterious Guardians, too. "To return to Eden," they cried in a common voice, "Was unthinkable 'til now. But the day we accomplish this will be marked for all time in human history—as will that man be marked who stays at home, unmindful of his duty!"

This last brought on a quite emotional scene, for the contingent to be organized was to be held at a thousand men, no more—yet every sword in Ellenrude was offered.

I'd asked only one question, and this of Hulok. The map he'd drawn resembled quite accurately the one I'd seen aboard the ruined *Scot's Leap*. But he'd placed Eden at a hundred miles or more to the *east* of where I'd seen the flasher-beacon. And so I told him.

But he wouldn't budge. "Dwarves knew where Eden is, my lord," he told me smugly. "And that is that!"

His comrades solemnly concurred.

Twelve

We left before dawn on the following morning. A light snow was falling, which, Sir Percy suggested, was not at all a bad thing—unless it got worse, that is. For with such a snow, the temperature at least stayed up; without it, we'd damn-well freeze our asses.

A good half of our thousand was made up of the chivalry of Sierwood, the other half, from Weils. Besides this number, however—and the nobility of any feudal system *anywhere* simply does not list lackeys, ostlers, cooks and the like in its ventures—we had a hundred of these plus a hundred and fifty young vicar-warriors. These last, totally committed; totally trustworthy, were used mainly as fore and flanking scouts, the hardest job in any army. . . . In Lothellian it was surely a suicidal post—if the moodans were not sick and dying. A final agreed-upon dispensation by the War Council of the two countries was for an additional five thousand made up of every volunteer knight and sergeant who'd failed the first group. At best they'd be two days behind us!

Among myself, Hulok and Finley, who took an interest in such things, we'd agreed that we would have to average something like sixty miles per day, for we now had but three weeks and two days before planetfall by the oncoming CT-Nova. With spare kaoles waiting along the way there would have been no problem. But such was not the case. Kaoles we had, in plenty. But they, too, would have to do that same sixty miles per, with or without a rider. And, as before, they would be acting as provision carriers and the like.

All-in-all it was a risky business; just as it had been from the beginning.

As the grayness came to denote the dawn, Hulok, who rode at my side, said disgustedly of the snow, "If this keeps up, my lord, our mounts will be up to their withers in it by nightfall."

I frowned, remembering the remarks of the ubiquitous Sir Percy. "And if it stops?" I asked.

"The temperature falls."

"Which is worse?"

"Snow, sir. Obviously. If the drifts get too deep, we'll be lucky to do *twenty* miles per day."

Damn Sir Percy. I groaned.

But the snow became quite intermittent so that the drifts were held to a minimum. Indeed, we managed almost seventy miles before we camped, and this in a spot which, according to Shan Duglass, was but ten or so miles from another great ruin. When I think back on it, its very proximity was the cause, if not the reason for the *third* visitation.

It came immediately after dinner. I'd taken a small harp from one of the vicar-neophytes and was singing the ancient Terran "Riddle Song," or, "Song of the Days," whose lyrics and tune were older than time. . . . I ended upon a somewhat gloomy and somber note, the exact line being, "And I am the tomb of all your hopes," and found myself the object of many a jaundiced eye from the great lords around Shan Duglass' fire. That this happened to coincide with the reappearance of the whisperer didn't help.

We'd camped at the head of a ravine, with ourselves but a hundred yards from the road and the remainder of our contingent, plus our kaole remuda, much farther into its depths. . . . It was almost as if it had walked there from wherever. For suddenly there it stood, a great shadowy figure resembling nothing so much as a ten-foot Terran monk all cowled, robed, quite dead—and semi-transparent . . . Duke Finley, I think, was the first to spot it. Being Duke Finley, he'd proceeded to observe it calmly, preferring not to alarm the rest of us. But we'd seen it too; as one oft' times sees from the corner of one's eye that flicker of unnatural movement, where none should be! As stated, we'd set our fires just below the mouth of the ravine. Indeed, from where we were the field between us and the road was *the* skyline. I turned to look because I'd seen others looking. Then, when I saw it too, I think the most important thing to me was that no one of ours seemed to feel or to exhibit fear. They were just curious.

A faint wind had cleared the skies of clouds. None of the moons had made an appearance. There was just the snow-field, the wind—and earth-light. Even as I watched, however, the wind seemed to gather into itself, to become a sort of controlled whirlwind, a *manipulated* vortex—an instrument for the creation of sound? The shrouded figure, I'm sure, was but the projection of a visual substance; the form was arbitrary. As it was, it served the *whisperer's* exact purpose in that it conveyed precisely what it wanted us to see—and perhaps believe? Interesting; as was the fact that I now knew that the wind was necessary for the sound. Indeed the wind, properly used *was* the whisperer's voice, or rather, the created semblance of *a* voice to be heard and understood. But how else could it communicate? Thoughts? Why not? And there had to be a reason, why not. . . . Whatever. By some power it, or *they*, for it was most certainly not alone in this, knew where I was at all times. Again, what of telepathy? If it had it, it would not use this means of communication. Hulok had said that they oft' times appeared in the ruins and *whispered* to whomever had the courage to observe. It would appear then that if they could communicate telepathically, they would. But they *didn't*—ergo, they *couldn't*!

Their power, apparently, was of another kind. I, in the meantime, had pressed a belt stud for instant taping. Hulok tapped my shoulder, said softly, "It's different than the other."

"Which other?"

"At the inn."

I frowned. Then the wind rose, played directly upon the roughened outcroppings of rock so's to produce the exact sound of — "Jaaaaarrrrrnnnnn— Ohhhhhhhhhhh, Jaaaaaa-rrrrrrnnnnnnnnnnnnnnn! Tiiiiiiiimmmmmmmmeeeee— Goooooooooooo— Nnnnnnnoooooooowwwww! Gooooooooooooooo— Jaaaaaarrrrrrrnnnnnnnnn—"

And this time there was a lot of other stuff. As a matter of fact, there'd been a lot of other stuff the first time, on Drusus. But I'd taped none of it. The second time, at the inn, I'd missed a lot before I'd switched on. And the third time, in Hools, well I doubt that it had time for extra curricular observations. It had to get us the hell out of there and not scare us to death in the process.

It kept it up for a while and then ended as it had begun—

with the use of my name and its limited instructions to "come," or to "go," or whatever. . . . The effect on our thousand was also minimal. Lors Raddle had begun some sort of chant, involving a dozen or so of his vicar-priests which, as Finley told me later, bordered on the rites of *exorcism!* All of our chivalry who'd born witness to the happening, had simply risen to their feet, crossed themselves profusely, narrowed their eyes and watched until the voice died and the shroud-like apparition had faded away.

I still held the harp, so I strummed a few chords and reseated myself before the fire. But their eyes were hard on me, all of them, expecting me to say something. I shrugged and offered the simple comment that the thing was apparently as worried as we were by the passing of time, the lateness of the hour, figuratively, and the distance of our goal.

Lord Finley screwed up his eyes and asked wryly—"And how does it feel, Warlord, to have such a thing as a sponsor?"

I laughed. "I've signed no contract, no 'pact,' as it were. Indeed, I owe them nothing. Indeed, the one in Hools did save us from a sticky death, remember? It showed us the escape path. Moreover, if we succeed now in what we do, we'll be truly in its debt."

"But why now?" Lord Tideman asked. "Why did it appear *now*, rather than in all the days before?"

Hulok spoke up, saying, "One cannot know the way of spirits, sir. To that thing, even the time factor could be different. 'Tis said, you know, that a ghost who's haunted a site for a hundred years, when challenged, will confess to the knowledge of but a *passing of days.*"

Something in my subconscious told me that Hulok had hit, perhaps, at the heart of the matter.

"So you know of ghosts, too, dwarf?" Shan Duglass spoke up. "What other knowledge do you possess beyond our ken?" He was at it again in his baiting. He couldn't help himself. Odd, I thought, since he was so controlled in other ways.

Showing no concern for Shan's deliberate sarcasm, Hulok said calmly, " 'Tis conjecture only; in this case, mayhap, a thing derived of 'old wive's tales'."

"Old dwarves' wives' tales?"

Hulok frowned. "My lord?"

"Nay, nay!" Shan Duglass shook himself. "My apologies, sir dwarf. You are a brave and steady comrade and I have no right to mock you . . . 'Tis that I grieve, for her. . . ." He turned away and walked into the darkness.

No one attempted to stop him. In this, he was his own man; though to walk alone was perilous for him—and for us, too.

Our fireside lords and knights then began to discuss all sorts of stories they'd been told of such 'visitations' in the past; if not of whisperers, why then of the shades of those who'd "gone beyond." It made for pleasant conversation. To me, however, the important thing was that no one at that fire had had the slightest aftershock to the whisperer's coming. They'd taken it all in stride, as it were. Even our High Priest-Vicar, Lors Raddle, continued to be pleasant to me afterward, asking me about the possible effects of his rites and whether I thought it had helped to stay the thing's intentions.

The ensuing four days—the time it took us to reach the Lothellian border, a distance of three hundred miles—was a period wherein the temperature went to below-zero, Fahrenheit. Ice rimed our eyebrows and the mustaches and beards of those who had them. In the mostly heavily forested areas between villages and the like, huge packs of avaks dogged our flanks, and here and there along the march a kaole was pulled down and dragged away, fighting and screaming its fear. On more than one occasion, our armed lackeys dashed out and into them, spearing and slashing so that their bodies lined our path for many a mile. Still they came on in their desperate hunger.

Except for the last day before the border, our only surcease had been when they stopped to ravenously devour their own dead. Other animals, too, attacked us: Great striped caatys, ferocious cave bears and a cat the size of a leopard that ran in packs of a dozen or so, were extremely intelligent in their method of seizing a fighting kaole, and usually made it to safety with their prey. A last thing, and this, to me, was hard to believe until I saw it: The remuda was attacked at one point by two bisonlike creatures, horned and *pawed*. Like the kaoles themselves, these last were omnivorous. They would simply eat both kaoles and the forage that some carried.

Great forests, snow-fields and villages. In all those we passed through, though we never stopped a single time, peasants or craftsmen would come running to shout that the Lord Dagar had passed that way. Our young Lord Chancellor would nod stiffly and his face would grow grimmer still. I'd cause to worry about myself, since I, too, had lost my Meagan, yet I could not react the same as Shan. I think I internalized it more. Or, perchance the two thousand years of colony training had truly made of me something *else*, a humanoid who was no longer *exactly* human.

It was not good to dwell upon the situation, and so I didn't. Yet, at the heart of it lay a simple fact which could not be denied. It went like this: If I fought through to Eden Base and found and used the key to the CT-Nova's destruction, I would then be for all of time the greatest of heroes. . . . But if the young queen-to-be, Meagan Anne, were to die by some mishap, or at the hands of Baron Hordee Dagar, and I, her lover, in the most romantic sense, was not there to help her; to *save* her—why then I'd still be the pariah of all time, the lowest of the low; and this in the eyes of all Avalonians—and not just down to, say, the tenth generation—but forever and ever. . . .

To be forced to dwell on that paradox was to destroy one's effectiveness. And so I didn't. Instead, I played the harp and sang harmless ditties—and watched my sturdy Hulok and his companions glare viciously back at those who dared to glare at me.

Within the first hours of our crossing the border into Lothellian, we saw the reason for the waning attacks of foraging beasts. It was a party of dead moodans, hundreds of them; dragged down, killed and eaten where they'd fought to save themselves, but were too weak to do so. And that was just the beginning of horror. Moodan villages, collections of hovels, really, were crammed with the plague-ridden bodies of the dead and dying beast men. And they were indeed the stuff of nightmare.

Most of ours, as the days passed, became inured to it. Others, unaccepting, could only raise the edges of their furred sleeves to hide their eyes against the blasphemy that such things should ever have lived—and with no two of them alike!

The shock was not all that great to me. I'd seen alien life before, most of it acceptable; some, well, the objective axiom of beauty, as being in the eye of the beholder, doesn't always work. For there are things in the galaxy so ghastly as to instantaneously sicken a humanoid to the point of death. As for the moodans? Well, around the fires at night I did confess to Shan and the others of the council that I'd thought they'd been treated shabbily, *hellishly*, by the so-called "givers of life."

In this last respect, our good Lors Raddle and his warrior-vicars *did* say prayers for them and sprinkled the blessing water from small vials upon all the villages through which we passed. A thing, I was given to understand, that had never been done before.

There was no letup to that monstrous happening of death on death. Moodan villages were, in the main, on, or next to the roads. Amid death by plague, starvation and *cannibalism*, and this, against a background of pure forests and bright snows, a full half of these villages had also been burnt to the ground by untended fires in hovels where the owners had simply died. Most were still smoldering as we passed through. Small groups of the still living would come to stare at our great remuda of kaoles, and at ourselves, their erstwhile enemies. Some held out scabrous hands for bread to feed a ragged hole with rotting teeth beneath a single ghastly eye; this, in a face where lesions, born of the deadly virus which had killed the *Old Ones*, ran red with pus and blood.

And there was an odd sameness about the dying: It was as if they felt no pain; an odd, but merciful phenomenon. The Guardians must have known of this, I told Hulok, else, perhaps they would have gone about their genocide quite differently.

"Genocide?" he queried instantly, angrily. The daily sixty miles of hell, death and snow had begun to truly reach him. "Who are you, Jarn Tybalt, to question the acts of the Guardians? You, who come from a people who have so casually condemned a whole great world with all its beasts and trees to instant death. Sometimes I do not like you Warlord. *Believe* me."

I shrugged. "I believe you."

He was, indeed, in one of his darker moods.

Halfway to Jarkbund, we were attacked by as many as two thousand of the creatures. A foolish venture. The night was again, moonless and snowless. We lost three men, whom we hastily buried, and slew moodans till our arms grew tired.

The drive toward Eden Base continued, though I knew, as Shan Duglass knew, that the road would lead past dark Jarkbund Castle and a date with destiny which he, at least, could not disavow; nor would he. . . . In my mind's eye, I saw Meagan always now as I had seen her on that last day: blue eyes laughing, chin high and a back as slim and straight as any arrow. She'd worn a heavy mono of Tremaine tartan; this over a thin velvet pants suit. Half-boots, socks of tartan, too, and a winter tam with a topknot—and a furred greatcoat to set it off. And the young warrior-vicar who'd seen her as captive described her thusly, too. Except he'd said they had tied her hands to the saddle horn. This last was the thing that got me. That so strong a life as Meagan's should be tied to anything; especially by our *bête noire*, our seeming nemesis, Baron Hordee Dagar, was a thing to boil one's blood.

I don't know what Shan Duglass thought. I didn't ask. No one else dared. Dagar's fancied love for Jocydyn was basically physical, brutish even. This last, Meagan had confessed to me, was the reason for the fight in the inn that first night. He'd beaten Jocydyn. At which Meagan had put the point of her short sword to his throat and would have killed him then and there had not Lors Raddle—the least likely of all to do it, or so she'd thought—struck it aside. All things considered, Shan's thoughts could not help but dwell upon the physical facts of Dagar's possession of Jocydyn. I'm sure it haunted his days as well as his nights.

Indeed, the closer we drove to Jarkbund, the more silent he became.

The moonlit nights were the worst. The *things* would come crawling, dragging themselves, bereft now of what little they'd had that was human. They cried and moaned for food. We drove them off. And always there was the howling in the distance, the insensate monstrous quasi-human howling. They even fought our kaoles for their fodder. The kaoles fought back. And, since they themselves were omnivorous, our morning scenes were in no way pleasant.

But nowhere in all Lothellian had we seen a sadan!

On the thirteenth day we came to a place wherein a narrow valley opened to the south from the foothills of a chain of low mountains around which the main road now curved and undulated. A side road leading into it stood starkly revealed along its winter length as being ancient, ruined and destroyed. The trees that were its normal cover were mostly deciduous, so that only boles and ghostly branches stood now against the dark earth and the white snow. The road with its stone slabs up-ended and broken by the dead roots of great trees and vines, ended visually in the dead ruin of Cloos, the gateway to Hools, and more. . . . We could actually see it, being slightly above it and looking down. Like the ruined road it seemed as a monstrous pile of rubble, with here and there a broken, crumbling wall, or a half-destroyed tower to remind one of what it had been. And yes, it was still crisscrossed by slitted paths resembling the half-seen streets of Hools; some even seemed like deep canyons. The mystery of Cloos, the very essence of its being, evoked an hypnotic calling within all of us. I could sense it, evil—watching. I felt drawn to it, as to a lodestone.

But our Lord Chancellor, seeing and staring, came instantly to the same conclusion I had. Either Hordee Dagar was at Jarkbund Castle with the sadans—or he was right down there, in Cloos! But he couldn't be in Cloos for he simply hadn't had the time. At best he'd been twenty-four hours ahead of us. There was no way he could have gone to Jarkbund, made a deal, left with the sadans for Cloos and, once there, concluded a new alliance so that he'd be even now on some great underground river on his way to serve a new master. No way! Which didn't necessarily mean that they were at Jarkbund either. Time, for the sadans, was as short as it was for us. If they were to leave at all it would have been yesterday, or the day before—or today; especially with Dagar to warn them of our presence!

Our *Rubicon* would be the juncture of the main road with that of the side road that led to Jarkbund. What would Shan do when we reached it? *What would I do?* Considering, I doubted that there was a man of our thousand who hadn't asked himself the same question. I'd known it, sensed it everywhere, and especially when I looked into Tideman's, Quigley's, or our Lord Finley's eyes.

Finley had even told me the previous night—and he was quite serious: "Whatever happens, *you* must go on to Eden, warlord. I'll be your proxy. I swear it, on my soul. I owe you, sir, and Meagan, for it was I who brought the two of you together."

At the time, I could only nod and mumble my thanks.

Duglass then did exactly what I would have done had I been in command. He tightened the train, moved the remuda to the absolute rear, placed the retainers and lackeys, now armed to the teeth between the sumpter kaoles carrying our provisions and ourselves, and ordered a second line of scouts to the fore. Should an enemy be sighted, the first line would fall back through the line of the second with all data, while the second advanced to become the first, and vice versa. Again, he'd even guessed the same as I, that whatever we found on the road ahead, it wouldn't just be moodans.

At two miles from the junction with the secondary road to Jarkbund Castle—and our two heroes who'd accompanied us back to familiarize us with the terrain, especially *this* area—had warned us of this likely spot, I got a quick pic from the Whatzit; indeed, it was a simultaneous flash of immediate peril from four of them, for each dwarf had one. The pic was startlingly clear. Just beyond the break in the two low hills ahead were between seven and ten thousand moodans. For the moment, I'd seen no sadans, or, for that matter, any humans either.

The time was midday. We still rode the contours of the foothills. Despite patches of conifers which helped to break up the awful whiteness, reflected sunlight from off the slopes slashed like knives at our eyes. Again we were forced to wear our slitted eyepieces. Our scouts—they'd spotted the enemy simultaneously with the Whatzit's pic—came pounding back through the drifts with the news. Our advanced units dashed forward. Then we too were on the crest and looking down at what I'd known would be there.

The view was that of a long shallow valley with sloping sides and a fairly level floor. To our immediate front and stretching from slope to slope was the mass of the moodan warriors. Strangely silent, they simply watched and waited, stoically—pathetically. Beyond them the road ran free and clear. To the left, well to the rear of the moodans and at a point some hundred and fifty yards above the valley floor, were as many as a thousand maniacally screaming sadans.

Apart from these by as much as a hundred yards was a group of sixty humans.

All eyes around me searched instantly for more moodans on the high slopes, ready perhaps to roll great boulders down upon us should we attempt the flanks as opposed to the valley. But the icy slopes were bare; just stunted brush and with but here and there the usual granite outcroppings.

We pranced our mounts, evaluating what we saw. Cries of rage had immediately risen from our ranks at the sight of Dagar's banners and those of as many as ten great Weilsian lords. Drawn swords clashed on heavy shields to inform them of our wrath. The sadan phalanx was something else. At Hools, we'd fought their counterparts by moonlight. Here, with the blazing sun directly overhead, their wild and colorful banners were a hodgepodge of insanity to blind the eyes in other ways. Colored glass baubles hung from their armor. Crystals, too, caught at the sunlight, captured it, sent it off like shafts of rainbow iridescence. Small mirrors hung from their noses, ears and helmets. Again, the reflected points of light were dazzling. The quite evident madness was in itself a thing to marvel at. I'd time to wonder too if the strange symbols on their shield-fronts had a meaning after all—a writing, perhaps, beyond our knowledge.

But my eyes, like Shan's, were ever drawn to that group of humans to the north of the sadan phalanx, to where Meagan Anne and Jocydyn sat their mounts and watched us, too. Poor Jocydyn seemed more downcast than ever; this, despite the obvious—that even now her lover, Shan, was preparing *the* charge that would take her from Dagar's grasp for all time. Mayhap she dwelt on the physical aspects of what had happened. She'd been accepted back before. Could it truly be so again? If it had been Meagan there would have been no problem with me, for we of the colonies possess no such hang-ups. Whatever. That, too, like the actual *winning* of this battle, was Shan Duglass' problem. Meagan was as I'd pictured her in my mind's eye. Her hands tied roughly behind her back, she sat her mount arrow-straight, contemptuous of everyone and everything around her. I felt her eyes exactly on me where I sat great Huaclan next to an acrobat squire of mine who now carried my banner. And I *knew*, for she seemed to say it right inside my head, that given the slightest chance, she'd break from that traitorous group—and to bloody hell with all Dagar's spears.

A muted rattle of drums had begun behind us. They'd stay that way until our charge. And should I say that I truly feared for Jocydyn more than Mcagan? Well I did. . . . That she had been used again and against her will was a thing that some of her temperament cannot survive. At best she was a strange one. I'd exchanged but a few rambling words with her in all the weeks I'd known her. We'd talked, I think, of the flower garden she hoped to plant at Kilellen when it was over. . . . She was afraid of me, as she was afraid of everything, excepting Shan Duglass—the bravest of the brave!

Lord Oldus Finley, counting noses, suggested gravely that we had as many as six or seven thousand moodans directly to our front. Lord Tideman and Sir Rex Thomaas, Sierwood's warlord, agreed, as did everyone else with a military knowledge of numbers.

Tideman said sternly, "Yon sadans and our Lord Baron and all those other sons of hell will attempt to skirt the valley's top and escape to our rear the moment we're engaged. You can count on it."

Shan Duglass said sharply, "I would—*if* Dagar thought as you, my lord."

"You think he won't?"

"I think that Dagar knows that we could as easily attack *him* along the crests, and so avoid those moodans. Does he know our strength? I doubt it. A few banners placed against him to the left should hold him. Nay, good Tideman, if he seeks to flee along the crests, we'll catch him. If we attempt to *attack* along the crests, he'll simply cross the valley and escape around the moodans to our right. Moreover, sir, there's this to think about—Is Dagar in command there—or is he captive?"

Finley laughed aloud. "By the gods, Sir Duglass. You've really touched a nerve there, and that's a fact. I doubt we'll ever know, really." And his pale eyes twinkled.

Shan's eyes caught mine. He grinned. I winked, and never said a word. He'd nailed it all right on the head, so that in my mind he'd damn well earned the title of chancellor *and* warlord!

"No!" he shouted then, standing in his stirrups to address all of us. "There's but one road to both Dagar *and* Eden. 'Tis through those poor bastards there. If we win through, Dagar is dead. If we do not, well mayhap the world and all that's in it is dead. Be that as it may, I intend to smash through those moodans and to then wheel and drive on the sadans and Dagar's seventy—and slay them all! In this, our final battle, there must be no quarter, sirs. And mind you, I speak not of moodans—for they are dying even as we talk—but of men and sadans. I repeat, no quarter, sirs. . . . All that has happened, the two thousand years of horror, the attempt by Dagar to destroy the two lands, this new effort to seek allies of the very devils of the ruins, inclusive of the obvious pact with sadans; and this by men who've lost the right to use that name, will end just here—upon this field, *forever!*"

"As for you, Warlord!" he shouted to me, "since you're the key to the final battle, you'll stay to our center-rear when we charge. When we break through, you'll ride straight on for *Eden.* You'll have your four dwarves, your standard-bearer and twenty knights, 'neath Sir Percy's command. That should be sufficient protection for the road. And do not fear for your lady, *Jarn.* I love her too—as does every man who'll draw a sword this day. Even our Hulok loves her. Believe me, friend Tybalt"—and he grinned a wry and evil grin beneath cat-slitted eyes—"we'll not have her suffer a second longer than it takes to bring my sword to Dagar's neck!"

And thus he'd used the queen-to-be to tell us of the vengeance that he'd wreak—for *Jocydyn!*

"NOW LOOSE THE DRUMS!" he roared. "AND GIVE US A PIPER'S TUNE. AND YOU DO IT RIGHT AND WE DO IT RIGHT, AND 'TWILL ALL BE OVER BY SUNDOWN!"

To me he said. . . . "And mind *you*, Warlord. We'll follow after, too. For I've a mind to *see* those Guardians."

One thing was true. Shan Duglass was a man's man. They loved him—all of them; even greater lords than he, such as Duke Finley, our lone intellectual, a man who by design, intent, or sacrifice, could take the world a small step forward—a thing that Shan could never do.

The beat of the drums sounded. Pipers winded their instruments on our right—and the skirling began. The kind, as one old ancient put it, "that would make the very dead fall into line." Squadron after squadron of knights moved into posi-

tion, pranced their war mounts and lowered their spears behind their shields. Other than the fact that they were the
finest warriors that Weils and Sierwood could produce, I
sensed an élan that I'd never seen before, something of another time—and another world.

Sir Percy, proud of the honor of commanding my escort,
but also cursing the luck that kept him from taking the head
of the rascal who'd stolen his Primrose, rode prancing to my
side to shout: "What now, Sir Warlord? We've a race with
time, I understand. And a devil of some sort to fight when we
get there. Fear not, comrade. We'll make it. Indeed, with myself and these brave little people as your shieldmen why, I
swear, were it just us alone, we'd still cut a path sufficiently
wide for all the army . . ."

"You have my hand on it," I told him.

"And mine." Hulok rasped. He then held our gallant Percy
with his eyes while he said forcefully, "But mind you, Sir
Percy, our job, when you get right down to it, is to prevent
this warlord of ours from joining *this* battle in any way. He's
not to be risked, understand? More. We are to keep him, by
force if necessary, from risking himself, too."

"By the gods!" Percy panted—he'd been struggling to hold
great Primrose in place, for the smell of blood, something
that forever inspires a kaole to gnash its teeth, spit wildly and
prepare for battle, was in its nostrils—"Is it true? 'Tis hard to
believe."

"Believe it!" I roared, suddenly angry at both of them.
"But by the gods, I charge you not to try it!"

At which Hulok ground his square teeth in helpless rage,
while Sir Percy harruummphed and said, "Well, now."

But the Duglass colors had been brought to the fore; a
truly formidable "wedge" had been formed of the hardiest
and most redoubtable knights and lords, and the single, piercing trumpet blast that would continue for at least the first
hundred yards, had been sounded.

"It would appear—" the befuddled Sir Percy began again.

But he got no further. With a rolling *huuurrrraaaahhhh*! to
snap the icicles from every hanging bush, we charged. The
massed moodans lifted spears that they rightly could no longer hold, they were that weak. As Shan had so rightly said, the
majority were actually dying—right there, before our eyes.
Moreover, for our fighters to even spear them was instantly

counterproductive. For the time taken to get them off was obviously time wasted. Our single problem was simply that they were *in the way* . . . Even to hew and hack at them was a needless time-consuming blasphemy. When I could no longer stand it, I shouted to Finley (he was the closest), from my protected position within the wedge. "My Lord," I yelled, "for the love of your *Abram*, forget the weapons. They'll only stay you. Shields to the fore and sides. That's the ticket. Drive through the bastards! Just put your weight to it."

He'd listened even as his great war kaole had reared up to come down and pulp the faces and skulls of two more dazed moodans. He didn't hear me fully, but he'd understood. "You're right, Sir Greeneyes," he called back instantly. "There's no victory this way, and certainly no honor."

With the aid of his warlord and counselor, the two Thomaas brothers, respectively, he forced his way to within shouting distance of the raging Duglass. What was shouted back and forth, we couldn't hear. But the word came back almost as I'd given it—"A shield wall to flank and front! Drive forward—and put your weight to it!"

One has his inevitable nightmares, but when awake they're usually hard to describe, except in patches. The fighting along the road toward the Jarkbund juncture was precisely that—nightmare. As stated: The moodans *were* dying. It was hardly live flesh through which we were forced to cut or push our way. It was mostly dead. They were like maggots writhing in the sun, stolid meat, propped up by the very press of flesh. They'd answered the age-old, conditioned "call to battle," from their masters, the sadans, and had mustered here. How, I cannot imagine. What they had lived on during their ghastly journey and in that short hiatus until our arrival, pains me to even think about. But they were across our path and in a strength of phalanxes stretching, as stated, from slope to slope.

That we had deliberately plunged into them and then *slowed* to cut them down was our error. We'd actually given them time to press from the flanks to reenforce their center. If they had been even semi-healthy and in possession of their usual cunning and alacrity, we could have been in serious danger. But such was not the case. Indeed, the total effect of their pitiful, slow-motion attempts to hold us was simply a presentation of more meat, more *maggots* to force our way through.

And so the dead, killed by ourselves or the plague, remained standing, held by the mindless, ever-moving press of their comrades. We'd long ceased killing them unless we had to. This grace, however, did not extend to our murderous kaoles. Bathed in blood and gore to their very withers—maddened, too, by the cuts of a thousand blades—they made of our wedge a monstrous hydra with a thousand hideous heads, each striking viciously to bite through arms, legs, throats, to tear out entrails and on occasion to rear and to pulp the screaming horrors that barred our path.

We, too, were awash with gore. It was a ghastly spindrift, in the very air; one was almost forced to *breath* it. Indeed, at the time of which I speak, there was hardly a man of ours who hadn't managed to tie a kerchief over nose and mouth, else he would have eventually choked to death on the stuff.

Finley had put it rightly. There was indeed no honor in what we did, nor any victory in the accepted meaning of the word. It was a *living* nightmare, of which few men care to remember—even patches.

Then suddenly we were free. And for whatever reasons, the moodans stayed where they were and made no attempt to follow. What life they'd possessed, I think, had truly left them. Almost to a man they simply sat stoically down among the dead and the dying to await their own death. . . .

Would you believe that despite all I have said there were still those among us who, watching, could not help but shed a tear? Perhaps *that* was our victory; that in all that horror some men had found compassion where none had been before. My own eyes were streaming, and I was not ashamed.

Hulok's eyes, and those of his companions, brimmed, too. His three-fold shield to his arm, all covered with matted flesh and blood—for some of them had reached us despite all Shan's men could do—he sat his mount as some strange avenging ogre. To see him there, one would not think that of all of us he'd be the one to truly care. He saw me staring, breathed deeply, once, twice, grimaced and said, "Well Warlord, there lies our open road. You'll forgive me my anger and impatience. That there could have been another way is past discussion now. That we've come this far and *did* it this way, is a fact for which I now congratulate you."

"Hulok," I replied with some stiffness, "I thank you for your words. But I thank you more for your steadfastness in staying at my side when you thought me frivolous, mad, and selfishly incompetent. More, sir! I thank you for your gift of courage in the face of adversity. Without you and your comrades it's not at all certain we'd have made it—and that, too, is fact. *However*, it would seem to me by yon stirring of sadans, that the true battle, for Shan, that is, is just beginning."

And even as I'd spoke, he'd completed the wheeling of our lords and knights to present a solid front to the sadan phalanx which had now flung their shields to the fore and were readying their war spears. Our line had done the same.

Duglass, looking back, saw me. "TYBALT!" he roared. "Why are you waiting, sir? GO! GO!" To the chivalry of Weils and Sierwood, he raised his war spear and yelled— "NOOOOO QUAAARTERR!"

I raised an arm, too, looking around for Percy, who'd lost his knights in the last minute of the breakthrough. Fixing on my banner, I saw him coming on with, perhaps, a dozen men. At the same time *everything* seemed to fly into motion.

The sadan phalanx, in possession of the high ground, was not about to sacrifice momentum by waiting until Shan's spearfront reached them. A strange yodeling began all down their lines; upon which a half-dozen sadan lords to the center raised their great standards, screamed hysterically, threw them forward to "point"—and charged Shan Duglass' thousand.

On the hill's upper slope, Baron Hordee Dagar's "seventy" held back. So, too, did at least a hundred of the wild sadan lords. A subliminal thought touched on my subconscious: To what purpose? But that was the extent of it. My eyes were on Meagan; so were my thoughts.

And then, as if in part, she'd read my mind, our queen-to-be of Weils, my arrogant, gutsy and downright courageous Meagan Anne did the one thing that even I'd not thought of—She threw herself foward to scream like a banshee being put to the impalement stake, seized on her great kaole's left ear with her teeth, and held on for dear life. . . . There was no stopping that kaole. Like a shot from an ancient Terran cannon, he headed straight north—the direction she'd pointed him before the act. Oh, cleverest of women! That red-eyed bastard was even slanting toward the road.

There was no way for Duglass' force, or any part of it, to be deflected for Meagan's rescue. Indeed, I'm sure they knew nothing of what had happened. In effect, they'd been committed. The die was cast, an excellent cliche. . . . But the sadans with Dagar, reacted automatically, as hounds to the hare. Apparently Dagar had *promised* them something. All other plans were instantly forgotten. A full thirty flew off in fast pursuit.

And I, not waiting for Sir Percy, whirled Great Huaclan, clapped my shield to my saddle horn, tossed my war spear to my standard bearer, swept the great kuri-sword from its sheath across my shoulder—it had literally leaped into my hands—swung it madly around my head, and sank my spurs deep into Huaclan's sides.

He literally boiled out upon that ice-bound road. After me, axes swinging in their right hands, great shields to their forearms, my four dwarves came riding like the death minions of the Erl King. Sir Percy, I learned later, was hardly a hundred yards behind.

Meagan's maddened kaole, free at least to choose his own path, followed the least dangerous angle to the road. His pursuers stretched in a long line after him. Mathematically, the angle was almost perfect to our own, in that the distances were the same. The single point in the sadan's favor was that they'd started a second or two earlier.

But no waaay!

With Great Huaclan's reins in my teeth and with only my knees to guide him, we ate up the distance between us as a lighted fuse to the charge. I literally cut the first sadan lord in half at the waist as I came up to him. His mount, however, shying in terror at this attack from the rear, almost knocked Huaclan from the flat stones that made up the road bed; upon which, Hulok and his three streamed through the breach. Their whirling axes smashed into backs, spines and skulls all along the strung-out line of the surprised enemy. Their dying shrieks alerted the others, who turned hastily at bay—only to have myself, Sir Percy and his twelve knights and my four dwarves drive into them.

They were good spearmen-swordsmen in that they lasted two minutes longer than the three I'd given them. For all we'd gone through; for all that was at stake, we, too, could give them no quarter. Indeed, they expected none. Taking the head of the last sadan lord who'd dared to put himself in my path, I continued on after Meagan. I feared for what could happen if she fell from the saddle. She could be caught and dragged, for one thing. For another, well one simply doesn't chew a kaole's ear to ribbons and expect it to retain a presence of sweetness and light.

Fortunately the damned thing had held to the road, once he'd reached it, and Meagan, perfect rider that she was, had refused to be shaken off, even after a mile or two of mad galloping that would surely have thrown the ordinary person. . . . I found them around a far bend beneath the bare and wintry branches of a lifang tree—the kind that produces sweet syrup for wheetie cakes. Seeing her sitting there, her mount all blown, or browsing, I slowed to a trot. I did *not* want to frighten it further.

She still sat spine-stiff. But her eyes were closed tight. More. She'd bitten her red lips so that blood had congealed on her throat and chin. Dried tears, too, had made rivulets down her cheeks. Except for the fact that she'd lost her great furred coat and her woolly tam in the dash of her maddened kaole for freedom, she wore the same outfit she had when she left for Jocydyn's quarters some thirteen days before. I quickly and silently cut through the bonds that held her hands. The flesh of her wrists were swollen, purplish and ugly. I lifted her carefully from the saddle, bundled her in my own cloak and laid her beneath the tree with my saddle bag for a pillow.

It was only then that she chanced it, for she'd never once opened her eyes. She asked, "Is it you, my lord?"

"Hey, now," I exclaimed softly. "Who else?" I took her in my arms.

She simply murmured, "Ahhhhhh," opened her eyes to make sure, closed them again and snuggled against my chest. I began to massage her wrists and forearms with snow. I even popped an antibiotic from a belt pouch into her mouth and saw that she washed it down with a shot of white wine from my canteen.

Hulok rode up with Fergus, Torgus and little Colin ap Werliggan in tow. Colin was at least a foot shorter than Hulok and seemed a great deal older, too. To our rear—and we'd come at least three miles—we could still hear the roar of the battle.

Sir Percy came dashing up then and began to apologize all over the place for having lost us in the last stages of our having freed ourselves from the moodans. "It was those damned extra mounts," he swore in confusion. "My first squad lost them in the press and I sent the others after them—only to lose them, too! But all's well now, Warlord," he announced heartily. "True, we're still missing ten knights—two of whom were slain in that fracas back there—but we still have ten of the best. And that's the thing, right?"

"Right," I agreed.

Hulok, ignoring Sir Percy, asked quietly, "How is our lady, my lord? Can she ride?"

A bright blue eye opened wide to stare at him. She then snuggled against my chest again to murmur, "Tell our brave Hulok, whom I admire above most men, that I need but five minutes; then I'll ride . . ."

At which he doffed his cap in her honor, a gesture I'd never seen him make before. He said, "Thank you, my lady. If it were not for the urgency, I'd not have asked."

To me he said, "Let's ride till sunset, Warlord; as far as we can from this place. We must take no chances now as to who's won or lost."

"Hey, comrade. Shan's not lost. Believe it!"

A small thing: I knew even then that Hulok preferred, for whatever reasons, to reach the Citadel *without* the Duglass, or for that matter anyone else but ourselves, for company.

"My lord," he continued querously, for he was still a dwarf, "We've five hundred miles to go yet, and but ten days to do it. You know nothing of a real winter's storm. Should one catch us between here and there, well we'll have lost the true battle, no matter all Shan's victories."

But I'd been thinking of something else. "There's a thing I've read of," I told him. "It's called a *travois*." I then explained the particulars of the Terran Indian, baggage-smashing trick of poles and frame. "Make one for her. She'll rest for the remainder of the day. *Tomorrow*, she'll ride."

Listening, she literally purred against my throat.

And that's what we did. With the cloaks of the two dead men from Percy's twenty, we made a traveling bed for Meagan to rival the Princess and the pea. . . . We trotted for four solid hours; indeed, till an hour past sunset. Then we camped, made a stew of dried meat and vegies, and heated sufficient wine to warm our bones, and slept.

Meagan slept in my arms.

Thirteen

On the twentieth day from Ellenrude we arrived at the Citadel of EDEN, or Eden Base, to give it its historic title. Whatever its name, it would always hold that singular place in human history where the survival path of a great race had *almost* been brought to a terminal halt.

One needs a sense, a *feel* for history to truly appreciate a ruin, an old building, an artifact, a statue, created, perhaps, by some long-dead artisan of a long-dead race. I've always had it. And, when I think about it, it's rewarded me magnificently in the area that counts the most—peace of mind. To have a sense of history, one must also, of necessity, love life and see it as one's true immortality. All else is nonsense. Inclusive of man-made gods. That there are gods, or lifeforms at much higher levels of development, who's to doubt? But there's no mystery there. For all things can and *will* be known; if not now, well then, tomorrow. And if not then, well sometime—surely!

We'd been met on our arrival with the rare phenomenon of a "snow rainbow." Arising from the blue-green depths of a great forest of conifers, it touched down, and this according to Hulok, in almost the exact spot on the table-land toward which we rode where Eden Base had been. As to how he knew this, he didn't say and I didn't ask. We'd long reached that point where such questions were unnecessary. Indeed, it was better that way. For we still had secrets, he more than I, or so he thought. That he felt strongly about them was evident in his reluctance to be truly open. But he'd been a good friend and, more than anyone else, was equally responsible for our being here at all.

Still, if I'd been a religious man, in the truly *limited* sense of the word and, considering all that had happened—why then, what stories I could write about that beauteous rainbow!

The mesa, or table-land, was an absolutely flat protrusion of earth from the southwest slope of a small mountain; one of a chain that swept off toward a west whose horizon was rimmed by brooding snow clouds. It encompassed as many as ten square miles, was threaded by small streams and laced with a patchwork of giant conifers and gulleys. In a northern sense, it was more a savannah, an expansive snow meadow. To reach it we rode up a shallow incline carved from the mesa front, so Hulok told me, by moodan labor. It wasn't all that high, though—a hundred feet at best. Bright Persei again glanced off the snow in such a way as to make us switch to our slitted eye pieces.

After a mile or so, we came to two large rock cairns and trotted between them, not around them, following Hulok's lead. To a man, every knight; indeed, each rider, inclusive of my quite excited princess, crossed themselves dutifully with the *tau* cross.

They knew the meaning of cairns.

There were no ruins, just a broad expanse of fused and glassy lava rock to mark the site of Eden: Point-zero of the raging nuclear fires. The greater part of this lay to the west of a lengthy tongue of solid basalt which, thrusting from the mountain itself, came out to partition the plain. Eden had been precisely there—to the west, Hulok said. And it was precisely *there*, on that supposed site of Eden, that a small pyramid now stood. By the looks of it, it was post-nuclear. Indeed, the very blocks of its substantial bulk had been literally carved of the fused obsidian stuff that the raging heat had created.

A doorway on the northern side was the only entry. To its front, and looking south; and this at a distance of as many as two hundred feet, there was a great semicircular arc of stones arranged *à la* Terra's Stonehenge, excepting these stood just breast-high. It was a barrier, Hulok explained, beyond which no moodan or sadan had been allowed to go. Evidence for this last lay in the literally hundreds if not thousands of lifeless, dehydrated sadan and moodan bodies which were spread over the great field beyond the barrier. Informed of their coming death, they'd apparently chosen to die right there, in the presence of their gods!

Trotting around the pyramid's four sides, in the wake of our guide, we then swung north and around the great tongue of rock. Its height was at least four hundred feet. *It had been higher!* At a quarter of a mile along the eastern side of this projection, we came to the heart of the matter. . . . For there before us, and set into a flat and gleaming plane of solid basalt, was a large round portal. Seeing it I smiled both inwardly and outwardly; indeed, I relaxed all over. It was the usual, protected-from-everything, colony-type entry to a human base.

Hulok watched me closely. So did his indomitable three. He asked, "Well, Warlord. What do you think?"

I laughed. " 'Tis what I *know*, not what I think, Hulok."

"And that is?"

"Why, that though you have entry to the temple-pyramid, still you do not have entry here."

"Do you, my lord?"

"Yes."

"They'll be here shortly, you know."

"Shan Duglass?"

"Aye, my lord. They are out there now, just beyond the mesa."

"Well, now. And how do you know this?"

"Merlin's Eyes."

"Ah," I said. "It can do that, too. I supposed as much."

He said suddenly, loudly: "Well, Warlord, you know of course, that the time has come for us four of the Dark People to place our lives into your hands."

"*That's* why you wanted to be here, first, with me?" I nodded toward the glistening basalt and the entry.

"Yes."

"And if I had no way to enter?"

"Why then, we'd have no choice but to prepare to answer differently to the lords of Weils and Sierwood. You must understand, Greeneyes, and you too, my lady"—he bowed his head to a wondering Meagan Anne—"All would be eventually explained and understood. But there would still be that first moment of danger; of unreasoning fear. A moment fraught with an irrationality wherein anything can happen. Now," he grinned, "I confess that I feel much better."

We'd turned to look toward the mesa's rim. A long line of

kaoles and riders had just topped it and were streaming in our direction. They'd be with us within a half hour.

I said softly, "Hulok, this is *not* the site of the blinker-light."

He paled visibly. "It's not?"

I smiled. His very fear was reassuring. "No. But no matter. We'll know it shortly."

Sir Percy, as puzzled and bewildered by it all as the least of the knights given him by Shan, had in the meantime, nudged Great Primrose close to ask fiercely, "Is that where the devil hides, my lord? Behind that metal door?"

"Nay." I soothed his ardor. "But you'll see him later, I promise you—tomorrow, or the next day."

"You know, of course, that someone's coming?" He looked to the bluff's rim across the snow plain.

"Indeed I do. It's Duglass and your own Duke Finley."

"Ahhh!" He sighed his pleasure. The other knights sighed, too. For though they felt honored to be our personal guards, they were still more at ease in the company of their own. That they had made such a journey, and in the company of four dwarves, a green-eyed foreigner, and the queen-to-be of Weils, was a thing they'd remember all their lives. . . .

We rode quickly back to the area of the Pyramid. We hadn't long to wait; indeed, once they'd topped the mesa, we could follow them all across the snowfield with our eyes. There were sixty of them. To the fore was the great banner of Tremaine, in honor of Meagan; then those of Duglass, Finley, Tideman and Thomaas.

They finally skidded up to us in a wave of splintered iceshards from beneath the feet of their war mounts. Shan Duglass, his eyes gleaming with the pleasure of a sportsman who's simultaneously found his game *and* his long-lost father, cried emotionally: "My Jocydyn sends her love!" and threw himself across his saddle to take Meagan in his arms and to kiss her soundly.

We then dismounted, all of us, to shake each other's hands and do the abrazo thing—pound each other's backs and weep wet tears. Such is the way of men who practice the martial arts and who have won a most difficult series of battles.

"How *is* she?" Meagan cried, and her face was as wet as a face can be.

"Well, sister. I sent her home to wait for us."

"What of the Baron?" our thick-skinned Percy blurted out.

Shan Duglass frowned darkly and looked away. "What else?" he cried suddenly. "The bugger's dead, sir. I split the bastard to his liver. Enough! Another time. And you, Brother Grccneyes," he cried. "What of our mission? What's happened? And have you found the light thing?"

I made a great pretense of drinking from my canteen so as to slow things up a bit. I wiped my lips and passed it on. "Well, now. One thing's for sure," I told them all solemnly, "you've arrived in time to be at the beginning. By that I mean that I intend entering that pyramid there and after that another place, which you will see. We beat you here by just two hours. Now that we're *all* here, however, there's no point in waiting longer. Are you ready, sirs to know the mystery of your past?"

They responded with a chorus of muttered Ayes.

I asked, "In courtesy, sirs, it may be crowded in the two places I will take you. If this proves to be true, then I'll ask that only the Council remain and that the others retire for a later showing of whatever there is to see. Agreed?"

Again the Ayes.

"A last thing I will ask: For this one time, please question nothing. Save it all for later. Make notes, if you will. But do not interrupt whatever I may do, I beg of you. My reason: Our time's still short and I've yet to find the blinker light."

We dismounted and, led by Hulok and Colin ap Werliggan, walked the hundred or so paces to the pyramid entry. I'd discussed what we'd do quickly and briefly with Hulok and Colin. They were to take us in and out of the pyramid and were to answer no questions from anyone except myself. . . . Megan stayed close to me. A small hand gripped my arm. Ill-concealed sighs and snorts were loosed all around us. I had only to remember their limited feudal background and the two thousand years of their history to understand their superstition and *fear* of this particular unknown. Only Finley was more curious than fearful. And so is it always with the inquisitive mind.

My wizened little Colin stepped forward to produce an oddly shaped key, insert it, and to swing open the rounded portal. He pressed a button in the inner wall—and, lo! Lights were everywhere and there was a low humming of hidden motors.

We then followed Hulok and his three down a long hall and into what seemed to me to be a simple control room for quite simple purposes. It would seat, at best, a working crew of twelve. Even the control panel before the major swivel was simplistic in the extreme.

From there we visited three great warehouse rooms taking up, or so I imagined, a considerable part of the cubic area of the pyramid. They contained spare parts for various kinds of servo-mechanisms, plus servo-mechanisms, deactivated; blocks and sealed containers of fuel of various kinds—everything to keep a pyramid going for the required two thousand years. The largest storage area contained food in the form of packaged, balanced meals of all kinds, vitamins, mega-vitamins, minerals, liquid and solid nutrients to be mixed with whatever, and plenty of dehydrated meats and vegies so that the enterprising could, if they so desired, prepare their own food. There were even square containers of wines, liquors and beer and ale.

In the control room again, Hulok's companions distributed square tins of two-thousand-year-old beer. Fergus showed them how to flip the tab to open each tin. Colin, grinning more like an elf than a dwarf, handed me and Meagan one.

I arose from where we'd seated ourselves, sampled it and said lightly, so as to put them at their ease, "Well, it's damned good beer and that's a fact. And bear in mind that it was *your* ancestors who brewed it. Perhaps they've left the recipe somewhere. There'll be plenty of time to look for it, after. Now, a few words before we leave for the second place. This pyramid, sirs, was built by the Guardians, also your ancestors, *after* the great magic. It's purpose was to portray itself as the House of the Gods to the moodans and sadans. It is my understanding that twice each year moodans and sadans together made a pilgrimage to this temple. Their objective, to hear the word of the gods, or Guardians, and to pledge themselves to the 'laws' of the Guardians. And, if you remember Hulok Terwydd's words at Ellenrude before we left—among these 'laws' was the pledge to keep all humans from the lands of Lothellian and the Deadlands. . . . Hulok!" I called. "Will you give us the first few sentences of the commands of the Guardians . . . Let us all be silent," I told the others, "for the voice you will now hear is that of a Guardian. If you were outside, standing before this temple as the moodans have stood for hundreds of years, this voice would sound—*as from the very heavens!*"

I need hardly have told them that. They were already popeyed, in their awe of where they were and what I was saying.

Hulok had moved to the command swivel. The lights dimmed. He'd done it deliberately, for the added effect. He then pressed the stud for the Guardians' stentorian delivery—which, I'm sure he'd heard a dozen times; and if not this one, then others.

A few seconds passed. Then the words filled all the pyramid.

"Moodans. Sadans. To all you gathered here. Listen well to the voice of your gods, the Guardians. The time has come after two thousand years for our ascendancy. The time is, indeed, *now*, for us to go and for *you* our faithful servants, to follow. Be not afraid of that which will seem as death. For it will not *be* death, but rather the entry into the life you've longed for, in human form; in another world free of the sorrows of this one. Listen now to what we say and prepare accordingly. Listen now to the life we promise—after death! . . ."

And the voice went on to tell us what Hulok had told us; that the time had come for all the moodans and sadans to die—for all the land was now free of the taint (read, radioactivity), and those who had suffered most from that same blight—*would be rewarded first!*

Listening, I did not envy the Guardians their task. But, considering, did they actually have a choice? I doubted it. Perhaps there'd been another way. But we'd never know now, would we? All that can honestly be said is that once again good men, in this case, the Guardians, had been forced to use the tricks of deceit and subterfuge to cancel the quite negative results of but one more *human* error.

When he'd thought we'd heard enough—and Hulok was as conscious of the passing of time as I; even more so—he switched off the Guardian's voice.

Upon which Shan arose to instantly call out, "If that was a Guardian of the Old Race, Warlord, then what now are we to call our dwarves? I recall, sir, that the sadan captive called them 'the keeper of the keys.' Whatever. I think it best that we know who and what they are right now."

He'd needed to assert his position. Understandable. After all, he was Lord Chancellor of Weils. But the fact that he still felt some fear of Hulok—as one fears an alien thing—contributed nothing to our problem.

"You speak too hastily, Cuz," I answered softly. Still, you and all here have a right to know about our Hulok—and all dwarves. Allow me then to introduce to you the *caretakers* of the temple—the most thankless job that man or beast has ever had since time began. Instead of anger, brother, you should honor them all for the task that mere humans such as you and I would have found quite difficult to do."

He grimaced at that and took a deep pull at his beer. But the silence was then broken by the grave voice of our respected Lord Tideman, who said placatingly, though I swear I saw a twinkle in his eye—"Well, now, Sir Greeneyes. With beer such as this forever in ones reach"—and he waved his tin—"I'm bound to think the job's not all that difficult. Still, *I* truly honor them." And he nodded toward Hulok, in salute.

Exhibiting the cool that he always possessed when he tried hard, Hulok grinned and hoisted his own tin to salute Sir Tideman.

Laughter then swept the room. Shan Duglass, off the hook, said brightly, "Well, now. I've been answered right. And to show I've no hard feelings, I, too, will pledge our dwarves, and honestly." And he did. But I still sensed his reservations.

Outside we trotted the short distance to the entry portal.

There has never been a secret to the entering of any human base—for another human, that is. This singular fact, a constant, applied even in the midst of our "Colony Wars." For entry portals are the same everywhere, and deliberately so. All humans who traveled the star paths were taught this from the beginning, as they are taught in the colonies today. Indeed, the number-one pack on a suit-belt has the dual bar of six notes which will signal any portal to open. In effect, entry to any base, as a haven of refuge from what is outside that base, is *guaranteed* to all humans, just as it is *denied* to all nonhumans!

Therefore my confidence that I could open the portal!

I dismounted, advanced and stood before its thirty-six-foot circular width, thinking the while that perhaps *this* portal was the single exception. I took a deep breath and touched the activator. At once six measured notes rang out, clear and pure. And, without a second's delay, the great portal, immobile for as many as eighteen hundred years of the two-thousand-year hiatus, moved ponderously out of its full twenty-foot thickness—and then swung open. . . . The inner airlock was sufficiently large to allow entry to even a *floater-skimmer*.

I invited all seventy-five of them to join me. The kaole wardens would guard our mounts. They stepped in, as if on egg-shells. The portal closed, the great *inner* door slid smoothly into its molybdenum-hardened casing. A control center, in explanation, is but one single gigantic unit. In this case it was embedded, literally, within the basalt of the mountain.

Moving quickly across the broad expanse of the immediate interior, a maintenance and parking area for small floaters and snow-skimmers, plus a number of mobile-servos, I led them directly to the master control room. And need I say that Eden's control center was the exact duplicate of that at Drusus Base in Eden Valley? Indeed, I felt at home, for I knew exactly where everything was—computer memory banks, screens, scanner viewers, sensors, audios, servo-controls, and the small breeder plant for nuclear power.

That power was working now, at the lowest possible expenditure of energy. . . . Accepting it all for what I knew it was, I went directly to the master swivel, seated myself, activated the banks, flicked on the scanner-viewers located directly before the entry and the temple—and heard the mutual gasps from all my lords and knights when they spotted their kaole wardens just as they'd left them, plus the terrain before the pyramid with its acres and acres of dead and dehydrated moodans.

But time was passing. Indeed, that was the first question I punched. The second question was based upon the activated sensors having picked up the mass of the oncoming CT-nova. Distance, speed and the like gave a final reading of forty-eight hours twenty-two minutes before planetfall. Which meant forty hours, at best; for there was simply no point in cutting things too slim. Indeed, the CT-warhead should be set off at a speed-of-light distance of ten hours. That's *deep* space. One simply doesn't play games with CT-warheads.

I'd also picked up the blip of the blinker light. The reading was what I said it was—approximately one hundred and eighty miles to the west of Eden's control center.

I announced my findings.

"I know of nothing in that area," Hulok said firmly.

I looked to the others. Their faces were utterly blank, and understandably so. I thought to put a scanner on the converted Ct-freighter and zoomed in to perhaps five thousands yards. "Sir Percy," I called, "have a look at your *devil*. . . . That's it," I told the others. "It'll hit us about six a.m., day after tomorrow. Unless I stop it."

Finley, Shan Duglass and the members of the war council drew closer, as if that way they'd see it better. I doubted even then, with all I'd told them, that they really understood what they were seeing. Excepting Finley.

He said, "It looks like a comet or a meteor."

"Aye," I told him. "It does that."

"Why does it shine?"

"Ion radiation from the motors."

"Ahhhh. Like our moons?"

"Nay. Your moons reflect your sun's light. They have none of their own."

"By the gods," he exclaimed, "so that's the reason. You know, I've wondered. . . ."

"We'll talk about it," I said softly. "After. Right now I've got to find that ship with the blinker light."

Hulok looked up, startled. "You know that? That it's a ship?"

I said grimly, "It had better be a ship, else all that we've done, we've done for nothing."

There was more hawking and gasping then so that I announced, "Sirs and lords—and you, my princess—the temperature in here is seventy-three. Springtime, right? So doff your furs and make yourselves comfortable." I'd begun to punch various keys. "In a few minutes now, we'll have food and drink."

I then put one of the viewer-scanners to work, while activating the large viewing screen. Keeping the scanner at perhaps two hundred feet from ground level, we swept over the terrain at such speed that we were converging on the ship within a few minutes. I slowed so that we wouldn't miss it.

Hulok asked, "How did you know it was a ship?"

"Standard. All downed ships, including the one I came here on, have such signals—a rescue; whatever. The blip could as easily be operated from a motorized snow-sled. But the *blinker*, sir, is, with rare exception, *strictly* spaceship! For one even to view such a light at such a distance requires a *viewable* light. When a blinker blinks, it means that a single, almost invisible particle of CT matter has been set off. In effect, for one infinitesimal part of a second you are seeing the flash of a *sun*. Harmless, but efficient."

Again, I doubted that even Hulok knew what I was saying.

But I'd found the ship—plus *something else*! It was berthed on a flat stretch of snow-blown tarmac and protected by a great glassed dome; the standard storage bubble. And there was nuclear power there, for the bubble was heated just enough to prevent ice from forming, anywhere. The slim bit of tarmac was positioned between two fingers of granite hills. The ship, I could see, was a class-four Ross Destroyer; the very latest—at two thousand years ago, that is. . . . There was a *second* bubble, too; its nose flung out and open. Without a doubt, it had housed the *Scot's Leap*; which posed a question: Why did the Whisperers send the *Scot's Leap*—instead of the Ross Destroyer?

No matter. The *something else* was on the far side of the west finger. It was a *town*, in a delightful shallow bowl surrounded by low hills all covered with conifers and nut trees.

Fourteen

It was not a town as Shan Duglass, or Duke Finley would see one; nor was it a town with which even I would be familiar. It was a town the likes of which the Earth would have built as an experimental "colony town" for Avalon. Not a barracks; not a fortress citadel beneath some stinking, poisonous lake. But a town built for humans to live in, freely, and within the total environment. As I saw it, it could hold, perhaps, five thousand people. It was absolutely beautiful, even in its snow-bound, pristine purity. And though empty of life, it was *still* alive! And how did I know that? Well those streets, for one thing, were not buried in drifts. More. There was a small lake surrounded by a park with playing fields marked off for various games. The grass was still green, and *cut*! And the lake, as opposed to a natural skating rink in one corner of the park, was *not* frozen over.

My eyes brimmed at what I was seeing and what it could mean, not just for Avalon, but for the colonies, too. And, thinking of the colonies and especially Drusus Base, I did that which I'd hoped to hold till last—I punched the well-known coordinates for communications to the Bellerophon system. Nothing. My knees weakened. I tried for a readout on the reasons for the warp and communications disruption with the rest of the galaxy. The answer: insufficient data. . . .

But I had scanned the CT-freighter at a distance of forty speed-of-light hours. Surely that must mean that I could jump that far? I was suddenly filled with an irrational fear. What if, even though I had the Ross Destroyer, I couldn't make it jump, go through hyperspace. If that happened, I'd have to hit it *within* the Persei system. And Persei was a double sun with an oddball collapsar for a companion—plus eighteen planets and three times that many moons. There'd be space

207

debris all over the place. The whole damned system could go up. I knew this last was impossible; at least I thought I knew that. But with a collapser, a *black-holer* tossed into the kitty, who knows what could happen, really?

I shuddered. No more foot dragging. For a few seconds I cursed the gods that I'd ever seen that little surprise built by those entrepreneurs of the Anglo-Celtic Development Company as a gift to the Terran Federation to be. . . .

I stood up, my eyes still tearing. But I didn't care.

"Meagan." I spoke to her first, for she was my love and she was innocent—"And you, Hulok and Shan and my Lord Duke. I can not wait. Indeed, it's my wish that we leave immediately, for there's simply no damned point in sitting here asking the Guardians questions when all the answers could still be made meaningless by our deaths. I'll take a dozen with me, no more. Let's go!"

I showed then the center's comfortable living quarters, built to support a hundred; this, while the servos brought beer and sandwiches. I explained, too, how the showers worked and revealed the stored clothing, suggesting for their comfort that they should wear what I wore. . . . We left them, Meagan and I, to bathe and dress—she, in almost silent wonder of everything; me, with a "high" to beat the devil. Three times I reached to take her—she was so willing. But each time I but held her for seconds and let her go. Like Avalon, the Colonies, and all that was left of humankind, we, too, had a date with destiny.

I was the proxy, Ancient Mariner. The stinking corpse of the albatross that was the CT-Nova had now to be destroyed—once and for all!

All others besides our chosen twelve were ordered out of the Center. There was a chance that we might not come back, I told them. And, if so, why then they should at least be able to die on their own earth, in their own world, rather than in some hard, cold world of alien metal.

A military floater has a crew of twelve. A civvy floater is more an airbus, or a freight-rig. The two within the center were in the latter category. Once aboard, my baker's dozen, inclusive of Meagan Anne and Hulok, looked more crew than barbarian. Indeed, one would never have known them from their original ancestors except for the grim hafts of greatswords which still pepped over their backs. They had kept their surcoats, though. But the rest was *crew*—thermal underwear, metallic body-suit, soft boots. They'd also kept their tartaned tams.

I took it out and signaled the portal shut again. My crew waved good-bye to their peers and the kaole wardens. Shan gave them all a few words, reboarded, and we were off.

A floater's exactly that. It moves on anti-gravs and mag-lines. This automatically limits one's speed to at best a few thousand miles per hour. The potential's unlimited, actually, but since, as I said, the energy's from mag-lines, there's only just so much control. Anything *beyond* control could literally tear the floater apart.

Like everything, the experience of flight was awesome to my guests. Despite their wonder, however, they were quite stoic about it all. At one point I shot up ten thousand feet to avoid the potential horrors of a small mountain chain. They didn't so much as gasp.

Twenty minutes from control center, I eased the floater down to the side of the great bubble. The town could wait till later. The bubble's nose operated on the same principle of the control center's portal. As I activated the six measured tones, the nose pulled out and around. . . . A triple blip for the entry hatch and we were into the Ross Destroyer. Again, I went directly to the bridge and the command swivel; almost oblivious now to the presence of my companions, I simply waved them to whatever seats they could find.

The absolute pleasure of reactivating the Class IV Ross was akin to that of bringing the dead to life, and not just the "dead" in the limited *human* sense, but rather a great and finely tooled machine. There had been nothing like it in the entire galaxy. Only a dozen had been made. Heilbron Center, the site of the colonies' central council, had one. And that, I think, was it. The rest were lost—destroyed across the tragic hiatus.

I floated it out, took it up on its anti-gravs, waited the required period for warm-up, got the signal—and then hit the Benson ions. We'd already been free of atmosphere, at some two hundred thousand feet, to be exact. Grids and matrixes working, I risked punching the coordinates for the CT-laden freighter-warship—and there it was. I sat staring, fascinated. Could it be that the disruption factor was in the form of a barrier so that all *within* it would be unaffected? *But extending to twenty light-years?* The very concept was a thousand times impossible. One would almost have to have tapped the total power of a sun to do the job. . . .

But there was no other answer. So be it. We'd "hole punch" warp through hyperspace, and *do* it!

I gave the long dormant accumulators a full half-hour, during which I introduced my baker's dozen to their world and to the wonders of ice cream in six different flavors, coffee and a choice of various liquors, all dispensed by the ships' servo-catering system. The view through the Ross' translucent bow was fantastic, the starry void in all its diamond brilliance, a true "wonder to behold." They were beyond being frightened. Meagan confessed to me later that as far as they were concerned, they had all died and gone to Father Abram's heaven.

And, too, for the first time they truly *saw* their own world. I did a counter-clockwise circumnavigation to Avalon's clockwise spin. This allowed them to see everything, even their limited "world," as Hulok had first referred to their comparatively small continent on the vast expanse of sea and land.

Duke Finley, who came closest to grasping what it was all about, became quite faint so that I gave him a pill or two to bring him back. My Meagan Anne—and she'd been this way since she'd first entered the pyramid—was speechless. I made no attempt to change this situation, since I deemed correctly that it could be the one small hiatus in all her life wherein her awe of something would keep her quiet. To be silent, to be able to watch and listen, is not only good for the soul, but also adds to one's stature among one's peers.

Then I signaled them back to their swivels and off the sky-walk encircling the inner contour of the warship's nose. The accumulators, like everything else, were working perfectly. I took a deep breath, touched all the coordinates *and* the prime release for warp to ten hours, speed-of-light—and off we went.

The Waa-waas hummed beautifully, barely reaching the whining stage, while the stars disappeared and the kaleidoscope of colors and elongated snowflakes broke over the bow. This, too, was fantastic, though it lasted just ten seconds.

Then suddenly—and there is always that concomitant feeling of having lost a particle of time—we were there.

I keyed the scanner again to relocate the CT-freighter. *On the nose!* We were a hundred thousand miles to starboard. I quick tapped the adjustment for a speed-of-light parallel with the Bensons, and said as clearly and authoritatively as I could: "You will now watch the larger view screen above you and at the same time keep an eye out for what you'll see through the ship's nose."

I, in the meantime, had set up two batteries of three heavy photon-guns each to bear upon the CT-freighter. The effect of the heavy energy release would be an instant implosion to trigger the CT-warhead.

I gave myself a countdown, mentally said, "Why not?" and pushed the fire-release bar. The true countdown began—from ten. During which time I announced mildly to everyone, or no one, or perhaps just to myself: "Well, kiddies, here's a sight for your children's children to talk about—for *there*, but for the grace of who or whatever the Whisperers turn out to be, is—"

But the slim beams of blue-white radiant energy had already touched on the dreaded starship's breeders—and the CT-warhead had become a miniature *nova*.

Indeed, I thought we'd had it, for even at that distance and with just the matter of the ship and the contra-terrene, it seemed that the entire galaxy had become one blasting, hellish white of released energy. But that was indeed, *it*. And when our sight returned, so did the stars.

Even bright Persei, a small mote, twinkling softly at a distance of ten hours, speed-of-light. . . . I lowered my forehead to the bank of keys while a great shuddering seized on all my body.

Fifteen

Back at Eden Control Center, I advanced a first priority to the War Council under the heading, unfinished business. It was: to convince the lords of Weils and Sierwood to say nothing of what they had found in the north, except that the Guardians were dead along with the moodans and sadans, and that the extraneous threat, the *thing*, had been taken care of.

This being agreed upon, Shan Duglass then sent riders to order all contingents on the road and still heading north, to return to Ellenrude at once.

"And, as a friend," I explained, "I must tell you that from this moment nothing in your world can remain the same. Our problem will therefore be to control that change gradually so as to wreak the least harm to *all* of Avalon, your world, and to at the same time, create the most benefits. So far, the Guardians' ultimate views have escaped me (I'd tried to get specific read-outs on them from the data banks before I'd blown up the CT-freighter, and after, and failed). I will eventually find them. In the meantime *and from now on, sirs, you are the Guardians*: and this, whether you like it or not. 'Tis a responsibility I would not hand you lightly, nor should it be so accepted. Without a doubt there's a privy council among the dwarves who have acted thusly. I'm sure you can work together on this."

All this was said to my baker's dozen—Hulok being the odd doughnut—in the command control room, where we were relaxing over after-dinner drinks and such. The rest were enjoying the pleasures of the center's reaction room, the pool tables, ping-pong tables, bowling lanes and the like.

"What specific tasks were given you by the Guardians?" I asked Hulok suddenly.

"Why to check the read-outs on the equipment, punch the

212

listed buttons for repairs, when such was necessary, and to turn the voice of the Guardians on and off at the bi-annual gatherings."

"Weren't you taught anything at all about the mechanics of what you were doing?"

"No, Warlord, we were not. We were told by the Guardians that we could learn that in our own time—*after* the death of the moodans and sadans."

"What do you think they meant by that?"

"Why that we would eventually know. That somehow we would manage to—teach ourselves."

There was an involuntary narrowing of my eyes. I couldn't help it. "Hulok," I asked . . . "was there a tape for you and you alone to play—and by that, I mean the dwarves—*after* the death of the moodans?"

He frowned, looked guilty.

"Then there was one, or rather, *is* one."

"Yes."

"Where is it now?"

Again he frowned.

"Look! It makes no difference now. They had no way of knowing that others, myself, would come *before* the moodans died."

He said slyly, "Ah, but they did."

I grinned. "Oh?"

He grinned, too, sheepishly; that is, if a courageous, stubborn and more often or not, insolent dwarf, can properly grin that way. He asked softly, as a child would ask: "You knew?"

"No. But it almost had to be that way, right?"

He laughed. "If you say so."

I got up, poured drinks all around, reseated myself and then said gravely, but with a twinkle in my eye, "Sirs! *Allow me to introduce to you the villain whose comrades shot my Scot's Leap down!*"

"By the bloody gods!" Shan Duglass exploded. But his eyes, too, were laughing. "At last I've got him. How's about that, Sir Dwarf?" he demanded. "Speak up. Confess!"

Hulok, not liking at all to be exposed this way, looked sorrowfully at me, his betrayer, and said: "A last charge was given us dwarves, my lords, along with a weapon which continually points to the skies seeking alien intruders that we were told would one day come. The weapon, they said, would protect Avalon until that time when Terran humans, *our Avalonians*, would of their own free will grant access to other humans."

"And so you used it on me?"

"Aye, my lord. We made a mistake."

"Where is that tape, Hulok?"

He shrugged. "In the deepest vault of the deepest cave of all the north."

"Merde!" I exclaimed, and sighed. "Only a dwarf would rebury a treasured diamond in a place where even he can scarce find it."

He shrugged again.

"And what of the Guardians being the only ones to speak to a Whisperer? What of that, sir?"

"To them, it wasn't such a big thing; nor were the Whisperers a big thing, to them. . . ."

"All right," I said. "We'll cross that bridge, too. Right now." I then punched for all input data on the Whisperers. The readouts were slim indeed: Something to the effect that such apparitions had all the qualities attributed to Terra's ghosts, or spirits of those who have died, and were generally found in their proper homes, the ruined cities. To my final question: Had the Anglo-Celtic Development Company ever explored any ruin in depth? The answer was yes. Such an attempt had been made in the latitude 38-60, on one of the larger continents to the west. The particular ruin had been penetrated and found to be a veritable catacomb, with level after level, all leading down to great caverns beneath. The work had been finally terminated with the internal collapse of the area being worked. No one was hurt. All future excavation was postponed until a more appropriate time—after the creation of the first colony town.

I then announced that I'd play the Whisperer's tapes, placing the first *button* into the unscrambling device. Almost instantly, Hulok and his companions, white-faced, came to range themselves directly behind me. I wondered at their fear—and that their hands were never far from their axe hafts. . . .

More disappointment. Other than my name being mentioned as I myself had heard it: "Jaaaaarrrrrnnnnnnn, gooooooooo nnnnoooowwww!" and the like, the garbled, moanings, sighings and verbalized intonations, came out like this:

"Death!. . . . Death!. . . . A double death for life before it was ever truly lived! A thing comes now to slay us, who went against the true gods and were killed down to the last child . . . Aaaaaahhhhhhh, for our sins—the unleashing of the plague in war, the building of the monsters and the lighting of the fire that never dies. And now *it* comes, the death sent by you who were birthed like us, and who never did you harm. Aaaaaahhhhh! Yours is the shame. Yours is the guilt! And 'tis you who must save us, Jarn Tybalt. For you alone, the least of the guilty, still live and 'tis your duty to this world. Gooooo Jaaarrnn to the other shiiippp. Aaaaaaahhhhhh—'Tis ready now. 'Tis ready."

And that was the gist of the first tape, or rather the last, for I refer to the one made just outside of Ellenrude. Would that I had understood the reference to the ship. I'd have felt a lot better, to say the least.

I then played the tape made at Hools. But one hardly had to decipher that one, for all it had done was to scream maniacally and to point to the proper escape path. It explained nothing. Indeed, it seemed to automatically assume that we knew all about the amoeba-like monster that was coming at us. . . .

The last tape, or the first—for I'd never made one of the meeting on Drusus with the *Scot's Leap*—the one made at the inn, was somehow flawed; either that, or I'd handled it improperly. So. Nothing. . . .

"Well! That's it," I told them. "We know as little now as we did before. Tell me, Lord Chancellor: Did any sadans at all escape?"

Shan said, "None. But this is not to say that others have not made the trip to Hools, the same as the first."

"Why only to Hools?" Duke Finley asked. "Our very world could be honeycombed with caverns. As for other sadans making the trip, well, sirs, when you think about it—it's been two full months since your fight among those monstrous temples. It stands to reason that this has happened. The only sadan dead I've seen are the one's we've killed, and those out there before the pyramid. . . ."

"Our number-one priority," Shan smiled. "*After* we decide

the temporary handling of all *this*!" and he waved at the world in general. "And, in *this* respect," he continued, "I'll tell you now, Warlord, that I fear for Jocydyn, for she is not as well and strong as our Meagan Anne. And she's still on the road, remember? It took us thirteen days to get to the scene of the battle between ourselves and the moodans and Dagar. It took us but ten days to drive through to *here*. I would deeply appreciate it, Jarn Tybalt, if you would use one of the 'ships,' as you call them, to bring her here, under yours and perhaps Lors Raddle's care. What say you?"

"Why," I replied softly, "that I apologize for not having thought of it myself."

—And all the while he'd been talking, I found my eyes inadvertently focused on a small boxlike attachment connected to the left side of the master grid of the great computer. . . . I've said that I knew every screw and bolt of any command-control unit, for they are all alike. But now I continued to stare at it—as an addendum that I'd never seen before.

Lord Tideman was asking, "Does the smaller one fly at night, my lord? For it would appear to me that we could best retrieve her in the wee hours."

"The wee hours?"

Finley smiled. "The 'witching hours,' my lord. Betwixt one and three. They'll be encamped; asleep."

I looked to Meagan.

She asked simply, solemnly, "For our love, Jarn Tybalt."

"Consider it done. We'll leave on the first hour—But you'd better change back. If you don't, why in their eyes you'll really *be* the Guardians."

We had six hours to kill and the time passed quickly. The rec-room with its games, movies, music, *books*, ice cream, liquors, wine, beer and a Terran coffee to make one literally slaver, was like a total fairyland to all of them. Shan Duglass, to his everlasting credit in my eyes, invited the lackeys and kaole handlers in to share these goodies.

But at the back of my mind, as a needling part of my subconscious demanding to be recognized, was the on-and-off subliminal of the small *alien* box attached to the master grid. . . .

Relaxing with Meagan in our quarters, and this against propped pillows and with a bit of Berlioz in the background—at least I think it was Berlioz—she asked directly and honestly, "What happens now, Jarn? Will all our world die, as we have known it?"

She'd gone to the very heart of the matter without the slightest equivocation. . . .

"Would that be so unacceptable?"

"No."

"Meagan. Nothing will change at once. And when it does, it will be across the span of the years of your life. Let us thank your gods for the fact that the times are such that it is *you* who will be queen in Weils, in place of the tyrant, Dagar—and that Shan Duglass and Lord Tideman and Lors Raddle will head your privy council. Let us also thank those gods for such as Hulok Terwydd and for Duke Finley and the Council of Sierwood. Believe me, my princess, it could have been one helluva lot worse."

"Well now," she said against my throat, and I could tell that she was immensely pleased, "I may not know of sky-ships, love. But I am a woman who definitely knows the difference between truth and cozening. You will have all my love, my lord, and that's for sure. And know, too, that I am *glad* that I shall still be queen." Her voice fell off, became small, but insistent. "I promise, Jarn. I'll be a very good one."

Then, for one long and very magical hour it became like our first meeting on the broad divan of Kilellen's Oriole window. Later, she asked again from her favorite position, with her lips against my throat—"Will you teach me to fly, sir, and to speak to those great machines and to know the meaning of all the numbers, and like that—?"

And that's what did it, triggered it, I think, for my subconscious, reacting immediately to the simple symbolism of numbers so's to put me properly on the track, flashed a pic of an un-alien metal plate at the bottom of the *alien* box. The very fact that I'd actually seen it; had even unconsciously *scanned* it, was precisely the camouflage needed for me to dismiss it. Not, I'm sure, that it was intended that way. Terran engineers were not "games players." In my mind's eyes, I could see it now. It even had a model number and a serial number. . . .

I arose, saying, "Meagan. Come with me. I've one more thing to do before we leave. It could be important."

Picking up Hulok, Shan, Finley, Tideman and a few others on the way back to control-center, I then went immediately to the master grid. The small metallic box was just there, an outwardly inoffensive appendage of the computer control grid. I bent to the plate. It read: WARP AND COMMUNICATION DISRUPTER. PERSEI SYSTEM. . . . Model No. AA1. Serial No. 1. It had two buttons, red and green; the universal on-and-off. As of the moment, the red one shone like a rubied drop of blood.

Swearing between clenched teeth, I keyed for all disrupter data, giving the name, model and serial number. Back came the read-outs, the whole story—and it was as simple as that. Three basic points were made:

(1) *The origins*: That a direct energy tap had been attempted by Avalon's engineers on Persei's companion star, a collapsar, *black holer*. That though the tap itself had failed, a nominally harmless by-product of the attempt had proved most interesting. The reactive and compensating extension of the collapsar's mag-lines had introduced a disruptive shield at a radius of twenty light-years from center to effectively deny either entry or egress to any form of communication, or any attempt at deep-space warp by a ship using conventional coordinates. In essence, a way had been found to deny the Persei system for any contact with the rest of the galaxy. . . .

(2) *The effects—as outlined by the Guardians:* With Earth's destruction by the misuse of giant CT breeders that should never have been there in the first place, Avalon's instant dilemma was: Should it' open itself to occupation by those of the thousand worker-engineer exploitation units throughout the galaxy, or should they sit on it? A minority had opted for instant exclusionary control. A majority deemed this unacceptable and anti-human. Fighting broke out, ending with the accidental triggering of a breeder aboard a base fighter-freighter, with an ensuing domino effect. Six of Avalon's eight ships went up; thus the destruction of the entire Base and the contamination of all life within a thousand-mile radius. . . . All involved in the construction of Eden City were contaminated (to become the moodans and sadans). All, excepting the fifteen on duty at Eden's Base's control-center, were killed. Only the explorer groups in the far south escaped the holocaust.

(3) *The Problem:* When the control-center survivors, the *Guardians*, all males, were themselves approaching death; this, after most had already lived beyond their span of one hundred and twenty years, they then made their limited pact with the dwarves. They concluded too, at that point, that the communications disrupter should continue to function until Avalon was cleansed of radiation; i.e., only then should the field be terminated—*as has been explained to the dwarves in their final instructions.*

Hulok hung his head after I'd finished reading it all to them. Whatever. *This* time, and with solid reasons, I knew it was a bit above their heads. To liven things up again and to take advantage of our dwarf's contrition, I thought to question him once more. After all, he did have a lot to answer for.

"What about the first day we met?" I asked him. . . . "Did you know I'd be on the road to Tag-Afran?"

"How could I?" He grimaced and blew smoke at me. Frankly, I think he enjoyed the questioning too. "I'd been told that a great ship was down, no more. I had intended viewing the remains to see if anyone or *anything* survived."

"Then there is an instant communication between all dwarves, right? And, since you're telepathic, it has to do with Merlin's Eyes, the Whatzit. . . ."

He smiled. "True," he avowed. "But now that you know, it won't do you any good. Only dwarves know how to use the Whatzit."

"What is the Whatzit, Hulok? You might as well tell us. I'll know in the end. How do they function? How do they live?"

Finely and Tideman were listening intently now.

"We've reasoned," Hulok replied, "and we think rightly so, that they are like bees to the hive, or the ant to the queen; though a thousand times more developed. All Whatzits, for example, know what all other Whatzits know. More. They seem to draw from the memories of their ancestors—and this, from generation to generation."

"Are they in themselves intelligent? Or is all that just a great big, accidental memory bank?"

He shrugged. "We don't know, Warlord. We really don't."

"Then do this," I said softly, obeying a great welling question from inside my head. "Project what I give to you, to it. Then tell me what it returns to you. I'm aware, you see, that other than the warning 'pic' they are limited in their communication to but one person at a time. Agreed?"

"Agreed." He carefully removed a second tobacco pouch from his leather pocket and placed it on the small table in front of his swivel.

I then, and with all the power I had, gave him a telepathic vision of *Earth* as it had looked at 100,000 miles—and *Avalon*, as it still is, from the same distance.

Hulok focused upon the tobacco-pouch Whatzit. His great round face was bland, expressionless. But there was a light of concentration in his eyes that was hard to believe. I watched him intently. Time went by. A minute, two—three. Then suddenly his eyes softened, became filled with a rhapsodic delight, pleasure. Then, after what seemed some sort of a signal from him to the Whatzit to stop, he sighed deeply, closed his eyes, shook his head, as one does to get the cobwebs out, and said, *"There seems to be a lot of them."*

I felt the blood drain from my face. "Blue and white, with clouds—and some green and brown?"

He reached for his pipe, saying again, "A lot of them."

"How many?"

I had to stop him at *twelve.*

"Are you all right, my lord?" Like the others in the command room, he couldn't help but notice that my face was awash with tears.

Not wasting a second, I went directly to the master controls, and the innocent appendage and pressed the green button. Almost instantly a faint vibration, noticed only by its sudden absence, stopped. Indeed, the warp factor, that lost part of a second in time was apparent, too. And then, well, nothing. Everything was as it had always been—with a slight difference.

Back in the swivel again, I threw open all com-lines and punched the coordinates for the fourth planet of the Bellerophon system. The master-scanner cleared, became opaque, cleared again—and suddenly there was the face of a young communications sergeant, Roald Voors, of Drusus Base. Seeing me he couldn't help himself. He yelled, "By the gods! Commander Tybalt! We'd thought you dead, sir."

"Not yet. Where's Commander Donnert?"

"Sick bay, sir. . . ." Others were gathering to look over his shoulder.

"Sick bay?"

"Some bad hydroponics, sir. He's out of danger."

"Who's in command?"

"Aars."

"Then get him, dammit."

The relief I'd felt at not seeing the grinning smirk of Arne Telles, or of being told that *he'd* be with me in a minute, was evident, I think, in that my language had not been accompanied by a scowl. Indeed, I was grinning, too. Happily.

Within seconds the screen was filled with the round young face of Captain Epping Aars. His blue eyes snapped in his space tan. "By the gods, Tybalt," he exploded. "It's *good* to see you."

"I haven't much time," I told him, "so listen sharply. I've found a few worlds for you. Alert Heilbron Base. You can tell 'em that the long night's over. I'll be recontacting in ten days. Got it?"

"Sheeeeee—Tybalt. You telling the truth?" Aars' grin was from ear to ear. His eyes were as round as hockey pucks.

"No. I'm lying. If you knew where I was, you'd wet your pants. Stay with it, Epping. I'll be in touch."

"Hey, Tybalt. There's going to be dancing in the corridors at free-time."

"Oh, yeah. How's Arne?"

"In the goddamn brig where you put him."

"Fine. We'll let him out, but not just yet. The best . . ." And I made the age-old "V" sign and cut.

My whole body was streaming sweat, my face was flushed. I had a grin to match that of the biggest caaty that ever lived. Meagan Anne said later that I looked like a five-year-old at his first birthday party.

Hulok, sensing my needs brought a full stein of beer to cool me down. They gathered around me, Shan, Finley, Tideman . . . Even Sir Percy wandered in to stare curiously and wander out again.

Shan said, "That was your Drusus Base, I take it. And those were your friends."

"Yes," I said. "I'm sure they'd thought me long dead by now. Every man of our floater crews heard the *Whisperer* before I left. By the way—" I turned to Hulok—"when I began to play the tapes, you were all behind me—and seemingly ready to battle the devil himself, or *me*. What was that all about, old friend?"

Hulok flushed. He was becoming quite adept at it. " 'Twas the question of the Whisperers."

"I *know* that."

"Nay, Warlord. You don't know. Even the Guardians never knew."

"Knew what, Hulok? No more games!"

"That there is more than one kind of Whisperer. 'Tis like a splitting of souls, my lord; the existence of good and evil, side by side. We know now that 'twas the good ones who serve you. But the one at the inn, sir, was the other. Indeed, if the inn tape had not been flawed, you would have found this out yourself. And therein lay the peril . . ."

I hesitated, barely grasping the enormity of his revelation. "And how do you know this, Hulok?"

He laughed a guttural chuckle. "Why, sir. Ask the Whatzit."

Duke Finley's voice broke in. "Are you saying, Sir Dwarf, that the Whatzit knows what the Guardians, or the ancient Terrans, didn't?"

"Well think on it, my lord." Hulok turned to him. "At the time *before* the magic the Guardians, or Terrans, knew only that Whisperers existed; that they were 'strange and harmless wraiths.' But that was two thousand years ago! Much has happened since then; ourselves, for one thing—and the Whatzits. Is it therefore so strange that the Whisperers, too, have evolved?"

"Why," I asked, "was I more in danger at the time of the tape playing than before?"

"Because of what it might say. There's no harm if its words are not understood. But if they are well, to be quite frank, one risks being *possessed*; in this case, my lord, it would not be just you—but everyone in this room."

I smiled. "And you?"

He said gravely, "No. As with the plague, we are immune."

"Which means you've actually heard the words of the darker half of our schizoid phantoms—and survived."

"Aye, Lord. We have, through the Whatzit."

"What did it say?"

Hulok said sharply, "Now's not the time, Jarn Tybalt."

And suddenly I knew he was right. The immediate task of organizing that which we had was the priority. We'd won a double victory. All right. Consolidate it, and make haste slowly toward that other goal of whose particulars we scarcely knew and had barely touched on yet.

I'd jumped the gun in the other area, too; this in my self-inflicted, emotional "high." I'd work on that, with Hulok and the Whatzit—to pin down the actual planets and their systems, without which all the boasting in the world was meaningless. I hadn't the slightest doubt that we'd do it; perhaps even in time for the ten-day appointment with Heilbron Base. I hadn't the slightest doubt but that we'd solve the problem of the Whisperers, too. But as Hulok so wisely put it, "Now's not the time!"

I casually, as if I'd done it every night at this particular hour, walked back to the small box attached to the grid and pressed the red button. . . .

When the faintest of shivers had passed, I turned to them. "My lords, all!" I exclaimed, and winked. "Let us put aside all mysteries for a while. For we've a certain beauteous and kindly lady to attend to, our Lady Jocydyn—and we've a great victory to celebrate, and a most lovely and intelligent queen to crown. And so I say, 'let's to it,' and in the words of a bard of ancient times, 'Bedamned to him who first cries hold, enough!' "

And Hulok smiled and Shan Duglass and Duke Finley smiled, and my lady, Meagan Anne seized my arm and marched me toward the portal and our floater.

Outside we found a raging snowstorm. "The more reason," Meagan said, "for us to hurry."